BEAUTIFUL UGLY

BEAUTIFUL
UGLY

ALICE FEENEY

FLATIRON
BOOKS
NEW YORK

BEAUTIFUL UGLY. Copyright © 2024 by Diggi Books Ltd. All rights reserved. Printed in the United States of America. For information, address Flatiron Books, 120 Broadway, New York, NY 10271.

Isle of Amberly illustration by Rhys Davies
Designed by Donna Sinisgalli Noetzel

ISBN 9781250337788

For Christine, the editor of dreams.

"We are ready to transmit."

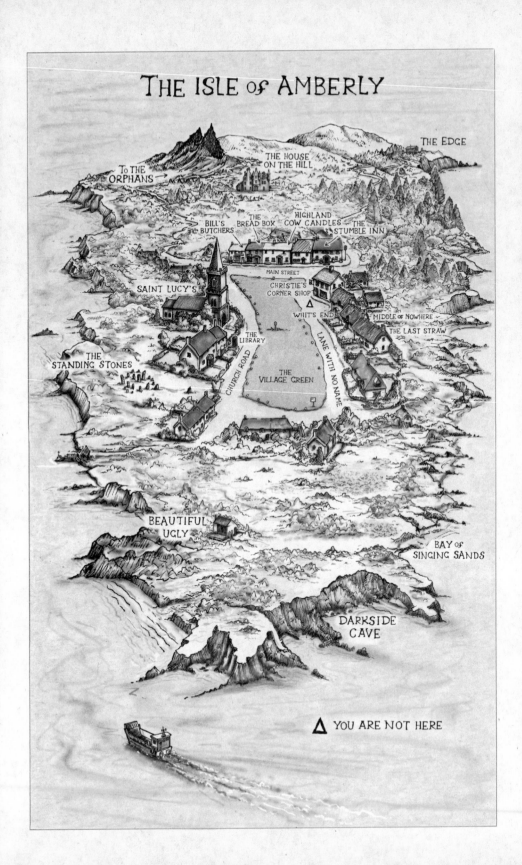

BEAUTIFUL UGLY

HAPPILY MARRIED

I f all we need is love, why do we always want more?

I dial her number. Again. Finally, she answers.

"I'm on my way, almost there," my wife says without me having to ask. I can hear that she is driving, so she *is* heading home, but *almost there* sounds like a lie. She has a habit of stretching the truth into something more agreeable these days.

"You said you would be here," I reply, sounding like a petulant child instead of a grown man. "This is important to me."

"I know, I'm sorry. I'll be there soon, promise. I've picked up fish-and-chips."

Fish-and-chips is how we have celebrated almost every major milestone. It's what we ate on our first date, when we got engaged, the day I got an agent, and when we bought our dream house. I'm a little in love with this old thatched cottage on the south coast, just over an hour from London but a million miles from the city. Our only neighbors these days are sheep. Tonight, fish-and-chips was how I hoped we might celebrate my first *New York Times* bestseller, washed down with a bottle of champagne I've been saving for five years. My editor in America said she would call if it was good news, but it's nearly 9:00 P.M. (4:00 P.M. in New York) and she hasn't been in touch. Nobody has.

"Heard anything?" Abby asks. I hear her turn on the wind-screen wipers, and I picture the rain streaming down the glass like tears.

"Not yet."

"Well, get off the phone or they won't be able to get through," she says and hangs up.

Abby was supposed to be by my side when I got the call, but she's late home. Again. She loves what she does—working as an investigative journalist and finding good stories about bad people. Men, mostly. My wife's whole life has been mapped out by her moral compass and an insatiable desire to expose wrongdoing, but I worry about her upsetting someone she shouldn't. Abby has been receiving anonymous threats sent to the newspaper where she works. She's become so paranoid that she's started recording all of her incoming calls, but she still won't quit.

My wife tells stories that matter, trying to save the world from itself.

I tell stories that matter to me.

My books have always been a place to hide myself inside myself when the real world gets too loud.

Marriage is made of a million beautiful and ugly moments stitched together into a shared tapestry of memories, all of which are viewed and remembered slightly differently, like two people staring at the same painting from opposite ends of a room. I didn't believe in love when I was younger. There wasn't enough love to go around in our house when I was growing up, so I spent my childhood hiding inside books and dreaming of writing my own. Based on my parents' relationship *happily married* was an oxy-moron, so marriage was something else I didn't believe in. Until I met Abby. She changed the way I looked at the world and she changed my mind about love. She made me feel things I didn't know I was capable of feeling, and I could never love anyone the way I love my wife.

When we first got together, we couldn't keep our hands off each other. If I close my eyes and concentrate, I can still remember the first time she let me touch her. Her perfect face, the softness of her skin, the delicate floral scent of her shiny dark hair, the taste of her mouth, the way she gasped when I pushed myself inside her. We used to stay up all night, sometimes just to talk, to tell each other our stories. Keeping the spark alive when you've been married as long as we have isn't easy. I try, but what's important changes as we grow older. At least, I think it does. It has for me. What we have now is all I ever wanted.

Columbo wanders into the room, wagging his tail as though he hasn't seen me for days, even though it has been less than five minutes since he fell asleep in the kitchen. He sits by my side and stares at the phone in my hand as though he is waiting for it to ring too. I prefer dogs to humans. *Dogs* are loyal. My wife bought Columbo for me as a surprise when he was a puppy. She said she thought I needed companionship, and we've been inseparable since. Abby worries about how much time I spend on my own and doesn't seem to understand that I prefer solitude. I need quiet to write, and if I can't write it feels like I can't breathe. Besides, I have my characters for company and I prefer them to real people too. My characters don't lie—at least, not to me—but before Abby, there wasn't anyone I could trust. People rarely do what they say they will or what they should. The only thing I don't like about being alone is the amount of time it forces me to spend with myself.

My path to becoming a bestselling author has been bumpy to say the least. I am the overnight success story that was ten years in the making, and for a long time I felt like the understudy in my own life. There were years of obscurity, shitty reviews, disappointing sales, and being dropped by multiple publishers. I was on the verge of giving up, but then I met my wife and she introduced me to my dream agent. Everything changed after that, so you could say I owe her everything. Writing books is the only thing that makes me truly happy. I know Abby's job is important, and that I just make things up for a living, but I so badly wanted her to be by my side tonight. If my latest book really is a *New York Times* bestseller she might be proud of me again. Look at me the way she used to.

My mobile buzzes, and my editor's name lights up on the screen.

My fingers are trembling as I answer the call.

"Grady, it's me," Elizabeth says. I can't tell from her neutral tone whether the news is good. "We're all here, the entire publishing team. Kitty is on the line too."

"Hi, Grady!" The glee in my agent's voice ends the suspense, and I surprise myself when I start to cry. Big, fat tears roll down my cheeks, and I'm relieved nobody—except a large black Labrador—can see me. The dog looks up as though concerned.

My editor continues, no longer able to disguise her excitement. "So, as you know, there's been a lot of buzz around this book and we're all so happy to have worked on it. We love you, and we love your books, which makes it even more wonderful to be able to tell you that . . . you are a *New York Times* bestseller."

There is cheering and screaming on the other end of the line. My legs seem to give way, and I find myself folding down toward the floor until I sit cross-legged, like the child who dreamed of being an author all those years ago. Columbo wags his tail and licks my face, and though I appreciate his unlimited affection, I wish my wife was here. My success still seems unreal to me and I don't recognize my own life in this moment. It feels too good to be true. Which makes me worry that maybe it isn't.

"Is this real?" I whisper.

"Yes!" my agent yells.

"I can't believe it," I say, unable to hide the wobble in my voice. "Thank you, thank you, thank you. This means so much to me, I . . ."

I can't seem to speak. I am filled with gratitude and astonishment.

"Are you still there, Grady?" my agent asks.

"Yes. I'm just so . . ." It takes me a while to find the right word. "*Happy*," I say eventually, trying on this unfamiliar emotion to see if it still fits. I think I might have to grow into it. "Thank you. All of you. I'm completely overwhelmed and so grateful."

I think this might be the best day of my life, and I wanted to share it with *her*.

Instead, it's just me and the dog, and he's already gone back to sleep.

I do my best to properly thank all the people who made this dream come true: my amazing agent, my wonderful editor, brilliant publicist, the fantastic sales and marketing teams. Then the call I've waited forever for ends, and suddenly everything is quiet. Too quiet. I am alone again. I pour myself a little glass of whiskey from one of the good bottles, then sit in silence, letting the news sink in. I want to treasure this special moment and hold on to it for as long as I can. When I have composed myself, I call my wife. I want to surprise her. I can picture Abby's mobile attached to the dashboard of her car, displaying her journey on a moving map just like always. The phone barely rings before she answers.

"Well?" she asks, her voice oozing expectation. I wish I could see her face.

"You are speaking to the author of a *New York Times* bestseller."

She screams. "Oh my god! I knew it. I'm so proud of you!" I can hear genuine emotion in her voice and think my wife, who never cries, might be crying. "I love you," she says. I can't remember when we last said that we loved each other. We used to say it every day. I like the sound of her words and how they make me feel. Like when you hear an old song you haven't heard for years on the radio, one you used to love.

"I'm almost home," she says, interrupting my mess of nostalgic thoughts. "Take the champagne out and—"

I hear the sound of screeching brakes, then silence.

"What's happened?" I ask. "Are you okay? Can you hear me?"

The silence continues, but then I hear her voice again. "I'm fine, but . . . there's a woman lying in the road."

"What? Did you hit her?"

"No! Of course not. She was already there, that's why I stopped," Abby says.

"Where are you now?"

"I'm on the cliff road. I'm going to get out and see if—"

"No!" I shout.

"What do you mean, *no*? I can't leave her lying in the lane, she might be hurt."

"Then call the police. You're almost home. Do not get out of the car."

"If you're worried about the fish-and-chips getting cold—"

"I'm worried about *you*."

She sighs and I hear the faint *click* as she releases her seat belt. "I think you've read too many Stephen King books—"

I think doing the right thing isn't always the right thing to do.

"Please *don't* get out of the car," I say.

"What if it were me in the road? Wouldn't you want someone to stop and help?"

"Wait, don't hang up!"

"Fine, if it makes you feel better." It has never been possible to change my wife's mind about anything. The more you urge her not to do something, the more determined she is to do it. Abby opens the car door. "I love you," she says again. By the time I think to say it back it's too late. She must have left her phone attached to the dashboard because all I can hear is the sound of her footsteps as she walks away.

One minute goes by, then another.

I can still hear the indicator and the windscreen wipers.

Five minutes later the call is still connected, but I can't hear Abby.

Have you ever known something terrible was about to happen before it did?

Or felt an overwhelming, inexplicable fear that someone you loved was in danger?

I am holding the phone pressed to my ear and have started pacing.

"Can you hear me?" I ask, but she doesn't answer.

Then I hear footsteps again.

It sounds as though Abby might be getting back into the car, but she still doesn't reply.

The only thing I can hear is the sound of someone breathing.

It does not sound like my wife.

A moment ago, I was happier than I had ever been. Now I am paralyzed with fear.

This is the worst best day of my life.

I know the stretch of road she is on. It leads directly to the coast, and is not far from the house. The nearest building is a mile away, there is nobody close by I can call for help. I start walking. Then I run. I'm still holding the phone to my ear with one hand, breathless but calling her name. She doesn't answer.

The night is too dark, too cold, too wet. There are no streetlights in the countryside, only shadows. All I can see is an anthracite sky speckled with stars, a silhouette of fields on one side of the road, and a moon-stained sea on the other. All I can hear are the waves slamming into the cliff, and my own labored breaths. I see her car parked on the verge, and I slow down, taking in the scene. The headlights are still on, the indicators are flashing, and the driver's door is open.

But Abby isn't here.

There is no sign of a person lying in the road either. No signs of life at all.

I spin around, squinting into the darkness at the empty lanes and rolling hills. I shout her name and hear my voice echo on the phone attached to the dashboard. She is still on the call to me. Except that she isn't. The fish-and-chips are still on the passenger seat, along with Abby's handbag. I look inside it, but nothing appears to have been stolen. The only unfamiliar thing in the car is a white gift box. I open the lid and see a creepy-looking antique doll with shiny dark hair and dressed in a red coat. Her big blue glass eyes seem to stare right at me, and her mouth has been sewn shut.

I take another look around, but everything is still and silent and black.

"Where are you?" I shout.

But Abby doesn't answer.

My wife has disappeared.

ONE YEAR LATER . . .

GOOD GRIEF

Y ou look bloody terrible. Good grief, I barely recognize you," my agent says as I enter her office. It seems like such an odd expression. Can grief ever be good?

"It's nice to see you too," I tell her.

"I'm not insulting you; I'm describing you."

Kitty Goldman never sugarcoats her words. She gives me a hug, then sits back down behind her desk where she has always looked most at home. I see that a few more wrinkles have dared to decorate her face since the last time we met, and I like that she doesn't try to hide her age. What you see is what you get, but not everyone sees her the way I do. Not many people get this close. I've never known exactly how old Kitty is—it's one of many questions I daren't ask—but if I had to guess, I'd say early seventies. She's wearing a pink tweed skirt suit and smells of perfume. Chanel, I think. She peers over her designer glasses.

"And I see you brought Columbo with you?" she says, staring down at the black Labrador making himself comfortable on her expensive-looking rug.

"Yes. Sorry. I hope that's okay. I don't have anyone who can keep an eye on him, and I can't leave him alone in the hotel during the day."

And there it is—the head tilt of sympathy. The pity I've become so familiar with makes itself at home on her face and I have to look away. It's been a year since my wife disappeared. Everyone who knows what happened looks at me this way now, and I can't bear it. I've grown weary of people saying, "I'm sorry for your loss." I'm sure they are sorry, for a while, until they forget all about it and continue with their lives. And why shouldn't they? They didn't lose their reason for living. That would be me.

I stare down at my shoes, unpolished and badly worn at the heel. Kitty speed-dials her latest assistant—sitting right outside the office—and asks her to get us some tea and biscuits. Since Abby disappeared I often forget to eat. I can't write either and I find it difficult to sleep. My nightmares are always the same, and it feels like I can't breathe when I wake up. I didn't just lose my wife. I had everything I ever wanted and I lost it all.

I still don't know what happened to Abby.

I don't even know if she's alive.

It's that, more than anything, the *not* knowing, that keeps me awake at night.

I glance around the beautifully decorated office, anything to avoid Kitty's stare and the questions I know are coming. It doesn't *look* like an office. It's far more stylish, like a mini library or something you might find in a boutique hotel, designed by someone with expensive taste. I take in all the bespoke wooden bookcases crammed full of her clients' books—including mine. I was Kitty's biggest client for a while. She has newer, younger, hungrier, frankly better writers on her list these days. Ones who can still write.

My eyes wander until they find the framed picture of Abby on Kitty's desk. I wondered if it would still be here or if she might have hidden it in a drawer. Some people think hiding their grief will make it go away, but in my experience it only makes it hurt more. Grief is only ever yours; it's not something you can share, but at least there is someone else who thinks about Abby as often as I do. Kitty is my wife's godmother, and I sometimes think I only have an agent because Abby begged her to represent me.

Kitty Goldman is one of the biggest literary agents in the country. She took me on ten years ago when I was still a young-ish author. My career was going nowhere except a series of dead ends, but she saw something in my writing that nobody else had and took a chance on me. The result was five bestsellers in the UK and several awards. Kitty sold the translation rights to my books in forty countries, then last year I had my first *New York Times* bestseller in America. It all feels like it might have been a dream now. Being unable to write for so long, and with all my belongings in storage, it is surreal to see a book with the name Grady Green on the cover again. I wonder if there will ever be another. The problem with reaching the top is that there is only one direction left to go: down.

"How are you?" Kitty asks, snapping me out of my self-pity. It's a simple question but I'm unsure how to answer.

The police gave up looking for Abby a few weeks after her car was found abandoned, despite finding the red coat she had been wearing. A dog walker discovered it half a mile along the coast the day after she vanished. It was soaking wet and badly torn. My wife has been "missing" for over a year but—according to the law—she cannot be presumed dead until seven years have passed. When other people lose a loved one there is a funeral or a service of some kind. But not for me. And not for Abby. The disappeared are not the same as the departed. People tell me I need to move on, but how can I? Without some form of closure I am trapped inside a sad and lonely limbo, desperate to know the truth but terrified of what it might be.

I've never been good with finances—Abby always took care of

that side of things—and when I checked our joint account after she disappeared there was a large amount of money missing. According to the statements I'd never bothered to look at before, she'd made several big withdrawals in the months before she vanished. We'd overstretched ourselves when we bought the house, and I couldn't afford to pay the mortgage on my own. With no new publishing deals, I was forced to sell it for far less than it was worth at a time when the housing market was crashing. Meaning I *still* owed the bank money. I sold most of our furniture too in an attempt to make ends meet, then rented a flat in London for a few months, paying a frankly extortionate amount to a landlord who knew I was desperate. I thought a change of scenery might help, but it didn't. Instead, it just drained away what little money I had left. Now I'm living in a one-star hotel, surviving on royalties from my previous books, unable to write another. Unable to do anything much at all except obsess over what happened that night. My life has been unraveling ever since.

"I'm okay," I lie, attempting a weak smile and sparing us both the truth. The smiling version of myself I used to present to the rest of the world is someone I don't recognize or remember. Pretending is harder than it used to be. "How are you?" I ask.

Kitty raises an eyebrow as though she sees the real me, despite my best efforts to be someone better. She has played the role of parent in my life more than once, especially in the days after what happened. I didn't have anyone else I could turn to, and as my wife's godmother, Kitty was just as devastated by Abby's disappearance. Agenting is a funny business and far more complex than most people imagine. It requires one person to perform many roles: first reader, editor, manager, therapist, surrogate parent, boss, and friend.

My agent is the only person I still trust.

"You don't look okay," she says.

I try to see myself through her eyes; it isn't a pretty picture.

I shrug, partly in apology, partly in despair. "I've been having trouble sleeping since—"

"I can see that. The dark circles beneath your eyes and the vacant expression are a bit of a giveaway. And you've lost weight. I'm worried about you, Grady."

I'd be worried about me too if I wasn't so goddamn tired. Months of insomnia has turned me into my shadow and I exist in a cloud of foggy slow motion. I don't remember what it feels like not to be exhausted, confused, lost. I'm in urgent need of a haircut, and my clothes all look like they belong in a charity shop. As if on cue, my jacket button falls off and lands on Kitty's desk with a sad *plink*. It's as though my clothes are trying to say what I can't: I'm broken. Kitty stares at the button, and her face says what she doesn't. Then her assistant taps on the glass door before bringing in a tray with some tea.

"I invited you in today because we need to talk," Kitty says when we are alone again.

We need to talk is never a good start to any conversation.

I think she's going to drop me from her client list.

I don't blame her. When she thinks about me she must think of her missing goddaughter, and that can't be easy. Plus, if I'm not making any money, then she isn't either. Fifteen percent of nothing is nothing. If I were her, I'd want to cut all ties with me too: A writer who can't write is one of the saddest creatures in the world.

I clear my throat like a nervous schoolboy. "I know I haven't written anything you can sell for a while but—"

"Your publisher wants their advance back," Kitty interrupts. "It was a two-book deal and since we've never delivered a second novel—"

"I can't pay them back. I don't have anything left."

"I guessed that much, so I told them to fuck off, but I do think we need to come up with a plan," she says, and I'm relieved to hear she's still on my side. Still fighting in my corner. The only one who ever has.

"It's not easy to write in the worst hotel in the city. I'm kept awake most nights by drunk people walking past my window, and during the day all I can hear is traffic and building works. The walls are paper thin, and there are constant interruptions and noise," I say, feeling as pathetic as I sound. I have never understood authors who choose to write in cafés or anywhere with other people or distractions. I need quiet.

"What happened to the flat?"

I shrug again. "I couldn't pay the rent anymore."

Her forehead folds into a worried frown. "Why didn't you tell me? I'm scared to ask, but how *is* the new book coming along?"

I've only written one chapter, and I've rewritten it at least one hundred times.

"It's . . . coming along," I lie.

"Is there anything you could share with me?"

I only have one thousand words. According to my contract, I need ninety-nine thousand more.

I nod. "Soon, I think."

"Or even a proposal or synopsis if you have one?"

I have no idea what happens beyond the first chapter, and I think I probably need to delete that and start again.

"Sure," I say.

Kitty's mobile rings, and she stares at it as though it has offended her. "Sorry, I have to take this."

"No problem."

She composes her face into one of pure displeasure, then picks up the phone. "If that's your best offer, then let's not waste any more of my time. I'm seriously jealous of all the people who have never met you. Six figures or fuck off," she says, then hangs up. Kitty likes telling people to fuck off. I've always been scared she might say it to me one day. "Where were we?" she asks, her voice composed and friendly again. She gently nudges the side of her glasses as though they aren't straight. They are. "Oh, yes. You were pretending that the novel is *coming along*, while I suspect you haven't written a word since the last time we spoke." I try not to smile. Or cry. Someone knowing me so well is still uncomfortable for me. "I think we might require something stronger than tea today," Kitty says, taking out a bottle of expensive-looking scotch and pouring two glasses. "We've been working together for a long time, and I've always tried to do what I believe is best for you, for your books and your career." This is it. Here it comes. The goodbye speech. She's given up on me and how can I blame her when I've given up on myself. Kitty has a reputation for being ruthless and for dumping authors as soon as they stop being successful, as though she fears failure might be contagious and infect the rest of her client list. That said, she's never been anything but kind to me. Until now. Kitty reaches inside her desk drawer, and I wonder whether she is about to tear up my contract in front of me.

"I've given this a lot of thought over the last few weeks and months—"

"I know I can write another book." I blurt out the words and they sound almost true.

"So do I," she says. "And I want to help you." Kitty puts a Polaroid photo on the desk. It's of an old log cabin surrounded by tall trees. "When a client of mine died a few years ago, he left me this in his will," she says, tapping the photo with a manicured nail. Pink to match the tweed suit. "It was his writing shed in the Scottish Highlands."

I fear the correct response is eluding me. "Lucky you?"

"I've not had a chance to visit it myself since he left it to me. Scotland is a bit of a trek and I haven't had a holiday for five years, but I'm told the cabin has beautiful views, and Charlie certainly found it to be a productive place." I frown. "Charles *Whittaker*," she says, as though I might not know who that is when the whole world knows who that is. Charles Whittaker used to be one of the biggest bestsellers in the business, but he hadn't published a new book for years. I often wondered what happened to him. "Charlie always said that his tenth novel was going to be his best, but he died before writing it, and he was a secretive soul, wouldn't even tell me the title. He wrote several bestsellers in that cabin when he was at the peak of his career, but now it's just sitting there, empty. You'd be doing me a favor, really."

I stare at her. "You want me to go to *Scotland*?"

"Not if you'd rather stay in that shit show of a hotel. And I should probably point out that this little hideaway isn't on the mainland. It's on the Isle of Amberly."

"Never heard of it."

"Which is one of many reasons why Charles was so fond of the place—it's very much off the beaten trail. There'll be *no* noise. *No* interruptions. *No* distractions. He needed the world to be quiet in order to write, just like you. Couldn't write a word when life was too loud."

"I . . . don't know what to say."

"Say yes. The cabin means free accommodation until you get back on your feet."

"I might just need to think—"

"Of course. Maybe this isn't a good idea." She nudges her designer glasses again, peering over them at me, and I fear I might have offended her. "It's very quiet and very peaceful— apparently—but by all accounts it is a bit isolated. And rural life is not for everyone. There aren't many *people* on the island . . ."

"Sounds perfect. You know I need things to be quiet to write and I just haven't been able to, with everything—"

"I'm not sure. Perhaps it was wrong of me to suggest it." She puts the photo back in the desk drawer, slams it shut, and pops a cigarette between her lips. "You don't mind, do you?" she asks, lighting it before I can answer. I shake my head even though I do and despite the fact smoking in offices has been illegal for several years. "I don't want to interfere or make matters worse," Kitty says, exhaling a cloud of smoke. "And I do worry that my other authors might feel jealous if they found out. I haven't offered the place to anyone else, and you know how some authors can get: Jealous. Paranoid. *Crazy.*"

"I won't tell anyone about it. I think it sounds wonderful."

"Good. That's settled then." She taps the ash from the end of her cigarette into a small silver AGENT OF THE YEAR trophy on her desk. "Take three months. Take the dog—he'll love it up there. Rest, walk, read, *sleep* . . . and who knows, maybe you might even be able to write. I'll tell the publishers to take a hike for now. There are plenty of other publishers out there, you write me a new book and I'll find you one. I know you can do it."

"I don't know if I can write without her."

Kitty stares at me, then at the picture of Abby on her desk.

The head tilt of sympathy returns and her voice softens.

"You've spent long enough grieving, Grady. As much as it breaks my heart to say this, I don't think Abby is coming back. She's gone and you need to try to move on. So do I." Her words hurt us both. I see the tears in her eyes before she blinks them away.

I do want to write another book. I just don't know if I can after what happened. Grief is a patient thief and steals far more than people who have never known it realize. My wife once said that I was only truly happy when I was writing, and I'm starting to think that might be true because I've never felt as broken as I do now. Being an author was the best job in the world until it wasn't. Maybe this is what I need to be able to write again.

I can't find the right words so say the simplest ones.

"Thank you."

Kitty nods then opens her desk drawer again, this time taking out a checkbook. I didn't know those things still existed. "What are you doing?" I ask.

"What does it look like? I'm writing you a check so you can buy yourself a new coat with buttons that don't fall off—it can get pretty chilly in the Highlands at this time of year—and I want to know that you have enough money to feed yourself and Columbo." She signs the check and slides it across the desk. It's for a very generous amount of her own money. "You can pay me back when we sell the next book. I'll email you all the details for Amberly and directions on how to find the cabin. Now get out of my office," she says with a wink.

I am forty years old, but there are tears in my eyes. "Thank you, truly."

"Success is often the result of a series of failures. Try to remember that. You never learn anything from success, but failure can teach you everything about a person. Especially yourself. I believe in you," Kitty says.

It makes me so happy to hear her say that.

It also makes me sad because she shouldn't.

ONLY OPTION

———◡———

A re there any benefits to losing it all? I think about that a lot. Your thoughts can change shape when you have too much time on your hands. Overthinking the things you *think* you need to worry about, under-thinking the things you should. The only good thing about losing everything is having nothing left to lose. I check out of the world's worst hotel, then load up the car with two suitcases filled with clothes, supplies, and books. I pack up my laptop and anything else I might need for a three-month stay on a remote Scottish island. Then I grab Columbo, and we set off toward a new chapter in my life. I hope it might be happier than the last.

It takes ten hours to drive from London to Scotland. Besides essential pit stops, I'm in the fast lane for most of the journey. My Mini is old and battered and has seen better days, but it still functions. Most of the time. Like me. Just past Glasgow, the view beyond my windscreen transforms into something spectacular. Trees in every shade of green, giant glistening lochs, and snow-capped mountains stretch out in every direction. My eyes, which had felt tired, are now wide open. Everything within my field of vision seems to be on a different scale. There is an infinite amount of unspoiled space, and the world seems bigger, or perhaps I am smaller.

A couple of hours later, beyond Glencoe and Fort William and still mesmerized by the spectacular views, I realize I haven't seen much of the world for years. I have locked myself away from reality, too busy writing—when I still could—but I wasn't really *living*. Merely existing inside my own head. Then grieving for everything and everyone I have lost. Not just my wife. Over the last ten years I let my relationships with real people drift while I obsessed over fictional ones. My work became my everything. I ignored invitations, and most calls, texts, and emails, because I was always too busy writing the real world away. Besides, I didn't need anyone else when I had Abby.

The realization deflates me a little, a new list of regrets writing themselves inside my mind. I drive on through this moment of grief, still in awe of the boundless beauty outside the window. I don't stop, even though I would like to. There isn't time. The ferry to the Isle of Amberly operates only twice a week, and I'm anxious not to miss the next sailing. According to what I read online, tickets cannot be booked in advance and can only be purchased on the vessel. From the few pictures I found of the island, it looks even more stunning than everything I have seen on my journey, so hopefully this epic road trip will be worth it.

When we finally arrive, late at night, the moonlit sea mirrors the coal-black sky in an unfamiliar bay. The satnav appears to think it has successfully led us to the "ferry terminal," which looks more like a bus shelter in front of a rickety wooden jetty. There is literally nothing and nobody else here. I climb out of the car and the cold air feels like a slap. I stretch my tired bones, easing the cramp caused by too many hours of sitting in one position, and let the dog out to do the same. All I can find to confirm that I'm in the right place is a handwritten sign saying AMBERLY FERRY with a list of sailing times scrawled beneath. They are entirely different from the times I found online, and the next ferry isn't due until tomorrow morning. I check my phone and see that I have no signal. There are no people, or houses, or any buildings at all, just a vast stretch of coast. There isn't even a vending machine. Columbo looks unimpressed.

"Sorry, boy. It looks like we're sleeping in the car."

The following morning, we are woken by the sound of squawking seagulls. I've barely slept and feel drunk with tiredness, but when I open my eyes I am greeted by the most spectacular sunrise. The sky is stained the color of crushed cranberries, looking like a painting composed of angry brushstrokes over a picture-postcard white sandy bay. When we arrived last night it was so dark that I was completely unaware of the stunning views, but now I can see rugged countryside dotted with purple heather on one side of the road, and a seemingly endless pristine coast on the other. I spot the outline of a small island in the distance, sitting pretty on the horizon—my first glimpse of Amberly.

We have been joined by two more cars and a black van, which has a quirky Highland cow logo on the side, and they are all parked next to the jetty. There is still no sign of a ferry—despite the handwritten timetable suggesting it is due—and I noticed there were no details for return sailings; all of the specified times are for one way only. Given that there seems to be no danger of an imminent departure I take Columbo for a short walk along the beach. The wind gently pushes me forward and ruffles my hair, the smell of the ocean floods my senses, and a taste of sea salt lingers on my tongue.

The sun is a faster riser than I am. Its golden yellow reflection dances on the surface of the sea, like a shimmering pathway from the mainland to Amberly. With the cloudless blue sky, calm turquoise water, and perfect white sand, this place looks more like the Caribbean than the Scottish Highlands. Only the cold gives our actual location away, stinging my face and creeping beneath my clothes. The air is so cool and fresh and pure compared with London. I greedily gulp it down, filling my lungs, feeling awake, alive, and a little bit excited for what might be a second chance.

The sea's calming sound is hypnotic and reminds me of where we used to live. Our old "not forever home." Then I think about that night, the sound of rain and the waves crashing on the rocks below the cliff road, the last time I heard her voice. My wife is always trespassing on my thoughts. Even now.

Memories of when we first met play in my mind like a scene from a favorite film, and I wonder if I might have edited them over time into something more meaningful than it was. I know some people thought she just decided to leave me when she disappeared. But even if she was going to leave me, I know she'd never stage something so dramatic. Abby isn't like that.

I try to pack my feelings away in a box inside my head. Like I always do.

They tend to let themselves back out.

As I walk, Columbo runs back and forth kicking up clouds of sand, chasing any loitering seagulls. I pick up a smooth dark gray stone and skim it across the surface of the sea. It bounces three times before disappearing and the dog runs into the shallow water. He's chasing something he'll never find, but we're all guilty of that. I turn and spot an old Volvo with a horse trailer pull up to join the other cars in the distance, back where we are parked. A hatch opens, and I see that the horse trailer has been converted into a small food truck. The smell of cooking soon mingles with the scent of the ocean and my stomach rumbles. I haven't had much of an appetite lately but I am suddenly ravenous.

"Come on, Columbo. Breakfast is served."

Back in the car, with coffee, a bacon sandwich, and sausages for the dog, I stare out at the sea. It's not as calm as before, and the once perfect blue sky is now covered in bruises. The ferry was due half an hour ago, but all I can see on the horizon is what looks like an old fishing boat. The other drivers turn on their engines as it approaches the jetty, and I feel a little nauseated as I read the name on the side of the vessel: AMBERLY FERRY. As ferries go, it's *tiny*. I'm reminded of a Fisher-Price toy ferry I owned as a child, which only had room for two plastic cars. Admittedly, this is slightly bigger, but it's old and rusty, and looks so unseaworthy that I'm surprised it floats.

The other drivers—who have clearly done this before—move their vehicles to form an orderly line at the front of the old wooden jetty. The sight of it makes me think of a scene from *Jaws*. One by one, they drive onto the ferry before I've even managed to put on my seat belt or turn on the engine. I see someone up ahead checking the cars before they board, leaning down to peer inside each vehicle before allowing anyone onto the boat as though looking for stowaways. I think it's a man at first, mainly because of their height and the way they are dressed—faded baggy blue jeans and an enormous yellow jacket that looks like it could double as a life raft. But as she walks toward the Mini, I can see it is a very tall woman. She's a good twenty years older than me, and has shiny black hair tied off her face in a short ponytail. She leans down and I lower my window.

"Can I help you?" she asks in a thick Scottish accent.

"Hope so. I'm trying to get to Amberly."

She stares at me for a long time as though she doesn't understand what I said or thinks I am dangerously stupid. "Sorry, I canny help. It's out of season."

I stare back. "What does that mean?"

"It means the Isle of Amberly Trust owns the island. It is home to thousands of protected trees and a community of just twenty-five people. *Visitors* are permitted on the island only from May to

July. Even if I could let you on board—which I can't—you'd have no way of getting back again for days and nowhere to stay—"

"But I do," I insist. "I've been invited to stay for three months."

Her makeup-free eyes narrow into suspicious slits. "By who?"

"Kitty Goldman. She owns a cabin there."

She shakes her head. "Never heard of her, and I've lived on Amberly all my life."

"She inherited it from Charles Whittaker."

The exceptionally tall woman stares at the island in the distance before studying my face, and her expression is hard to read. Then she smiles.

"Charlie's bonnie old writing cabin? Good for you. Well, you'd best grab your things and get on board then. Your car should be safe parked up here for a wee while at least."

"Can I not take the car on the ferry? It looks like there's room."

"*Visitors* are not permitted to bring vehicles to the island."

"What? But I have all my stuff . . ."

The woman's weathered face folds into a weary frown. I see myself through her eyes and try again. I need this woman to help me.

"I'm sorry. I've had a long journey—"

"Haven't we all," she interrupts, as though I have already taken up too much of her time. "You can bring as much as you can carry, *or* you can stay on the mainland. Them's the rules, and that's the only option, I'm afraid." *Only option.* What a ridiculous expression. *Only* means one, and *one option* means none. "The choice is yours. You've got as long as it takes me to get a sausage sandwich from the food truck to make up your mind," she says, then walks away.

I have always been rather slow at making quick decisions, but this one seems simple enough. I grab a rucksack filled with Columbo's food and things, a suitcase filled with mine, and throw my satchel containing my laptop and notepads on my shoulder. I can't carry anything else, not even the bag of food I packed, but I grab a packet of milk chocolate digestives and shove it in my jacket pocket. That will have to do for now. I lock the car and hurry toward the boat, Columbo trotting at my side just as the ferrywoman returns with her breakfast. She takes a large bite of her sausage sandwich and ketchup oozes out, landing on her chin. She curses, wipes it with a white paper napkin, and the resulting stain looks like blood.

"Decision made?" she asks, and I nod. "Then welcome aboard," she says with a smile, before taking another bite.

The seagulls squawk and scream, flapping their dirty white wings as if protesting, and circling above the ferry as it breaks free from the jetty. Their wingspan is vast, casting swooping shadows across the deck, and when I look up, I see that the tips of their beaks are red, as though dipped in blood too. They descend and dive so that I have to duck out of the way, and the ugly noise they make almost sounds like a warning:

Go back. Go back. Go back.

I'm sure it is just the exhaustion and my imagination playing tricks on me, and I notice the birds do not stalk us for long. They retreat toward the mainland when the ferry pulls away, slowly sailing out of the bay.

The sun has fully risen now, and everything is a dazzling shade of blue. It's hard to tell where the sea stops and the sky begins. The Hebridean Sea is rough and the other passengers all stay inside their vehicles, but that isn't an option for us. Columbo and I make our way to the front of the ferry and I sit my things and myself on a metal bench on the exposed deck. It's cold, and we get showered with an occasional mist of sea spray, but the view of the Isle of Amberly is utterly mesmerizing. A halo of white sand and a turquoise sea surrounds the tiny island, making it look like a mirage and this feel like a dream. A pod of dolphins leaps from the waves the ferry has created as though they are escorting us on our voyage, and my face stretches into an unfamiliar smile.

Our adventure might have had a tricky beginning, but this is beautiful, and I experience something like hope for the first time in a long time. Perhaps Kitty was right, and this *is* the fresh start I so desperately need, a second chance to get my life and career back on track. My agent is almost always right. I look around the deck, wondering if anyone else has spotted the dolphins, and that's when I see her. She's wearing the same bright red coat she had a year ago, the one she was wearing the night she disappeared, and is standing at the back of the boat, staring right at me. I shiver, not just from the cold, and it feels like time stops for a moment. Columbo barks, breaking the spell. I glance down to see what he is growling at—it turns out he was looking in the same direction as me, at her—but when I turn back, she is gone. It all happened so fast that it feels like I might have imagined it, but the woman I saw was the spitting image of my missing wife.

AWFULLY GOOD

Reading people used to be something I was good at, but lately I don't trust my own judgment. I don't even trust my own eyes. Insomnia sometimes causes the edges of my reality to bend and blur, but the woman really *did* look like Abby. I grab the bags and Columbo's lead and hurry toward the other end of the boat, weaving through the parked cars. The rocking motion causes me to lose my balance and stumble and I grab hold of a grubby railing to steady myself. When I look up whoever I saw is still gone. If she was ever there in the first place. When you lose someone you love you see them everywhere.

She looked so *real*. I spin around and hurry between the cars again, peering inside the windows. I study every face I see but none of them are her. The black van with its tinted windows is harder to see inside and I step away, feeling like a fool. I am delirious with exhaustion, confusion, and grief. Maybe driving all the way to Scotland and spending a night sleeping in the car wasn't a good idea when I'm already so very tired. I can't remember what it's like *not* to feel completely shattered. And broken. And alone. I convince myself that I must have imagined it. That I must have imagined *her*. It's a human affliction to see what we want instead of what is really there.

My mind wanders inside the memory of another boat we were once on together. A much nicer one than this. It must be almost a decade ago, but I still remember that day so clearly. I had booked a three-night cruise on the Dalmatian Coast as a surprise anniversary gift. We boarded in Croatia, and despite a mix-up with the booking resulting in a cabin with twin beds, it was supposed to be a romantic getaway. Abby was already behaving strangely and sent me to the bar to get us some drinks. When I returned to our tiny cabin with a couple of overpriced cocktails, I could hear music inside, the familiar sound of Nina Simone. I opened the door and discovered Abby dancing to "Feeling Good." The kind of slow dancing that was funny and sexy at the same time. She had her back to me, as though she didn't know I was there, and she was miming the words and swaying her hips slowly from side to side in time with the music. All she wore was a smile, very short white shorts, and her bra, and I still remember how the white lace looked so bright against her tanned skin. I can picture her face when I close my eyes, and it's her eyes I remember most. They were the bluest I've ever seen. It was like staring into the ocean and wanting to drown.

"There you are," she said when I put the drinks on the bedside table.

"Here I am."

"I hope you die in your sleep."

I looked up, thought perhaps I'd misheard. "What?"

"I hope you die in your sleep. I've been thinking about it lately—death—and it's got to be the best way to go. If you truly loved someone, *that's* how you'd want them to die, and I love you more than anything. So I hope you die in your sleep."

We said that to each other every night before we went to bed from then on.

I hope you die in your sleep was our way of saying I love you.

"And because I love you so much I got you a little something for this trip." She produced a white captain's hat and put it on my head before wrapping her arms around my neck and pressing herself up against me. "You're my captain of everything," she whispered, unzipping my jeans. Her hand made short work of getting me hard, and then she stopped, looking over at the twin beds. "Would you prefer to take me port or starboard, Captain?"

We made use of every surface in that cabin when we made love that afternoon. I took my time and gave her what she wanted; pleasing her always turned me on. Then it was my turn. It was the only good part of the trip. As soon as we set sail she said she felt seasick and didn't leave the cabin for three days. She didn't admit it, but Abby seemed terrified when we were out at sea. I felt so guilty for booking the cruise—I had no idea that she was afraid of the ocean until then—but we always avoided boats after that holiday. I know my wife well enough to know she would never set foot on a rusty old ferry like this. I must have imagined seeing her. It wouldn't be the first time.

I'm saddled with sad memories and bags and a growing sense of uneasiness, but there is no point in returning to my seat. The ferry is fast approaching another wooden pier. The Isle of Amberly—which was once just a smudge on the horizon—is now almost close enough to touch. I'm not sure what I was expecting, but it wasn't this.

I researched the place online before I packed up what was left of my life and made this journey, but there isn't much about the Isle of Amberly on the internet. The first thing I noticed when looking at a map is that the island is shaped like a broken heart. A spiky ridge of steep granite peaks appears to cut off one half from the other. The island is also tiny, only six miles long and five miles wide, situated ten miles off the Scottish west coast. I did see some pictures online of an ungroomed landscape, craggy hills, and dense forests with incredibly tall trees, but none of them did justice to the reality of the place. It's more spectacular than anything I've ever seen.

This side of the island is a tapestry of lush green grass with drystone walls forming uneven seams. There is a shimmering loch in the distance and lilac-colored fields full of wild heather, all framed by deserted white sandy beaches. There are no buildings that I can see from here, or people, just something beautiful.

I believe life rations happiness. People who get more than their fair share get fat on joy, those who don't get enough forget how to feel it. I fear I had forgotten, but I want to remember this moment, so I search for my phone in my pocket to take a photo. I notice that I still have no signal, not a single bar.

As the handful of cars drive off the ferry, I disembark on foot with a large dog and too many bags. The black van with the Highland cow logo is the last vehicle to drive past me, and I don't think I imagine how slowly it moves, or how long the silhouette of the driver stares at me through the tinted window before turning their attention to the road. Soon everyone else has gone. I wasn't expecting to find an Uber—and I thought I'd have my own car while on the island—but there is no sign of any form of public transport. Not even a bus stop. The only vehicle left is a dust-covered, battered old silver pickup truck parked on the dock. Without any mode of transportation, I'm a bit stuck. I know the cabin is *at least* a mile away, and I don't think I can carry all this stuff that far by myself. I'm not even sure what direction I need to head in. Then I spot a large wooden noticeboard with WELCOME TO AMBERLY carved into the top.

Behind the glass I can see a hand-drawn map of the whole island. It's like a 3D work of art. I take in the broken heart shape with trees covering at least a third of it, but it appears there is much more to see than that. There are rivers as well as the loch, multiple beaches, and a cove on the south coast marked on the map as Darkside Cave. There are buildings on the island too, I just can't see them from here. I spot a church, a farm, and The Stumble Inn, which I'm guessing—hoping—might be a pub. There is a row of small thatched cottages, something called the House on the Hill, and then, far away from all the other buildings and surrounded by trees, I spot The Edge—which Kitty told me is the name of Charles Whittaker's writing cabin. My phone still has no signal, but I take a photo of the map. There are several peculiar things about it, including the small red triangle that says: YOU ARE NOT HERE.

"Do you need a lift?" says a voice behind me. I spin around and see the ferrywoman standing a tad too close. I frequently disappear inside a daydream—I suspect most writers do—but it's unusual for Columbo not to have heard someone sneaking up on us. "I think you might struggle to find Charlie's old cabin, and there's a storm coming," she says, glancing at the cloudless blue sky. "You'll not want to get caught in it." She nods to the silver pickup truck that has seen better days. "I can take you where you're going if you'd like?"

The truck looks like a death trap, but I don't have any other options.

"That would be amazing, thank you," I say, pleased as punch that the first person I have met on the island is so kind.

We set off on the bumpy track of a road, and I make a point of saying how grateful I am numerous times, while also holding on for dear life. My bags are in the back of the truck while the dog and I bounce around on the back seat. The ferrywoman is so tall that the top of her ponytail touches the truck's ceiling as she drives, not that she seems to notice, or mind. Her large hands grip the steering wheel, and despite the moth-eaten woolen mittens, I can see the cuts on her fingers and dirt beneath her nails. Everyone has a story to tell and I find myself wanting to know hers. I wonder how old she is—up close I think maybe in her sixties. Then I wonder how long she has been single-handedly sailing a small ferry to a remote Scottish island. And why. I try to think of a way to ask that doesn't make me sound sexist or ageist, but then she selects a cassette tape—something I've not seen for several decades—slots it into the dated-looking stereo, and smiles to herself when the music starts to play. It sounds like bagpipes. A lone piper perhaps. Like something you might hear at a funeral.

"It'll help get you in the mood!" she says, staring at me in the rearview mirror with a grin accompanied by an odd little wink.

I do not ask what for. And I do not ask her to turn the "music" down even though it is a smidgen loud. The truck is extremely noisy too, coughing and spluttering its way to the top of the hill, and I wonder when it last had a service. I check my seat belt for a second time and try not to worry about it. Abby often said that I needed to learn to go with the flow, and at least the locals seem friendly.

The road twists and turns and the view outside the window constantly changes. The higher we climb the more I can see, and every glimpse of the island is more surprising and breathtaking than the last. It might be small, but from here, it looks vast—a giant patchwork quilt of wild-looking grassy hills stitched with drystone walls. In the distance I can see trees displaying all the colors of autumn, an elaborate rainbow of amber, brown, and gold. Farther still I can see a mountain the color of maple syrup, dripping with waterfalls. It is pockmarked with boulders, all dressed in blotches of bright green moss. Fall has always been my favorite time of year and October has always been my favorite month.

I spot a ruin of an old cottage—nothing left of it except four uneven gray stone walls, with long grass growing where the floor would once have been. I hope the cabin is in better shape—preferably with a roof—and I'm relieved when the ferrywoman keeps driving. We approach another loch, the water so still that it mirrors the sky perfectly, reflecting the bright blue canvas dotted in fluffy clouds. Until one of them hides the sun. Then the world instantly becomes a darker version of itself. The road looks as though it has been chiseled out of the mountain in places, with steep banks of moss-covered granite rising up on either side. We are now sandwiched between fields sprinkled with sheep. Angry-looking ones, with devilish horns and black faces.

"Our version of lawn-mower robots. They keep the grass nice and trimmed," my new friend says with another cheerful wink.

"This is awfully good of you. I'm very grateful," I say, thanking her again.

"How can something good be awful?" she asks without a hint of irony. "I'm Sandy MacIntyre, by the way. I own the island ferry but I'm also the sheriff here on Amberly. I should have introduced myself before kidnapping you and your dog."

"You sail the ferry *and* you're the sheriff? That must keep you busy."

"Not especially. The ferry only runs twice a week, and that's if the weather is good, which it often isn't. And there is no crime on the island."

That sounds like a ridiculous claim.

"No crime at all?" I ask.

"No. Everyone knows everyone. There could only ever be twenty-five suspects."

"What about visitors?"

"Luckily we don't get too many of those," she says, staring at me again. "I didn't catch *your* name."

Because she never asked for it.

"Grady Green," I tell her, instantly wishing I had made up something different, but if she recognizes my name she hides it well. I've always felt a bit uncomfortable with people knowing who I am and what I do, so it's nice to know I can still be anonymous.

"And what brings you to Amberly, Grady?"

I have nowhere else to go and my agent took pity on me.

"I'm a writer," I say.

"Are you now? Good for you. Good. For. You." She nods a few times then looks back at the winding road. "We've had a fair few writers stay on the island. I've lost count of all the creative souls I've met over the years who come here for a holiday and never leave. They seem to find the place inspiring. What sort of books do you write?"

I don't write anything anymore. I can't remember how.

"Oh, wow. *This* is beautiful," I say as we turn a corner revealing a spectacular view of a valley below. I've always been good at changing the subject when the subject is one I don't like. We are approaching a small village surrounded by craggy emerald hills. There is a forest in the distance and, beyond that, the sea. I notice that the sky has darkened to a threatening shade of gray, and I fear Sandy might have been right about a storm.

"Aye, it is the most beautiful place in the world," she replies, with a look of wonder as though she too is seeing Amberly for the first time.

There is an ancient-looking old stone church called Saint Lucy's in the middle of the village, with an elaborate wooden lychgate. An immaculate village green with striped grass separates the church from a row of three small, pretty thatched cottages, and I can see that The Stumble Inn is indeed a pub. The black van I remember from the ferry with its Highland cow logo is parked outside a shop and several people are helping to unload it, carrying boxes of what looks like fresh food inside.

"The island might be small, but she takes care of her own, and I'm sure you'll find anything you need," Sandy says. "We all help each other out. I hope you're community minded; it's the best way to be. Everyone that can helps to unload the weekly deliveries, which is what you can see happening now. Many hands make light work, as my grandpa used to say. That's Christie's Corner

Shop, the only general store on Amberly. It's also the post office should you have something you want to send in the mail. The islanders own everything on the island—you won't find any supermarkets or fast-food establishments here—only *local* businesses run by *local* people. If you have any special requests for food—or drink—during your stay, Cora Christie can order them for you, and they'll be on the next ferry over—"

"About the ferry, I noticed that the timetable only showed sailings *to* Amberly. There didn't seem to be any details for sailings going back to the mainland. Is there a timetable for the return journey somewhere?"

"You're not leaving so soon, are you?" she asks.

"No. But—"

"Well, once you've been here for a little while, you'll probably . . ."

I stop hearing what she is saying because I see her again.

My wife.

"Stop the truck," I say, interrupting Sandy mid-speech.

"What?"

"Stop the truck. *Please*."

As soon as she does, I fling open the rusty door and run back toward the black van I saw Abby climb out of. I hurry inside the shop, but she isn't there. Everyone who is stops and stares at me as though I am a madman.

"Where did she go?" I ask nobody in particular.

"Who?" asks an elderly lady in a shopkeeper's apron standing behind the cash register. Her eyes are too big for her face, and her pale skin is heavily lined.

"My . . . there was a woman. She just got out of the van and came in here wearing a red coat and carrying a box—"

"You must mean Meera," the shopkeeper says, looking increasingly perplexed. She squints at a woman holding a box of vegetables—who I am guessing is Meera—who is indeed wearing a red coat. Just like the person I saw on the ferry. Just like Abby the last time I saw her. She has the same dark hair too, but other than that, she looks *nothing* like my wife. I glance around, but nobody else inside the shop fits the description. This woman must be who I saw.

"I'm sorry, I . . ."

I feel as though I might be losing my mind, and everyone in the shop is staring at me in a way that suggests they agree. The police found Abby's red coat not long after she disappeared. Nobody is walking around wearing it now. It's all in my head.

"Sorry," I say again, retreating as fast as possible. "I thought you were someone else."

I have to stop doing this.

I imagine seeing Abby everywhere.

And I still think about her every day and every night; I don't know how not to. I lie awake wondering if she is dead or whether she might be alive somewhere, living a life without me. If she is alive, I wonder where she is and if she misses me as much as I miss her.

She is a wound that won't heal.

"What was that about?" asks Sandy when I get back in the truck.

"I thought I saw someone I knew."

I don't want to say any more than that. I already feel like a crazy fool. She starts to drive out of the village, sighs, and shakes her head.

"People always see ghosts on this island."

SAME DIFFERENCE

This is not a great start. We spend the rest of the journey in awkward silence; awkward for me at any rate. I'm so embarrassed. Sandy has shown such kindness and must think she's offered a ride to a crazy man. I wanted to make a good first impression, but I fear I have made the opposite.

The truck hugs the coast for a while, and I stare out of the window at the endless beaches, all deserted. Every time we turn a corner the coast changes into something new and even more beautiful. A relentless sea rushing to meet shimmering sand, gray pebbles, or crumbling cliffs. The road gets progressively steeper until it eventually levels out, winding its way around the top of a craggy hill. A line of silver birches appears to be growing out of the rock, leaning away from the sea, and they look more like witches' broomsticks than trees, blown sideways by the westerly wind. One of the trees is so close to the edge of an eroded overhang it looks like it might fall into the sea below at any moment. Clinging to the cliff for dear life.

It starts to rain and Sandy turns on the windscreen wipers. The sound they make translates into words inside my head:

Screech and scrape. Screech and scrape. Screech and scrape.

Run away. Run away. Run away.

I shake off the negative thoughts and try to replace them with positive ones, but I am out of practice. There is *nothing* not to like about this place, and I am lucky to be here. I tell myself the same thing over and over until it sounds like the truth.

We turn off what passes for a main road, drive down a dirt track, and it isn't long until we're surrounded by a canopy of tall trees, which seem to block out almost all of the sun. I'm guessing this is the forest I saw on the map. They are the most enormous trees I have ever seen, taller than a house, and some of the trunks are wider than Sandy's pickup truck. I'm guessing they must be hundreds of years old and will still be here centuries after I am gone. The thought makes me feel small and insignificant.

"Redwoods. Nature's giants," Sandy says.

"Sorry?"

"These ancient trees are special. The island is one of the few places you can find them in the UK. They can live for thousands of years and weather almost any storm, but they're a rare sight thanks to mankind. That's why we protect them, and everything else that is magical about this place, from people who might do them harm. These magnificent trees are why visitor numbers are restricted and why we don't normally allow visitors on the island at all out of season," she says, staring at me in the rearview mirror.

"I thought redwoods were native to America."

"You thought right. I'm impressed. Nice to meet an educated chap for a change. A few hundred years ago, an explorer called Agnes Amberly brought some saplings back after a voyage across the Atlantic that almost killed her. Agnes spent a lifetime sailing to all the different corners of the earth before coming home to Scotland and declaring this little island the most beautiful place in the world. A cautionary tale if ever I heard one."

"Why cautionary?"

"People rarely know what they have until they lose it. They spend their lives searching for a better one, wanting more, needing more, blind to the fact that they already had it all. I think sometimes it's only when something gets *taken* from a person that they appreciate what they had. Agnes spent almost her entire life in search of the perfect place to call home before understanding it was here all along. The Isle of Amberly was renamed in honor of the woman who planted the first one of these magnificent trees and the redwoods have been here ever since, not that anyone on the island calls them by their formal name."

"What *do* you call them?"

"Ghost trees," Sandy says. "I don't know why," she adds before I can ask. "Agnes Amberly was ahead of her time. She understood how important trees were to the future of the planet and the future of us, but the men in charge back then didn't listen. Those in charge of things today still don't. You soon learn, living in a place like this, that we're all connected. Trees grow down as well as up and I think it's the same with people. The more we grow up, the more we learn to feel down. Do you know what I mean?" I'm not sure that I do but nod anyway. "Some trees shed their leaves and lose almost everything every year, but then they grow again. Side by side. People could learn a lot from trees. Are you married?" Sandy asks, staring at me again in the rearview mirror.

"Yes. But . . ." This isn't a conversation I'm ready for or know how to have with a stranger. "I'm here on my own."

"No need to say more. I hear you. Wives! Can't live with them, can't live with them. Am I right?"

She laughs at her own joke and I force my face to attempt a smile. I am used to this now, people making comments that make me want to scream.

I lost my wife, the person I loved most in the world, and without her life feels meaningless. Abby was my person. She was my everything and when you lose your everything there simply is nothing left. I want to tell Sandy that when it comes to the people you love, you can't live without them. But I don't.

I keep my thoughts to myself because silence cannot be mis-quoted.

Sandy takes another turn, persuading the pickup truck to squeeze down an even narrower, bumpier, muddier track. The heavy rain stops as abruptly as it started, as though someone just switched it off, and the dark clouds are soon swept from the sky by a determined breeze. I can see the sun again.

"We have our own microclimate on the island," she says. "The weather here is fickle and changes its mind an awful lot. Best be prepared for anything."

"This weather really is something."

"No, I mean you. Now. We're here. This is the Edge of the World, as Charlie liked to call it," she says. "The rest of us just call it The Edge." I peer out of the windows but see nothing but trees. "You're on your own from here, I'm afraid. This is as close as I can get; the cabin can only be accessed on foot these days. Charles Whittaker liked to be alone, and he took his privacy seriously. It's been a few years since he passed away in what he called his 'writing shed' and it was a wee while before anyone knew. Nobody has lived here since and I imagine the place might be a tad dusty and in need of a clean, but you're a grown lad. I'm sure you're not afraid of a few cobwebs or a bit of dirt. The cabin is as rural as they come and ridiculously rustic on the outside, but don't let that fool you. Old Charlie boy liked his creature comforts, so the place has power and hot water thanks to solar panels and . . . well, you'll see. It gets very cold out here at night, just to warn you. Very cold and very dark. But you'll be fine. Or you won't, and you'll be wanting to get the next ferry back. Head north from here, and you'll find the cabin soon enough."

"Right, thank you," I say, clambering from the truck. Columbo leaps out behind me and runs off to explore the forest without a backward glance. I wish I were as fearless as my dog. I grab the rest of the bags and turn 360 degrees. "So . . . north then?" I say to Sandy, hoping for a clue as to which way that might be.

"Do you not have a compass?" she asks, as though it is something everyone should carry at all times.

"Didn't know I'd need one."

She shakes her head again. "It's little wonder so many people feel lost these days. You can't find your way if you don't know where you're supposed to be going."

"There might be one on my phone," I say, taking my mobile out of my pocket. I feel my cheeks burn when I see nothing but a black screen. "The battery is dead . . . I haven't been able to charge it since—"

"Phones rarely work on the island anyway. There's no mobile signal. No internet. Here, take this," Sandy says, reaching for the glove compartment. She unfolds a small pamphlet revealing a map of Amberly, the same design as the one I saw when I got off the ferry. Then she speaks to me in a tone more suitable for an intellectually challenged child. "North, south, east, west," she says, stabbing the map four times with her finger. "And here's a compass you can borrow," she adds, handing me a contraption I haven't seen since I was a Boy Scout. "This island is only six miles long and five miles wide . . ." She looks me up and down. "Even for someone like you, it's easy enough to walk from one end to the other in a few hours. Also easy enough to get lost, so I suggest keeping the map and the compass with you at all times. Stay away from The Orphans; those hills are steeper than you'd think. There's no mountain rescue here, no police or 'emergency services.' Just *me*. And I'm already busier than midges on a nudist beach. I'll pick you up for dinner at seven P.M. tomorrow."

"Thank you. What?"

"Dinner. You do *eat*, don't you?"

"Yes, but—"

"Good. My sister is very fond of authors. She runs the island library. Me, I couldn't care less. Writer, bus driver, same difference. But she'll want to meet you, and I'll never hear the end of it until she does, so best for all concerned to get it over and done with. Just don't tell her I had a sausage sandwich for breakfast; she worries about my cholesterol."

I realize I brought the dog's food, but not my own—anything I had with me is still in the car back on the mainland, and it didn't occur to me to grab a few supplies from the shop on the way here. Maybe dinner with some friendly locals isn't such a terrible idea.

"Seven o'clock tomorrow night it is," I say. "Looking forward to it already."

"I wouldn't if I were you. The food will be shite. My sister can't cook to save her life, but she does like to try, and the world loves a trier. Good to meet you, Grady Green," Sandy says out of the truck window before driving away.

I fiddle with the compass and start heading north. The trees seem to shiver as I approach them as though trying to communicate. The leaves take it in turns to rustle and whisper, and when I look up the sun seems to sparkle through the gaps between them, offering tiny glimpses of blue sky. I experience a comforting and unfamiliar sensation and it takes me a while to identify the feeling.

It feels like coming home.

Which makes no sense.

Because I've never been here before.

PASSIVE-AGGRESSIVE

wander through the woods and start to question what I am doing here. Perhaps my decision to pack up, leave London, and drive to a remote Scottish island I've never heard of was a little hasty. There is nothing resembling an actual path through the trees, but I follow the compass and try not to trip over the bumpy network of exposed roots covered in moss. The forest feels magical. If I wasn't so tired, and if my hands weren't full of bags, I'd stop to take it all in. Try to capture this moment. The start of my new life, the one I am determined to live.

Dappled light occasionally illuminates places to pass between the trunks and branches, and when I look up I can see glimmers of blue sky. Spiders' webs decorated with tiny raindrops sparkle in the redwoods, which are even more impressive and intimidating up close, their sheer size reminding me of how small I am. Columbo, who normally runs ahead, comes to stand by my side. I stop too, worrying that we might be lost. The woodland scene looks the same in every direction, and the trees are all starting to look identical.

But then I see it. An old log cabin in the woods.

There is an expensive-looking slate sign protruding from the muddy earth. When I read the words THE EDGE, I feel an overwhelming sense of relief to have found what I was looking for. I don't know a huge amount about the author who used to live here. I'm not sure anyone does. Charles Whittaker rarely gave interviews or attended events. He didn't have any social media accounts—other than those run by his publishers—and was once quoted as saying that authors should be "read and not heard." By all accounts, he was a man who liked to be left alone. Kitty said he was always like that, even at the start of his career before he was a big deal. She said he wasn't rude, just private. I'm not so sure. He refused to attend book festivals, never accepted an award in person, and once failed to turn up for his own book launch. The man took the writing recluse stereotype to the extreme.

The cabin looks old and rustic, but it has a certain charm about it. At least, that's what I'm telling myself. A door separates two windows, making the front of the cabin look like a face. The roof is covered in turf and moss with a scattering of wildflowers growing on top, and it has a black chimney sticking out of it. I also notice a neat stack of chopped firewood by the front door accompanied by a rusty axe. There is an old timber shed in the distance—almost as big as the cabin—and I wonder what can be inside, but first I want to check out The Edge. It's a strange name for somewhere in the middle of a forest.

The wind has completely died down but the tall trees continue to sway and creak and groan. I hear something else too. It *sounds* like the sea but it can't be; I'm surrounded by trees in every direction, their branches stretching high above and all around me. I follow the unexpected sound of crashing waves to the rear of the cabin and see that it is perched on a cliff. Almost on the edge. The name suddenly starts to make sense. There is a small decked area with a wooden bench, and the ocean view is spectacular but I daren't get too near to the verge. Even from where I am standing I can see that it is a steep drop down to the rocks below, and there is no safety barrier to prevent a person from falling to their death.

"Stay close, Columbo," I say.

The dog does what I tell him to do. He is the only living creature ever to do so.

The rear of the property is very different from the front of the cabin, which looks traditional and old. The back wall is almost entirely made of glass doors, presumably designed to showcase the sea view. Like at the front, all of the curtains and blinds are drawn, preventing me from seeing inside. This seems like the most idyllic spot, hidden away in a secluded corner of a forest *and* with spectacular sea views. But from the state of the crumbling cliff, I don't think this place will be here forever.

And that's okay because neither will I.

I search inside my satchel for the list of instructions Kitty sent me. Apparently the key is under the doormat so I head back to the front of the cabin, but when I look beneath the welcome mat there is nothing there. I try the handle and the door swings open with a spooky creak. It wasn't even locked. Perhaps there is no need in a place like this; Sandy did say there was no crime on the island. What a comforting thought if it is true.

I feel a strange sense of apprehension as I peer inside. Not just because of where I am, and the fact that Sandy mentioned nobody has lived here since Charles died, but also because of what I came here to do. What if I *can't* write another novel? I don't know how to do anything else. My bank account is almost completely empty and I have nowhere else to go. Writing has saved me from myself more than once, and I hear Kitty's words inside my head: *It's the not giving up that separates the winners from the losers.*

And she's right. I mustn't give up.

Can't waste this opportunity to get my life back on track.

I step into the cabin slowly. It's too dark to see inside with all the curtains and blinds still drawn, and I'm unsure what I might find given that the place has been empty for several years. The floorboards creak and groan a half-hearted welcome and I dump the bags. Then I blink, trying to adjust to the gloom while my fingers feel for a light switch. When I find one, I am relieved that it works. Then I'm pleasantly surprised by what I see.

What looks like an old log cabin on the outside has been completely renovated and transformed into something beautiful and modern inside, but still retaining the original features. It's one big open-plan space, with a small kitchen on the left-hand side, a large metal-framed bed on the right, and a comfy sofa in the middle facing the huge glass doors at the back. I open all the curtains and blinds, which reveal an incredible 180-degree view of the ocean. This place takes the notion of a room with a view to another level and, from here, it really does look as though we are on the edge of the world.

When Kitty first mentioned an abandoned writing cabin, I pictured something rustic filled with dust and cobwebs. This is nothing like that. Smart-looking bookcases line any spare wall space, their shelves neatly crammed full of books—paperbacks, mostly—and arranged according to color, which surprises me. The bare, sanded floorboards are hidden in places with a series of sheepskin rugs, and wooden beams run the length of the ceiling. It smells of scented candles and open fires and . . . coffee, I think to myself, spotting an expensive-looking machine on the kitchen counter. There are fresh flowers on the dresser, and the bed has been made. Everything is neat, tidy, and spotlessly clean. Not a cobweb in sight. The penny drops. Kitty must have paid someone to come in, clean the place, and prepare it for my arrival. That woman thinks of everything. I should send something to thank her. Ideally a new novel. I find my charger and plug in my mobile. Even if I can't use it to make calls, I'd like to take some photos of the place.

There is something unfamiliar looking on one of the pillows on the bed, and I take a closer look. At first, I don't recognize the round black object, but then I pick it up and see that it is a Magic

8 Ball. I had one when I was a child, it's not something I can imagine someone like Charles Whittaker owning, but people are full of surprises. I try to think of a question to ask it.

"Will I ever write another book?"

I turn the ball so the window faces upward and read what it says.

ASK AGAIN LATER.

At least it didn't say no.

Columbo is busy exploring our new surroundings and I do the same, heading straight for the old brass drinks trolley I spotted in the corner. I've had to downgrade my taste in alcohol since the money started running out, so I can't help feeling a bit excited to discover what must have been Charles Whittaker's whiskey collection. All the finest—and most expensive—bottles of scotch are here, and most are unopened. I tell myself it would be rude not to, then choose one of the crystal tumblers from the trolley and pour a small glass. When I taste it, I pour myself a large one. Then I open the sliding glass doors, sit on the sofa, take in the view, and enjoy the sound of nothing. Nothing except the sea. My wife would have hated it.

Abby thought I had a drinking problem. She demonstrated her disapproval with passive-aggressive silences and a series of tuts. It was one of the few things we always argued about, and we *did* disagree because it *isn't* a problem. At least, not for me. I started drinking when I was a teenager and I never really stopped. My nana died when I was still at school, I didn't have anyone else, and alcohol became a companion of sorts. Something to help me feel like me again when I couldn't remember who that was. It didn't make the overwhelming hurt go away, but it numbed my feelings of abandonment. I've been partial to a drink ever since and it was something Abby openly disapproved of. I confess that sometimes if she came home late—which she often did—I would be passed out on the sofa with a bottle and book beside me, but there are far worse things I could have been doing. She called me a cliché. I don't remember what I called her because I was drunk, but I always apologized when I was sober. I dished out *sorry*s like sweets at Halloween and she gobbled them all up, even the ones she didn't like the taste of.

Everyone is addicted to something because we all need a form of escapism, and alcohol is my drug of choice. I only drink in private—a happy consequence of having no family or friends—so nobody except the dog sees the state I sometimes get into. And it's not like I sit around drinking all day, just a little something in the evenings. To take the edge off. To help me sleep. To stop me from thinking about her.

There is a retro wooden record player in the corner of the room, and I wonder if it still works. I glance through the impressive vinyl collection, select an old favorite, and can't help smiling when the sound of Nina Simone fills the cabin. There's something Abby would have loved. I miss the way she danced when she thought nobody was looking. I miss so many things about her.

I find myself drawn to Charles Whittaker's writing desk. It's quite small, more like a child's desk, and the only things on it are a key, a red harmonica, a pretty box of matches with a robin on the front, and a square silver frame, which I pick up to take a closer look. I've never seen a framed paper napkin before. A message is scribbled on it in black Biro: *The only way out is to write.* It's an odd thing to find on the desk of an author, but I think I understand what it means. There are small wooden drawers, and I can't help wondering what is inside. It feels wrong to look in someone else's desk, even if they are not around anymore, but I do it anyway. Dead people are the best at keeping secrets. The first drawer I open contains crisp, thick, white paper. The kind for writing important letters. The next drawer contains envelopes. The third contains pens. Perhaps that's all a good writer needs; paper and pens. I check out the wall of books next; it's like a library of the best novels ever written. They're all here, and I select a classic I think I might like to reread.

I pour myself another drink, lie on the sofa, listen to the beautiful sound of sea infused with Nina Simone, and feel myself start to relax. The whiskey melts on my tongue, slides down my throat, and warms me from the inside out. I could get used to this: the views, the solitude, the whiskey collection. Three months isn't long to write a novel, but if I can, perhaps I could stay longer. Maybe I could live on the island and never have to see or speak to anyone ever again, surrounded by books and writing my own. I think that might be an almost perfect life. Kitty is so clever; this place is exactly what I needed.

I close my eyes, savoring the moment, until Columbo ruins it by barking.

"Shh, Columbo," I say, keeping my eyes closed.

He ignores me and barks twice as loud.

"What is it?" I ask, standing up to see him scratching furiously at one of the sheepskin rugs. "Stop that right now." I lift the rug to prevent him from damaging it, but he just starts scratching at the wooden floorboards it was covering instead. "Stop," I say again, and this time he lies down with his head between his front paws, staring at the same spot on the cabin floor. I look closer and see that the board he was pawing at is loose. There are no nails holding it in place and it comes up without much effort. There is something there, under the floorboards. It's too dark to see clearly so I use the light on my phone. Then I take a step back.

It's a collection of small bones resting on a red velvet cushion.

And the bones are in the shape of a hand.

RANDOM ORDER

A m I really looking at human bones? I don't know for sure, and I don't know what to do about it if I am. They've been arranged on a cushion as though the skeletal hand is pointing at something, but I can't see what.

There are a finite number of things I turn to when life is too stressful, and my life is always too stressful, so I pour myself another drink. I imagine Abby's disapproval as I fill my glass. I can still see her face when I close my eyes, still feel her hand in mine, still hear her voice inside my head. Sometimes I think she is lying next to me in bed at night, and when I wake and remember that she isn't, it feels like losing her all over again. People say time is a great healer, but it only seems to hurt more the longer she is gone.

The whiskey helps calm my nerves—it always does—and I take another look at what I have found, telling myself that there is no need to panic or let this unexpected plot twist spoil things. In my experience, there is no such thing as a random order of events; everything happens when it happens for a reason, even if the reason is hard to see at the time. I'm sure there is a perfectly logical explanation for all of this, and that the bones are nothing to worry about. They're probably not even real.

Constantly lying to yourself requires a special variety of stamina.

I grab one of the metal tools from beside the wood-burning stove and use it to lever up the next floorboard. Then I stand and stare at what is hidden underneath.

I haven't discovered any more bones—which is a relief—but there is something else.

At first, it just looks like a pile of A4 paper covered in dust and dirt. But when I blow the cobwebs away, it's clear that I'm looking at a manuscript. I take my reading glasses from my jacket pocket and crouch down until I am close enough to read the title page:

BOOK TEN
By Charles Whittaker

I remember what Kitty said about Charles never finishing his tenth book, the one he thought was his best, but here it is. She also said that he never told anyone anything about it, including her, not even the title. I pour myself another drink—it helps me think—and consider the options. Charles Whittaker was once a bestselling author, a giant in the mystery and thriller genre in his day, but he hadn't published a book for years. If he had written what he thought was his best novel, why would he hide it beneath the floorboards in his writing cabin? As always, I wonder what my wife would do and wish that I could ask her.

I pick up my mobile even though I know there is no signal. I paid to keep Abby's phone working all this time in case someone called with information about what happened to her, but also so I could hear her again when the calls went to voicemail. Abby's number has always been saved in my contacts as THE WIFE. It was something we used to laugh about. I dial it now, just as I often do when feeling lost, but it doesn't go through. I feel so alone as I stare down at the manuscript again.

There is no harm in reading it.

That's what I tell myself as I carefully lift the book as though it were buried treasure.

I can't think straight with the bones in my eyeline, so I cover them back up with the loose floorboards, then cover the floor with the sheepskin rug. What I need now is coffee. I don't have any milk so it'll have to be black. Most of the cupboards are empty, but I find some pods that are still in date and—with a little jiggery-pokery—figure out how to use the machine. Then I settle down on the couch and start reading.

It is 3:00 A.M. when I read the final page.

I have barely moved from the sofa except to feed the dog his dinner and feed myself—the entire packet of milk chocolate digestives I shoved in my jacket pocket earlier. I stopped reading only to lock the door with the key I found on the desk, and to light the wood-burning stove—Sandy was right, this place does get chilly once the sun goes down. I'm grateful to whoever left the pretty box of matches with a robin on the front for me to find. The crackling fire, Columbo's gentle snores, and the sound of the sea outside combine to make a soothing soundtrack for my tired, befuddled brain. I lean back and close my eyes, just for a moment, my mind too restless to entertain the possibility of sleep. I'm still trying to process what I just read, but it's undoubtedly one of the best books I've ever had the pleasure of reading, and nobody else even knows it exists.

The only question now is what to do with it.

DEFINITELY MAYBE

One Week Before She Disappeared

ABBY

Trapped. That's what I am. The woman I have come to speak to calls me by my maiden name, and the sound of it surprises me. As though it is something I have forgotten. At work, I am a different version of myself—someone confident and well respected—but at home, I am just *the wife*. It's like I am playing a role I didn't audition for, but nobody tells you that the script of your life sometimes changes when you say "I do."

I feel like I lost part of myself when I got married.

As though once he had me, he didn't want me anymore.

It's as if I'm invisible.

I've always been a private person. I know a lot of people believe in counseling and that talking to therapists *helps*, but I've never been one to share my problems. Until now. The woman I've made an appointment to speak to doesn't look like a therapist. She has long blond hair and is dressed in black, as though she might be off to a funeral once she has finished listening to me. I don't know if I can tell her the truth, but I'm so tired of pretending. She *looks* like someone you can trust, and she *sounds* kind, patiently waiting for me to tell her why I am here.

"Take your time," says the woman in black.

Then she checks her watch.

It's okay. I'm just as good at pretending not to be offended as I am at pretending to be fine. I take in my surroundings. This is not a nice-looking office. There is no stylish furniture or calming paintings on the wall. It is a place that has never seen better days.

"I'm sorry, I'm not sure where to start," I tell her.

"It's okay." She smiles and leans forward, tilting her head so that her long blond hair falls over her shoulder. "I'm here to listen whenever you feel ready." The smile doesn't quite reach her eyes, and I wonder if listening to other people's problems makes her feel better about her own. "Maybe start at the beginning," she suggests.

Which seems wrong because this feels like the end.

We are not the same people we were when we met.

I think you're in my seat.

Those were the first words my husband ever said to me.

I wonder what will be the last.

"I think you're in my seat," said an unfriendly voice.

I looked up from my book and saw a man staring down at me. He was a little older than I am. Attractive, but not in an obvious way, with dark hair and intense eyes. He was in good shape, well enough dressed, and wore the expression of a man who knew what he wanted from the world and how to get it.

"I don't think so," I replied and returned to my novel.

I've been traveling on planes since I was a child. My mother first sent me away on one—alone, because she said she could no longer stand to look at me—when I was ten years old. I was not a novice traveler and I knew I was in the right seat. But he didn't move, just stood there staring at me, pulling the face of a person not used to being ignored.

"Sorry, you're obviously reading something good . . ."

Trying to, I wanted to say but bit my tongue.

"My boarding pass says twenty-five A," he blathered on, holding up the whole queue of people trying to board the plane behind him. "And that's where you're sitting."

Why do some men always think they are right, despite having so much previous experience of being wrong? I glanced up from my page, again, to look at the boarding pass he was holding irritatingly close to my face. I had a curious urge to grab it, tear it up, and throw the pieces in the air.

"You're in twenty-five F. This is twenty-five A," I replied and returned to my book.

So it was definitely not love at first sight.

There was no apology as he took his seat on the other side of the aisle. Other passengers continued to file past looking for their seats—hopefully the correct ones—but nobody sat down between us, and I could *feel* him still looking at me.

"I've read that book, by the way," he said from the other side of the plane. I ignored him and pretended to carry on reading. "It has a very disappointing ending."

"Thanks for letting me know," I replied, still not looking up.

"I could tell you if you like; save you some time?"

I deployed the look I reserve for people who irritate me more than is tolerable. A look I only use when I *want* someone to know that I hate them.

"No. Thank you," I said, hoping he would get the message and that would be the end of it. Finally, someone sat in the seat next to mine, coming between us and blocking seat 25F's view of me and my reading choices.

"Excuse me," I heard him say to my new neighbor. "We're actually traveling together." To my surprise, and horror, he meant me. "Would you mind swapping so I can sit beside my friend?"

I was not his *friend*. I was not his anything.

"Of course," said the man who had just sat down next to me, already unfastening his seat belt.

"Oh no," I protested. "You really don't have to do that—"

"It's no bother; I don't mind."

I *did*.

My *friend* strapped himself into the seat next to mine and held out his hand, expecting me to shake it. I didn't. Instead, I glared at his hand and then at his face as though I found them both offensive. "I think we may have got off on the wrong foot," he said. "Can we start again? I always think traveling is a great way to meet new people."

"I could agree with you, but then we'd both be wrong."

"Ha! That's funny. Are you a comedian?"

"No," I said, staring back down at my book.

"What *do* you do?" he asked. When I didn't reply, he said, "I'm a writer."

And those were the words that changed everything because writers were my rock stars.

He instantly transformed from an irksome stain on the planet into a creature of wonder. We started chatting, and he was charming and witty and clever. The book I was reading went into the seat pocket and wasn't opened again. I have always had a soft spot for storytellers. I fall in love with their words; then I fall in love with the people who wrote them. I sometimes wish I could crawl inside their heads, hear their innermost thoughts, and see the world through their eyes.

It isn't as though I'd never met an author before. The woman who raised me—when my mother gave up trying to—worked in publishing. I spent my teenage years living in a home that was often filled with writers. She would host these amazing dinner parties in her London flat, and they would all sit around for hours talking, eating, drinking. I would sit on the top step of the staircase, secretly listening, wishing I was allowed to be down there having fun with them. Those "dinner parties" often went on until the sun came up and I had to get myself ready for school. I'd go to class exhausted but happy. It didn't matter to me whether they were million-copy bestsellers or award-winning novelists—though many of them were—they were all magicians of words, and that was my favorite kind of magic.

We talked so much when we first met on the plane that I barely noticed when it took off. When the flight attendant arrived with a trolley full of drinks, he ordered three: a cup of tea, a whiskey, and some water. I don't usually drink on flights, but I had some wine. I watched him pour a dash of cold water into his steaming cup of tea.

"I've never been a patient person," he said, by way of explanation even though I hadn't asked.

It was a night flight to New York, and before long the cabin was in darkness. Most of the other passengers seemed to be asleep already—travel cushions tucked under their heads, eye masks on—but we continued to whisper, like children excited to still be up long after bedtime. We spoke for hours, and I felt like I could talk to him forever about books, travel, life, anything. I wanted to know everything about him, what he thought and felt, to know if his view of the world was the same as mine. Have you ever met someone and just clicked? As though you had known them for years even though you had just met? That's how it felt. So I confess I was a little disappointed when he yawned, tilted his seat back as far as it would go, and said he might try to get some sleep. I worried that maybe I had imagined the chemistry between us.

Nobody was sitting in the aisle seat next to him, it was just the two of us on the row of three, and he offered me the spare blanket he had swiped from the empty one earlier. I took it, even though I didn't really want it, and tried not to sulk when he switched off the reading lights above our heads, plunging us into semidarkness like the rest of the plane. I attempted to get comfortable in the uncomfortable seat, turning my head to face him and closing my eyes. I kept feeling like he was watching me, but whenever I opened my eyes, his were closed. When I thought I saw his eyes start to open, I squeezed mine shut.

His face was so close to mine I could feel his breath. I opened my eyes a fraction and studied his features, his hair, his thick eyebrows and dark eyelashes, the shape of his nose, the shadow of stubble around his mouth, his lips. He seemed to be sleeping already, unlike me, so I turned away. It's strange how we sleep next to people we do not know on a plane, how we can allow ourselves to be that vulnerable when surrounded by strangers.

I thought I was imagining it at first.

A hand slowly slid beneath the thin blanket that was covering me. It came to rest just above my knee, and I didn't know what to do or how to react. I kept my face turned toward the window. The hand moved again, warm, strong fingers finding my skirt beneath the blanket and gently gathering up the material. Then the hand started to slide up my thigh. My eyes were shut, but I couldn't hide that I was breathing faster, my chest rising and falling. My thighs were closed together, blocking the hand, but I opened them just wide enough for it to go wherever it wanted. I only opened my eyes once, to check that the blanket was hiding what was happening beneath it and that nobody else could see. I opened my legs a little wider, and the fingers found their way inside my underwear. I didn't tell him to stop. I didn't want him to stop. The only time he did was when I gasped as his fingers slipped inside me. Only when I was silent did he carry on. His fingers moved tantalizingly slowly at first, stroking, exploring, plunging deeper until he reached the perfect rhythm. Ripples of pure pleasure made me want to cry out, but he stopped if I moved or made even the smallest sound. So I kept quiet, and I kept my eyes closed—even though I was sure his were open and looking at me— because I didn't want what he was doing to end.

Several hours later, when the cabin lights came back on and the flight attendants began serving breakfast, he acted as though nothing had happened, so I did too. We chatted—just as we had before—and when the plane landed we parted company with a simple,

"Nice to meet you."

There was no exchange of contact details.

No plans to meet again.

I felt confused, numb, and incredibly foolish for thinking I had met someone who liked me. Someone I could maybe learn to love. I looked for him in the queue for passport control and again at the baggage re-claim carousel, but he was gone. Only when I walked out into arrivals, overwhelmed by the sea of happy faces waiting for loved ones, did I see him again. He was holding a large bouquet and a box of chocolates and smiling in my direction. I smiled too.

"What are you doing?" I asked.

"I met a girl," he replied. "I wanted to buy her flowers."

"That's nice."

"She is. Smart and fun, too."

"Well, thank you."

"Can I take you out for dinner? I want to do this properly."

"It's eight o'clock in the morning; it's a little early."

"A second breakfast then?"

"Definitely maybe," I said and he grinned.

We spent an entire day walking around New York hand in hand and never ran out of things to talk about. He was late for a book event, and I was late for a meeting, but neither of us cared. We shared stories, laughed, ate, drank, and we made love that night in my hotel room. It wasn't just sex. It was something different from anything I had ever experienced before. Something more. We got married a year later.

It never occurred to me that I'd made a huge mistake. Until now.

I don't share any of this with the woman in black.

"I'm sorry. I think I might have wasted your time," I tell her. I stand up and gather my belongings, but she soothes and silences me with her kind words and her smile, and I realize just how good she is at this—getting people to trust her.

"I know it can be difficult to talk about the things that upset us," she says. "How about we start with one word to describe what brought you here today? The one thing that is troubling you the most."

"Trust," I blurt out.

"That's good," she says. "Is there someone you think about when you say that word?"

"My husband."

"You don't trust him anymore?"

"No, he doesn't trust me."

She frowns then, ruining her perfect face. "What makes you feel that way?"

"I've been lying to him, and I think he knows."

"Lying to him about what?" she asks.

"Everything."

MODESTLY AMBITIOUS

—◆—

GRADY

On the envelope, I scribble my agent's name and her office address. Then I seal it, and it feels as though the deed is done. I can't call or email her—there's no phone signal or internet—but I have put the writing paper and envelopes I found inside the desk to good use. It's late afternoon now, the sun already a little low in the sky. I could wait until tomorrow, but then I fear I might change my mind. I need to send the letter before I can talk myself out of doing what I have decided to do. So I grab the envelope addressed to Kitty, and Columbo's lead, and prepare to head out into the woods.

I open the cabin door and take a step back. It's as though the trees have crept closer overnight, surrounding the cabin and leaning toward it. It's eerily quiet as we trudge through the forest. Too quiet. An unnatural silence seems to permeate the space between the trees. A light breeze rustles the leaves of the branches high above my head almost as though the trees are whispering in a language I don't understand. Columbo repeatedly runs ahead then circles back, wagging his tail and panting so that it looks like he's smiling. His joy used to be contagious, but I'm completely exhausted having barely slept the last two nights.

The sunlight twinkles through the canopy of leaves, and I think I can see every shade of green. The forest floor is a carpet of moss and exposed roots and I soon learn to watch my step. I see what I think might be the entrance to a foxhole next to an enormous tree trunk and wonder what other creatures might be living here. The trees glitter with cobwebs decorated in droplets of dew, but something other than insects must have made this place their home. It's truly beautiful, but *something* feels not quite right. Almost as though the forest is holding its breath. Or hiding something. I remember the bones in the cabin but choose to forget them again. There is a reason why people paper over the cracks in their lives, or in this case, hide things beneath the floorboards. It's far easier to pretend your problems away if you can't see them. I feel as though I've been gifted the opportunity of a lifetime—I know I won't get another like it—and I can't let anything, or anyone, spoil this for me.

The sky darkens and the temperature seems to noticeably drop. The wind picks up and a sprinkling of tiny leaves fall from the sky like confetti. I watch one of them twist and turn and float on the breeze, an unwitting hostage to its surroundings. My own journey comes to a brief standstill while I check the compass and map Sandy gave me. As I stand in silence trying to see if I'm heading in the right direction, I finally figure out what is so strange about this forest. There are no birds. I haven't seen or heard a single one. But when I look up I do see another glimpse of blue sky, and note that Sandy wasn't kidding about the island's microclimate. The weather here alternates between sun, rain, and cloud, and none of them take their turn for long.

Columbo and I carry on until we emerge from the trees and reach a road I recognize from yesterday. It's the main road—though little more than a single-lane track hugging the coast—connecting one end of Amberly to the other. There are views of the island that I couldn't see from the truck yesterday. Tetris-like layers of pale gray rock guard this corner of the coast, like tall, uneven stepping stones, bleached by the sun and battered by the sea. The sort of thing children might want to play on but would fill me with dread. Funny how fear is something life teaches us. If we stick to the road we'll be safe enough, and eventually reach the village.

When we do, I stand on the ancient little stone bridge that crosses the pale gray ribbon of a river, and stare at the view. The map I've been using is almost an exact replica of what I can see now, and I look down at it again. The buildings are all drawn to scale and neatly labeled. Everything from Saint Lucy's church to the little thatched cottages is there. Even the landscape is remarkably accurate. When I look up at the real island the whole place has a feeling of . . . home. Somewhere I might like to stay. Despite being picture-perfect there are *no* people. No signs of life at all, which seems strange.

I see an old-fashioned red telephone box and feel a rush of excitement. I had forgotten about landlines in this age of mobile phones. I can call Kitty from the phone box! I rush over and pull open the red door, confused and dismayed when I see rows of shelves crammed full of secondhand books and a little wooden sign saying THE LIBRARY. There is still a phone, but when I lift the receiver there's no dial tone, only silence. I stab some of the redundant silver buttons but nothing happens, so I close the door and head across the road to Christie's Corner Shop. I remember Sandy saying it was also the post office, and I could do with getting a few supplies while I am here. A little bell tinkles above the entrance when I step inside.

"Hello again," says a woman I know must be Cora from the name badge pinned to her shopkeeper's apron. I guess she remembers me from our brief meeting yesterday when I thought I'd seen my wife walk into the shop. Cora Christie is old and a little frail-looking, and I wonder how she manages to run this place all by herself. She has a good crop of gray hair with corkscrew curls spilling out in all directions, and is dressed in green from head to toe, including green spectacles on the end of her upturned nose. Her eyes seem to sparkle with mischief, nestled beneath barely there eyebrows, and they are trained on me.

"There are no working phones on the island, I'm afraid," she says. "Not even the old-fashioned variety. A fishing trawler accidentally took out the communications cable on the ocean floor a few months ago; we've been even more cut off than normal since then while we wait for it to be repaired. But we're all very *community minded*. Anything you need, you just say the word," she adds with a smile. The old woman was clearly spying on me and doesn't even mind if I know it.

"I was hoping to stock up on a few things."

"Of course, be my guest."

She must have a hundred other badges pinned to her apron, and another catches my eye:

IT TOOK 80 YEARS TO LOOK THIS GOOD.

She sees me staring at it.

"Age is just a number!" she says with another grin.

I smile back, take a metal basket, and look around the shop. It doesn't take long. I grab a few essentials while I meander down the aisles—bread, butter, cheese, milk, eggs, potatoes—then I see the fridge full of "homemade" ready meals. The lamb hotpot looks tasty, so I put a couple in my basket. One thing I do need in order to write is food. Nobody wrote anything worth reading on an empty stomach. I add a couple of bags of ready-salted crisps and an extra-large bar of chocolate, which I intend to share with no one. I get some dog treats for Columbo too.

Cora tuts when I return to the till. "None of your five-a-day in there. We've got lots of lovely fresh fruit and veg, only came in on the ferry yesterday. How will you write well if you don't eat well?" I frown at this stranger, wondering how she can possibly know who I am and what I do. "You are *the author*, aren't you?" she asks.

I guess news travels fast in a place like this.

I used to be modestly ambitious, but I don't tend to volunteer what I do for a living these days. People are either overimpressed or completely underwhelmed when they meet me, and neither reaction is great for my fragile ego.

"I am an author, yes, and you're quite right; we are what we eat," I say, grabbing a bag of apples I don't want.

"I guess that makes you a lamb," Cora says, scanning the hot-pot. She chuckles and two dimples make themselves at home on her face, which reminds me of my nana, the woman who raised me. She was the only person I considered family and I still miss her, even though it has been decades since she passed away. Nana would have been around Cora's age had she not died so young. They are the same height too, and I find myself staring at this stranger as though she might be something more than that. Cora looks sad all of a sudden, a pattern of concern decorating her features. I realize that her face might be mirroring my own and tell myself to snap out of it. "Also, someone mentioned that this was the place to come if I wanted to post something . . ."

"It is indeed," she says, putting my purchases into a tote bag, something else I didn't want but seem to have been charged for. It says I LOVE AMBERLY on the side. "Do you want to send whatever it is first class or second?"

"First class please. It's just a letter," I say, taking it out of my pocket.

Cora snatches it from me, and I see that even her fingernails are painted green. She places the envelope on a small set of scales—despite it being a standard size and weighing almost nothing—then holds up a contraption with different-size holes. She slides the envelope through each one, starting with the "large parcel" opening first, even though it is obvious that the envelope will fit through the slimmest slot.

"Is it important?" she asks.

It might help me get my life back.

"Yes. I suppose it is," I tell her.

She looks at the envelope, eyes filled with suspicion. "Want to send it registered?" she whispers, as though someone else might hear even though the shop is empty.

"No. Standard first class is fine. I'm guessing it will go on the next ferry?"

"First class will go tomorrow. On the mail boat."

"There's a boat just for mail?"

I hear what sounds like the crackle of a walkie-talkie beneath the counter, and Cora—who has, until now, seemed like an unflappable woman—looks flustered. "Can I get you anything else?" she asks, checking the time and hurrying to put the rest of my purchases in the bag before thrusting it in my direction.

"No," I say, paying the bill and taking my things. "Thank you."

"You take care now," she replies as I start to leave the shop, and the kind words sound more like a threat. She follows me, practically chasing me out of there, still clutching my envelope in her bony fingers, which remind me of gnarled twigs in the forest. The bell above the door tinkles to mark my departure and as soon as I am out she slams it shut. At least Columbo, who has been waiting outside, looks happy to see me. He wags his tail so hard you would think I'd been gone for hours, not minutes. I give him one of the dog treats I just bought, throwing it in the air for him to catch, and we start to walk away. But then I hear the crackle of a walkie-talkie again from the other side of the shop door and, unless I am imagining it, the sound of someone laughing. A quiet, sinister-sounding cackle. When I turn around, I see that the sign in the window now says CLOSED.

DEAFENING SILENCE

The Stumble Inn looks inviting, and I wouldn't say no to a drink before the long walk back, but when I try the pub door, it's locked. The sign in the window says CLOSED, even though I'm sure I could hear the clink of glasses and the murmurings of people talking inside only a moment ago. I wander through the village and discover that the rest of the shops are closed as well, all of them, which seems strange for this time of day. Given that there is nowhere else to go, I cross the village green and start heading toward the cabin.

That's when I hear ringing.

It takes me a moment to translate the sound as I slowly spin around trying to locate its source: the old red telephone box.

The phone inside *does* work. I can hear it. Which means I could call Kitty.

I sprint across the grass, Columbo running alongside thinking this is a game, then I yank the door open. I'm out of breath, but the sound of ringing is even louder now and I grab the receiver.

At first I don't hear anything or anyone on the other end of the line.

Then I hear what sounds like the sea.

"Grady, it's me," says a distant voice I haven't heard for a long time.

"Abby?"

"Can you hear me?" she asks, her voice so quiet I barely can.

"Abby? Is that you?"

The line crackles and I think I've lost her but then she speaks again.

"Grady, I'm so cold. It's so dark here. Why won't you come and find me?"

She sounds so far away.

"Where are you?"

"It's so cold and so dark—"

The line goes dead.

But I can still hear a dial tone.

There must be some way to reconnect the call.

I stare at the receiver in my fingers. My hand is trembling. All of me is trembling. I hang up and when I lift the phone to my ear again it doesn't make a sound. It's completely dead now. I try once more and this time I do think I can hear something, the sound of the sea again. But then it starts to sound like the wind howling outside and I realize that's all it is. Did I imagine hearing a voice?

Someone knocks on the door of the phone box and I literally jump off the ground.

"Are you okay?" asks Cora Christie, peering in at me through the glass. She's wearing a green coat and a green woolly hat and appears to be heading home for the day. "This phone is broken, has been for months now, I told you that already," she says, pointing at the OUT OF ORDER sign with a green fingernail.

"I thought I heard . . ." From the look on her face I think it might be best to stop talking.

I'm already worried that the whole island will think I am crazy.

I remember that I haven't slept for a very long time. Maybe

my mind is just getting more creative with the tricks it insists on playing on me. I've imagined seeing my missing wife before, maybe now I'm starting to hear her.

"Thought I might just borrow a book," I say, picking up a random paperback.

Cora nods but her beady eyes are still full of suspicion. "Good for you," she mumbles before sticking her hands in her pockets and walking away.

When she is out of sight, I press the buttons on the phone one more time, just in case.

But there is nothing except a deafening silence.

I think I really am losing my mind.

The sky has already dressed itself for twilight by the time we reach the forest. I find my way without using the compass, and as soon as we are inside I pour myself a large glass of scotch. My hands are still shaking, my head is pounding, and I don't feel at all well. I know it's an old-fashioned concept, but husbands are supposed to protect their wives and I didn't. I know what happened wasn't my fault, but I still sometimes blame myself. I should have done more to keep her safe.

Everyone had their theories about her disappearance at the time. Her friends, the press, the police. The large amounts of cash that Abby withdrew from our joint account made other people—including Kitty—think that my wife left me. I still have no idea what she needed all that money for, despite searching every inch of our home for clues, but I'll never believe that version of events.

We loved each other more than any other couple I know.

I know that even if nobody else does.

Something happened to Abby, something bad. And until I know where she is and whether she is okay I don't think my life can ever return to anything resembling normal. I need to know the truth. I see the Magic 8 Ball and decide to give it another try, picking it up to ask a question.

"I must have imagined it but . . . did I hear Abby on the phone in the village?"

Two words appear on the screen: VERY DOUBTFUL.

I nod as though a toy has just confirmed my deepest fears: I *am* going mad.

Maybe it's the tiredness catching up on me.

Perhaps it's the result of still being so desperate to know what happened to her.

Or it's possible my mind has broken due to the stress caused by what I've just done.

Seems to me I had three options when I found Charles Whittaker's secret tenth novel:

Tell Kitty what I have found.

Tell Kitty I've had a great idea, then steal Charles's book and
    pretend it is mine.

Tell Kitty nothing.

I always tell my agent everything—writing can be a lonely business, and I don't have anyone else to talk to—so the third option wasn't really an option at all. And, until relatively recently, I've always told my agent the truth. I ask the Magic 8 Ball another question.

"Have I done the right thing with the book?"

Four words appear on the screen: MY SOURCES SAY NO.

I throw it back down on the chair, reminding myself that it is just a silly toy, and that whatever message it displays means nothing. But doubts are already starting to whisper themselves inside my head. It's too late to do anything about it now, the letter has been posted, but maybe it wasn't a smart thing to do. Regrets, by definition, are the least punctual of emotions.

Abby was always very good at doing the right thing. It was something I loved about her from the start. She was good at being likable too; everyone who met her adored her, including me. I feel jealous of people who are naturally outgoing and friendly, even toward people they can't possibly like. I would love to be that way, but for me all social situations with people I do not know are stressful and uncomfortable. Parties are my idea of hell. Even a brief encounter with an elderly shopkeeper has left me feeling exhausted. I decide to rest my tired eyes for a moment. I haven't slept properly since I left London. That's a lie—I haven't slept properly since my wife disappeared—but maybe sleep is finally going to find me.

I can't see a thing when the sound of someone knocking on the cabin door wakes me. I don't know where I am at first, or how long I've been sleeping, and I blink, adjusting to the low light. The darkness that had gathered at the edges of the evening sky has now wiped it black, so I must have been asleep for a while. I turn on a lamp as Columbo rushes over to greet whoever it is outside—Labradors do not make good guard dogs—then I hurry to the door myself but hesitate before unlocking it. I feel a little disheveled and disorientated having just woken up. "Who is it?" I ask.

"Who do you think it is? What other eejit would be traipsing through the woods in the dark to knock on your door? It's Sandy! We said seven o'clock, and it's already five past. If we're late and the dinner is ruined I'll never hear the end of it."

I completely forgot. I've been forgetting a lot of things lately, and brain fog is becoming a permanent weather warning in my daily forecast. I'm just so tired all of the time I can't seem to function at full speed.

"Sorry," I say, unbolting the wooden door. "I lost track of the—"

"Time? Yes, this island will do that to you," she replies, looking over my shoulder and peering into the cabin. "I haven't clapped eyes on the inside of this place for a wee while, nice to see it restored to its former glory. You've done a grand job cleaning it up."

"I didn't—"

"Did you not hear me? We're late. Are you ready?"

I grab my jacket. "As I'll ever be. Sorry, I should have checked, is it okay to bring my dog? I feel strange leaving him in an unfamiliar place so soon."

"Of course, the more the merrier! We love dogs. Anything you can't stomach you can feed him under the table. You'll understand once you've tasted my sister's cooking."

We step out of the cabin and everything is black. The tall trees, the night sky, the forest floor. It all looks the same to me in every direction, but Sandy has a torch and clearly knows the way. We walk in silence and I try to think of something to say. It's so quiet. *Too* quiet.

"I never hear birds in the forest."

"You won't hear birds anywhere on the island. There aren't any," she replies.

"What? Is that true?"

"It would be an uncanny thing for me to lie about."

"But . . . why? How is that even possible?"

"I'm no bird expert, and it all happened long before my time, but birds were banned to protect the trees."

"How can you *ban* birds? Surely they just fly back."

"In 1888 there was a terrible famine on the island. Almost all of the crops failed, not unlike the potato famine in Ireland a few years earlier. Nobody could understand what caused it, but then the islanders noticed that the redwoods were dying too. The bark on these giant trees was peeling away and huge branches snapped off like broken twigs. Trees talk to each other, did you know that? Through their roots they can send messages or warnings, and the islanders thought that something terrible happening to the trees had somehow caused the crops to fail.

"They noticed something in the redwoods they hadn't seen before: woodpeckers native to the Scottish Hebrides. Hundreds of them had made their nests in the branches and holes in the trunks. Those holes left the trees vulnerable to disease, and some redwoods started dying. The islanders were hungry and frightened, so the men on the island did what men always do when they are afraid, and started killing the things that scared them. Not everyone knows the difference between a woodpecker and other birds, and I doubt everyone had twenty-twenty vision back in the 1880s. Soon all birds were getting shot, regardless of what they were, but, when they were all dead, the trees recovered and the crops started to grow again. Problem solved. The next season new birds came to the island and they were killed too. Mother nature has a way of warning her children, and somehow the birds learned not to come back. There hasn't been a famine since."

"Or any birds?"

She shakes her head. "I've lived on Amberly all my life, for over sixty years, and I've never seen so much as a sparrow. Seagulls sometimes follow the ferry when it leaves the mainland, but they always turn back before it gets to Amberly. I don't know how they know, but they know. So we don't have any birds but we do have *thousands* of these precious, beautiful, life-giving trees."

"I can't get my head around it—an island with no birds."

"The trees take care of us and we take care of them," Sandy says.

"But—"

"But nothing. It is what it is. Besides, I think birds might be smarter than people. They're certainly more loyal. Did you know that ninety percent of bird species have the same partner for life? Not like humans. And, unlike people, birds know when they're not welcome and when to stay away."

SMALL CROWD

━━━━ ⌇ ━━━━

sland life is stranger than I imagined. So are the people I've
met so far. But maybe this level of isolation does that to a person? There are no phones, no internet, no social media, no news
apps, no cinemas, no museums, no art galleries . . . being this cut
off from society and culture must have an impact. Either way, at
least they seem friendly enough. Sort of. I can't think of many
people who would invite a stranger to dinner in this day and
age; it was a kind thing for Sandy to do. Maybe I can learn to live
without birds.

Sandy tells me to "hop in the back" of the truck just like earlier, so I do, with Columbo sitting by my side. I stare out of the
window as we head off, but it's too dark to see anything except
the ghostly silhouettes of trees whizzing past. There are no streetlights, or signs, only the same narrow winding road dimly illuminated by the truck's headlamps. Sandy grips the steering wheel
and I notice that she is wearing a very distinctive ring on her right
hand. The intricate design incorporates a silver thistle, and I've
never seen anything like it before. I look back at the road and start
to feel a little carsick when we take another bend at breakneck
speed, so it's a relief when Sandy hits the brakes.

"Here we are, the House on the Hill," she says, sounding cheerful again. "I was born in this house and my family were the sort of
folk filled with kindness but lacking in imagination. The house is
on a hill, so that's what they called it."

I climb out of the truck and am surprised by what I see. The
"house" with its gray stone walls covered in ivy is enormous, by
far the biggest I've seen on the island. It should have been called
the Big House on the Hill. And it's more than just a house. There
are stone turrets on either side of the double-fronted facade, making it look like a mini castle. With neat, formal flower beds lining
a path to the entrance it's a little intimidating.

"Not what you were expecting?" Sandy asks with a smile.

"Well, no, if I'm honest."

"Only you know if you're honest, pointless asking me."

Sandy does not look, sound, or behave like someone who is
wealthy—and I wonder whether I have misjudged her. We walk
side by side and I'm reminded how tall she is. She's dressed in
what looks like the same clothes she wore yesterday: jeans (presumably extra-long), a white shirt, and her giant yellow coat. No
makeup, no nonsense. She doesn't *look* like a lady of the manor or
a queen of the—albeit miniature—castle.

The place is impressive at first glance, but it's a bit run-down,
with paint peeling off the window frames and doors like burned
skin. The closer we get, the more imperfections I see; tiles missing
from the roof, dead plants in the window boxes, cracks in the walls.
It's an unhappy-looking house. Once picture-perfect, I imagine, but
now tired and unloved. The windows look like eyes, and I feel as
though they are watching me. There is also a strange-looking metal
tower behind the house at the very top of the hill. It *looks* like a
phone mast.

"What is that?" I ask, over the sound of our footsteps crunch-
ing on the gravel driveway. "I thought there was no mobile phone
signal on Amberly."

"There isn't. Although I'm told someone once managed to get one bar by the Standing Stones. What you see there is the old radio tower. Such an ugly thing, but this is the highest point on the island where it could be easily accessed for repairs, so here it is. We don't need mobile phones—nobody does if you ask me—but we do need radio. Can't do my job without the shipping forecast, for one thing. The tower is also how these work," she says, taking a walkie-talkie from her pocket. "Everyone on the island has one."

"I don't."

"They're only for permanent residents, people who are part of the community, and they're only really supposed to be used for emergencies."

There's that word they all seem to love again: *community*.

Sandy turns off her walkie-talkie before putting it away, which seems like a strange thing to do if it is for emergencies when she is the island sheriff.

"Your home is very impressive," I say, but Sandy shakes her head and a strand of shiny short black hair escapes her ponytail.

"It used to be a bonnie pile of bricks when I was a child, but big old places like this require a lot of maintenance, which requires a lot of money. It will cost more than I earn to return her to her former glory, but I'm working on it."

A large front door opens before we reach it and I see my wife standing there.

I stop and stare, blink a few times, and when I open my eyes again I realize it's not her.

It never was.

Never is.

A petite woman in a loud floral dress stands in the entrance. She waves and smiles at me like I am a long-lost friend. "This is my sister, Midge MacIntyre," Sandy says. Midge is as short as Sandy is tall, and has an immaculate blond bob of hair that doesn't move when she does. They look a similar age but they do not look like sisters.

"Come on in out of the cold; you'll catch your death," she says, ushering me inside, which is far more welcoming than the exterior. The place smells of scented candles, home cooking, and an open fire that I can hear crackling and spitting somewhere in the distance, and everything, and I do mean *everything*, is covered in tweed fabric. The chair in the hallway, the lampshade, the cushions, the curtains, the walls, the draft excluder. Everything.

Overly tactile people tend to make me uncomfortable, but I don't mind too much when Midge hugs me. Perhaps because I have forgotten what it is like to be embraced; my only source of affection these days is the dog. When my new floral friend has finished patting me, she starts stroking Columbo, who is instantly taken with her.

"I couldn't believe it when Sandy said *another* author had come to stay on our little island! We're a small crowd, just twenty-five permanent residents, but a lot of them love books. Including me. The news really has made my day!" she says in a thick Scottish accent. It's a beautiful sound. Close up, I can see she's a smidgen younger than Sandy beneath all the makeup.

"Are you here to write a book?" she asks. "Most writers who visit the island seem to find it great for inspiring their creativity."

"Well, yes, actually. I am here to write. Do you get many authors coming to Amberly?"

"A few, and we all miss Charlie, of course. Perhaps you could be our new resident writer? Wouldn't that be lovely?" She links her skinny little arm through mine. "Now come on into the kitchen so we can have a wee glass of the good stuff and you can tell me all about yourself. And your books, of course."

The kitchen is also decorated in tweed, a mostly pink pattern in here. And the good stuff, it turns out, is some homemade alcohol that Midge calls "poutine" served in miniature glasses. It burns my throat and tastes thoroughly unpleasant.

"It's good," I tell her.

"A little taste of yesterday's rain to help prepare you for tomorrow," she says.

I do not know what that means, but three tiny glasses of yesterday's rain later, I feel more relaxed than I probably should. I notice that Midge keeps refilling my glass but barely touches her own. I also notice that she is wearing the same ring as Sandy on her finger, silver with a thistle. It must be a family thing. She leads us through to a candlelit dining room—tweed in every shade of green in this room—and serves *something*. I'm not entirely sure what.

"I hope you like lamb," Midge says.

"It looks . . ."

Inedible.

". . . delicious," I tell her.

All of the rooms have open fireplaces and they all appear to be lit. I suspect it must be difficult to keep a big old house like this warm, but they've done a grand job of making it feel cozy. I can feel myself start to unwind for the first time in a long time.

"I'm afraid I haven't heard of you or your books," Midge says as I stare at my plate.

The relaxed feeling disappears. It's a comment that never fails to sober me up and dampen my mood. Being a bestseller doesn't mean people will know who you are. Being an author, even a moderately successful one, is an invisible sort of life. It used to be one of the reasons why I loved my job—I've always been shy, happy to stay out of the spotlight—but these days I just feel unseen. Past my prime. Forgotten.

"She doesn't mean to be rude," Sandy says before I can answer.

"I'm not being *rude*, just honest. I run the island library so—"

"When she says *island library*, what she means is the old red phone box next to Saint Lucy's. It's not been used for making calls for months—it got struck by lightning, hasn't worked since, and we're still waiting for someone to come from the mainland to repair it—these days the old phone box is filled with secondhand books."

I thought Cora said a fishing trawler took out the cable on the ocean floor.

"Are you okay, Grady?" Midge asks, a look of concern on her face.

"Yes. Sorry. I have a bad habit of daydreaming, one of the drawbacks of my job. I stumbled across the phone box earlier today. Thought I heard it ringing actually." They both stare at me as though I might be crazy. "But it was just my imagination."

"I imagine that must be another downside of being an author," Sandy says, pushing some more food around her plate. "Constantly living inside an imaginary world must make it difficult to tell truth and fiction apart sometimes."

"Sometimes." I take a large gulp of wine from my glass, which is on a tweed coaster.

"Have you written many books?" Midge asks, and I retreat inside myself a little bit more.

"A few," I say, desperately trying to think of some way to change the subject. A deep reservoir of sadness supplies my moods these days and it never runs empty. Sandy seems to pick up on my discomfort, and I am grateful when she moves the conversation along. Something about the church roof leaking and costing too much to repair. I tune out for a while and wallow in the depths of my own self-pity; it can be hard to drag myself up when I feel this down.

Is a writer still a writer if they can no longer write?

I have *tried* since Abby disappeared. I just can't.

Something got broken, and until I know what happened to her I don't know if I'll ever be able to write again.

That's why stealing someone else's book and pretending it's my own is such a good idea.

It's also the only one I've got.

ALMOST EXACTLY

P lease help yourself to more if you'd like some?" Midge offers.

"Thank you. It was *delicious*, but I'm full," I say as I put
down my knife and fork.

She smiles then stares at the ring on my finger.

"What does your wife think about your novels?" she asks. "I
imagine being married to a writer must be quite something."

That's one way to describe it, I suppose.

"My wife was my biggest supporter from the start. She believed in me even when nobody else did," I say, not wanting to
share anything further. It isn't a lie. Abby did always believe in
me and I am still married. Albeit to a ghost. My missing wife has
defined me these past twelve months—it's all anyone who knows
me thinks about when they see me—but maybe she doesn't need
to here. Perhaps, while I am on the island, I could just be me
again.

If I can remember who that is.

"She must be very understanding to let you go off gallivanting
by yourself, leaving her behind at home. Especially a handsome
man like you," Midge says, pouring me another glass of wine.

It's been a long time since anyone called me handsome and I feel myself blush.

Good wine makes up for the not great food—Sandy wasn't exaggerating about the horror show that is her sister's cooking—and the company is . . . interesting.

"You're sure I can't tempt you to a second helping?" Midge asks, eyes hopeful and wide.

"No," I reply a little too fast, and Sandy hides a smile with her napkin. "I couldn't eat another bite, but thank you. If the rest of the islanders are as friendly as you, then I'll have a hard time leaving."

Midge smiles. "There are only twenty-five of us on the island, but that's still a lot of new names and faces to remember. Where's that map of yours?"

I find it and hand it to her. Midge unfolds the map of the island and lays it flat on the wooden table, trying—and failing—to smooth out the creases in it with her palm. "So, the first thing to remember is that only a handful of us were born on Amberly, and Sandy is the only one who has lived here all her life."

"You haven't?"

It's hard to see beneath all the makeup, but I think Midge might be blushing now.

"No, I left for a while. I had dreams of being an actress, and my chances of becoming a movie star on a tiny island where half the population didn't even own a TV seemed slim. So I worked hard, saved hard, and booked a one-way ticket to Hollywood. But the dream I had spent my whole life chasing turned out to be a nightmare. After a lot of auditions I did get cast in a handful of small roles, but my name was never in lights. The world didn't see me the way I saw myself, and the reality of that—of not being good enough—crushed me. Soon producers were only offering me parts in exchange for things that I didn't want to do. All of them were men back then, and it was rarely my talent they were interested in.

I became very sad and very lonely very quickly. Sandy paid for me to come home, and I realized that everything I needed to make me happy was right here. On the island. The rest of the islanders feel the same. Almost everyone living on the island now came here in search of a new beginning and a different end. The eternal human quest for happiness. I wonder why you're really here?"

She stares at me. They both do. Then Midge laughs.

"I'm only teasing. We all know why you're here," she says. They both stare at me again and I feel so uncomfortable I think I'm starting to sweat. "To write a new book, silly!"

We all laugh then but I can't wait to leave. I don't get out much—or at all—but the people here really are a bit strange.

"Yes," I say, nodding and taking another sip of wine. "To write a new book."

She makes it sound so simple.

Midge leans closer and whispers, "And have you started? Writing the new book?"

I nod. "Early days, but I've got it all plotted out."

Sandy smiles, pats me hard on the back. A little too hard. "Good. For. You."

"Good for you, good for us," Midge says, clinking her glass with mine. "And we don't want you getting lost before you finish the book, so pay attention. You are *here*." She stabs the drawing of the House on the Hill on the map with a pink fingernail. I can't help remembering the YOU ARE NOT HERE on the wooden sign when I arrived. Midge starts to count on her fingers. "We're your nearest neighbors. Most people live in 'the village' as we like to call it. Let's see, who should you know? Cora Christie runs the corner shop—"

"He's met her already," Sandy says. "Made a first impression that she won't forget."

"Oh dear," Midge says, shaking her head. "I hope you didn't tell her too much. That woman loves scuttlebutt." I must look confused. "*Gossip*," she explains. Seems to me Midge may as well be describing herself. "The whole island will be talking about you now but never mind, everyone knows she's completely mad. You might have noticed she was dressed all in green?" I nod. "Cora has worn nothing but green clothes since I've known her. Like a little leprechaun ferreting about the place. *Green* sweaters, *green* skirts, *green* underwear—apparently—she thinks wearing any other color is bad luck. If you like a drink, and from what I've seen tonight, I think you do, Sidney and Bella King are the landlords of The Stumble Inn, Amberly's only pub. Then there's Jack, a master builder who trained on the mainland donkey's years ago but then came home to Amberly. It's been a long time since any new houses were built here, but we get a lot of storms and there's always something Jack needs to fix after. Good with plumbing, wiring, woodwork, thatching . . . there's nothing Jack can't do. Who else? Travers and family live at The Croft right on the other side of the island, away from everyone else. Travers is fondly known as our tree doctor and takes care of all the ancient redwoods."

Sandy nods. "Nice family. They have a little girl called Holly and a big dog called Ivy."

My mind wanders to Abby, as it so often does, and I wonder if I'll ever see her again.

Midge continues, oblivious. "There's the hairdresser, Mrs. Sharp. Her smile is as rare as a unicorn, but she's good with scissors. I've lost count again; who am I forgetting?"

"Surely there's a doctor?" I ask.

"Of course, Dr. Highsmith, but she doesn't live on Amberly. She visits every Tuesday from the nearest other island. Unless the sea is too rough for the ferry to sail. So I suggest you only get ill on a Tuesday, and only if the weather is good. Did Sandy tell you she was the island sheriff *and* the ferrywoman?" Midge asks. "She might be a handy resource for your next crime novel!"

"Sandy said there wasn't any crime on Amberly."

"Well, technically no and not *recently*," Midge says. "Not even a case of petty theft in over twenty years since Sandy took over. Where else in the world can you say that? But there was something strange that happened almost exactly a year ago—"

"It's late. We should let Grady go home," Sandy interrupts.

"What happened here last year?" I ask.

Midge leans across the table. "Well—"

"Come on, I'll give you a lift," Sandy says, but Midge continues.

"There was a visitor who came and never left. A woman—"

"*Midge*. That's enough."

"I've started, so I'll finish," Midge says, pouring us both another drink and ignoring her sister. "The woman came on the ferry—it was during the tourist season, so Sandy didn't think to ask too many questions—but, unlike the other day-trippers, she never went back to the mainland. On an island this small, one of us would have known if she was staying, but she arrived on the island, then vanished."

It can't be Abby. That would be too much of a coincidence and there's no such thing.

"And this was a year ago?" I ask and Midge nods. "What did she look like?"

"I don't know, I never saw her. But here's the thing, nobody else did either. Nobody except Sandy saw her after she walked off the ferry. And then Sandy found the body a few weeks later."

I feel sick. "The woman's body?"

"No. Keep up, she was never seen again. It was a man. No ID, nothing. Just a body washed up on the beach. But maybe the mystery woman had something to do with it."

"I thought you said there was no crime on the island?" I say, turning to Sandy.

She shrugs. "There *isn't*. He'd been dead a long time when I found him. I reckon whatever happened to him happened on the mainland. Tide carried him here is all."

"What did she look like, the woman who came here?" I ask Sandy.

"I don't remember her face, but I do recall she was traveling alone and looked very anxious on the ferry. Some folks don't like boats," Sandy says. "It was a year ago and, no offense, all people from the mainland look the same to me. Though I confess I won't forget the dead man in a hurry. The body was so badly decomposed from being in the water he was impossible to identify—"

"*And* he was missing a hand," Midge whispers with a strange sense of glee. "It was like something from a horror film. Are you okay, Grady? You've gone quite pale."

PERFECTLY IMPERFECT

— ⌣ —

One Week Before She Disappeared

ABBY

"Help can be hard to ask for," the woman I've come to see says. "You've done the right thing by talking to someone about your feelings, and I want to help if I can." She doesn't seem to understand that it's already too late. When life bends itself into a question mark you start looking for answers, and when you can't find the right ones, you go looking for the wrong ones instead. That's all there is to it.

"If you don't want to tell me what you've been lying to your husband about, that's okay," she says, pulling a face that suggests it isn't. I assess her, the way she has been assessing me. The blond hair, the black clothes, the sensible shoes. She's so calm, collected and sure of herself that I start to dislike her. She uncrosses her legs then crosses them the other way before flicking her lovely long hair over her shoulder again. I imagine hacking it off with a pair of shears, and the thought makes me relax a little. "Have you always found it difficult to be honest in relationships?"

It feels like an insult disguised as a question and I have to think before answering. "Not with everyone."

The woman in black nods as though she understands.

But she doesn't.

"We learn how to form and behave in relationships at a very young age," she says. "Like most things, we first learn by imitating others, from watching other people and copying how they interact. That often means learning from our parents. Did your parents have a loving relationship?" she asks.

I think about the screaming arguments.

The crying.

The axe.

"I was still very young when they separated," I say.

"I'm sorry, you did mention that another woman raised you. What happened to your birth mother? Tell me about her. What do you remember most when you think about her?"

I find it hard to suppress a sigh. Not everything in life is the result of mommy issues, and this is not going to help, but I indulge her anyway.

"My mother wanted me to learn how to play the piano," I say.

Figuring out which other parts of the story to share is a little more difficult.

My mother inherited the piano when her aunt died. It was very distinctive, with birds painted on its side. My mother would have preferred to have been left money; we didn't have any, but her great-aunt Veronica—who she said wasn't great, or even a real aunt, and who I had never met—left her a piano and a blue vase instead.

I don't know where my mother found him—the teacher we called the music man—but I remember the first time he came to the house. I was nine, and I thought he looked old, but everyone over thirty looked old when I was young. He was probably no older than that. The piano was in the dining room—we always ate in the kitchen, so it was a room we never used—and my mother left me in there with him. I'd been taught not to talk to strangers, but apparently if a stranger called themself a teacher it was okay. The music man closed the door "so as not to disturb her" and the first lesson did not go well.

I love music. I could listen to Nina Simone, Billie Holiday, or Ella Fitzgerald all day long, but I have never been gifted in that way. I can't even play a triangle. The piano stool was too low to reach the keys, so the music man placed a red velvet cushion on the seat for me to sit on. It made me taller but didn't help me play any better, and when he left that afternoon my mother was bitterly disappointed. She had been listening and didn't like what she heard.

The next lesson was the same as the first: a disaster. The music man always brought two things with him: a metronome and a flask of coffee. He would slowly twist the lid off the flask at the beginning of each class, then take noisy sips from his plastic cup before placing it on a lace doily on the top of the piano. I have never liked coffee, and I'm sure it is because of him. Just the smell of it makes me feel sick. He started the metronome as soon as I began to play the basic scales he was trying, and failing, to teach me. He said it was to help with my rhythm.

Click. Click. Click. Click.

When, by the third lesson, it was obvious I wasn't getting better, my mother expressed her disappointment in me *and* him. So he came up with a plan and things were a little different for lesson number four.

The music man closed the door as usual.

He opened his coffee flask just like always.

Then he sat down on the piano stool instead of me and started to play the scales himself.

"You want to make your mother happy, don't you?" he asked quietly. Nine-year-old me nodded. "Good girl," he said, looking pleased with me for the first time. Then he switched on the metronome.

Click. Click. Click. Click.

My mother was delighted after the lesson, she thought I had finally got the hang of it.

I hadn't.

I never did.

But there were other things the music man wanted to teach me.

The following week we did the same thing. I sat next to him and he played the piano pretending to be me. The metronome was already ticking away, producing a nice steady beat, when he unzipped his pants with his left hand then played a C-major scale with his right.

"Your mother would be so upset if I told her you lied and that you don't really know how to play," he whispered. "I won't tell, but I need you to do something for me."

I did what he told me to do. Afterward, I used to hear the sound of that damn metronome in my sleep. Months went by and my mother thought I'd progressed from scales to Mozart. She was so happy, I couldn't tell her the truth, and the music man said everything he made me do in that room had to be a secret, because if my mother ever found out she would be very upset.

He was right about that.

One afternoon she walked into the room without knocking, carrying a plate of freshly baked cookies. The music man's hands were on the piano keys, his trousers were around his ankles, I was on my knees. I didn't hear her come in. He didn't either. Neither of us knew she was there until she hit him over the head with Aunt Veronica's blue vase. He fell to the floor unconscious and the room was completely silent, except for one sound.

Click. Click. Click. Click.

I didn't know what happened after that because she sent me to my room and locked me inside until the following morning. I know I never saw the music man again and that the axe we used for chopping wood was missing. My mother locked the piano shut and said that I was never to talk about what happened. With anyone. And I haven't, because why would I? I don't want to be judged or defined by that. The thing that upset me the most was the way my mother treated me afterward. Things were never the same and she looked at me as though I were damaged. Broken. Unlovable. Which made me feel as though I was all of those things. I think that's why she sent me away, so that she didn't have to look at me anymore.

SILENT CONVERSATION

GRADY

"Me and you need to go back to the cabin right now," Sandy says, staring at me with a strange expression on her face. She and Midge exchange a glance. They share a silent conversation the way only people who really know each other can. "I need to see these bones for myself."

Before we can leave the room there is a loud bang on the ceiling, followed by several more in short succession. We all look up at the miniature crystal chandelier as it starts to creak and sway from side to side, casting an eerie pattern of moving shadows on the table.

"What was that?" I ask.

Once again they converse without words before answering me.

"It's nothing to worry about. Just Mother," Sandy says, glaring upward as the banging starts again. "She uses her walking stick to tell us when she needs something."

It doesn't sound like a walking stick.

"Is she all right?" I ask.

"Oh yes," Midge says with a nervous smile. "Fit as a fiddle, but with one or two broken strings. Our mother, Morag, used to run Amberly Tweed on the island before she retired, created some of the most beautiful handwoven fabrics you'll ever see." I think I might have seen some of them tonight, glancing around their tweed-clad home. "Sadly tweed isn't as popular as it used to be and the business closed down. She needs constant care these days—there are no facilities for the elderly on the island—but I don't mind looking after her," Midge says, sounding as though she does mind. The banging from above resumes. This time it sounds more like someone trying to force down a locked door. "I'd better go and see to her. I'll take her a wee glass of the good stuff, that normally settles her down."

Sandy drives faster than seems sensible on the dark and twisty roads. Given the amount she has had to drink tonight, I'm not convinced she should be driving at all. I wish I'd never mentioned the bones beneath the floorboards. All I can think about is Charles Whittaker's manuscript, which I left on the desk. Whatever happens, Sandy cannot see that. Nobody can. The letter I sent to Kitty was a proposal for a similar story. A *very* similar story. I'm obviously not going to copy it word for word—Charles had an extremely distinctive voice—so I need to edit the book. Make it my own. But for my plan to work, nobody can know about the original version.

We reach the forest clearing and it is a relief to get out of the truck. The night is still, silent, and cold. It's too dark to see anything except the silhouettes of trees. Sandy turns on a torch and starts marching toward the cabin, so fast that Columbo and I practically have to run to keep up with her. The branches of the tall trees sway, and lean, and groan, and the leaves on the forest floor swirl around us, almost as though the place is coming to life as we walk through it. I hear what sounds like screaming in the distance, but Sandy doesn't stop striding ahead.

"What was that?" I ask.

"Just nature. Haven't you ever heard a fox before? They're quite harmless."

I've heard plenty of foxes, even when living in London, but they never sounded like that. Something flies too close to my face at high speed and I wave my arms in the air before stumbling into Sandy.

"I thought you said there were no birds here," I say.

"That was a bat."

"A *bat*? I suppose they're harmless too?"

"There are two species on the island. One is, one isn't."

She doesn't elaborate and I don't ask.

We carry on walking and I hear the sound of twigs snapping somewhere close behind us. Columbo growls and I spin around but there is nobody there, only darkness. I wish I wasn't scared— even admitting it to myself makes me feel like a wimp—but I am, so I walk a little faster to catch up with Sandy.

"This'll be why the bats are out," she says. I've been too busy looking over my shoulder to see what she is seeing, but when I look up there are hundreds of tiny lights all over the forest. They're everywhere. In the trees and the air around me. I wonder if I might be dreaming.

"What are they?"

"Fireflies," Sandy replies. "I bet you've never seen *them* in London."

"I've never seen anything like this anywhere before." The glowing yellow lights seem to dance in front of me. It's magical.

"One of the benefits of having no birds is having more bugs," Sandy says. "We've got a lot of rare beetles, moths, and spiders as well as these special old trees to protect. The fireflies are a favorite of mine. These little fellas thrive here. Their bioluminescence is to attract a mate and to communicate with each other, but the light they produce also warns bats not to eat them."

"Why? Are they poisonous to bats?"

"No, they just taste *horrible*. Like Midge's cooking." She laughs at her own joke, then looks suddenly serious. "They light up when they're in danger too. If they get caught in a web, for example. If they're trapped and can't get away." Sandy stares at me with an expression on her face I don't like or understand. Her eyes narrow, and she takes a step closer toward me. Too close. "Some fireflies can still light up the world around them after dying. Not forever, of course." She smiles and looks more like herself again. "Nice to look at though, aren't they?" she says, continuing to walk through the forest. Her mood swings are unsettling but I try not to overthink it. Most people are contradictions of themselves.

When we reach the cabin I unlock the door and it gives a theatrical creak when I push it open. I turn on the lights and am relieved to see that everything appears to be exactly as it was. Including the precious manuscript on the desk.

"Where are the bones?" Sandy asks as soon as we step inside.

"Just under here," I tell her, pulling back the sheepskin rug. She bends down to take a closer look at the loose floorboards, then lifts them with her bare hands in no time while I attempt to casually walk over to the desk. Sandy shines her torch in the hole and I wonder if this means I won't be able to stay in the cabin. I'm guessing it might be a crime scene now and I wish I'd kept my big mouth shut. I turn the first page of the manuscript over so it cannot be read. A bit like Sandy's expression.

"*Do* you think they are human bones?" I ask, coming to stand by her side.

She looks up at me. "There's nothing here."

"What?" I say, crouching down to see for myself. She's right. There is nothing but wood and dirt. Even the red velvet cushion is gone. "I . . . don't understand. The bones were right there."

Sandy looks past me at the old brass drinks trolley in the corner of the room. Then she sighs, dusts off her hands on her jeans, starts to stand.

"You said your books had a hint of horror about them. I can see you've been working on something," she says, nodding toward the manuscript I was so desperate to hide. "Perhaps the tiredness from the journey, a little whiskey, being alone out here when you're more used to city life . . . maybe your imagination got the better of you."

"I didn't imagine it. I . . ."

But I can't explain it. Or understand how something I'm sure was there last night has vanished.

"Well, honestly, I'm relieved," Sandy says. "The island is very proud to be crime-free and—apart from one dead body on the beach a year ago, which Midge should never have mentioned—a safe place for everyone who lives here. Don't give it another thought. There's nothing there, so let's pretend it never happened."

I nod.

But it did.

"I meant to ask you earlier, but I forgot," I say. "When is the next ferry back to the mainland?"

Sandy frowns. "Not leaving so soon are you? I thought you said you liked it here—"

"Oh I do, very much so. It's just . . . there are some things I left in my car that I need."

"Well, give me the keys and I can get them for you next time I'm on the mainland. No sense in you losing precious writing time."

"That's very kind, but I would like to know when the next sailing is. Just in case I need to get back anytime soon."

She stares at me. "Hard to say with the weather. But I'll be sure to let you know."

I might have had too much to drink but her behavior seems a little strange to me.

After Sandy leaves, I pour myself another glass of whiskey. Then I stare at the empty space beneath the floorboards, in case the bones might have reappeared. They haven't. But there is something in the cabin that wasn't here before. Something I quickly picked up before

Sandy saw it. An envelope with the words *Read Me* written on it was slipped under the door while I was out this evening.

I open it and am shocked by what I see.

23rd March 2017   The Times   Page 5

WOMAN FREED AFTER THIRTY YEARS IN PRISON
A Wrongful Conviction and a Broken Justice System

Abby Goldman

Thirty years ago, on a cold October afternoon, Coraline Thatcher's daughter did not come home from school. Late that night, after reporting her missing and making several calls, she suspected that her fifteen-year-old child was at a party at a friend's house. The friend's parents were not home. On arrival, it was clear that the party had got out of hand. The house was filled with young people, loud music, and the smell of drugs. Coraline eventually found her teenaged daughter in a bedroom, unconscious, and being raped by a twenty-one-year-old man.

Coraline reached for a bottle of Jack Daniels that was on the bedside table and smashed it over the man's head. She was still holding the broken bottleneck when he climbed off her daughter, grabbed Coraline by the throat, and pushed her up against a wall. He was six feet tall and weighed fourteen stone. Witnesses concur he spat in her face and threatened to "end her."

Coraline's lawyer claimed that sticking that broken bottle into the man's throat and severing an artery in his neck was self-defense. But a jury, which astoundingly included a cousin of the rapist, found her guilty of murder and she was sent to prison. For life.

The courts have now ruled, thirty years later, that Coraline Thatcher should never have been convicted. The man she killed had been arrested numerous times, before he raped her daughter, for violent sexual assault and stalking. He was known to the police but he was never charged. A woman is killed by a man every three minutes in the UK, and yet when a woman tries to defend herself she is the one who loses her freedom. Our justice system is broken. Coraline did what she did to protect herself from a man the police failed to protect her from, and she lost everything as a result.

Her daughter was put into care and Coraline was not allowed to see her. She lost her home and her business. Her mother died while she was in prison. Her daughter, now forty-five, the same age Coraline was when convicted, refuses to speak to her, and she has grandchildren she has never met. Coraline now lives in a halfway house in London and is dependent on charity to get by.

I met with her in the hope of an exclusive interview. But she met with me only to tell me why she wouldn't give one. "There's nothing anyone can do to give me my life back," she said. "All I wanted was to run a little shop and take care of my daughter." Coraline was dressed in green and looked older than her years. The dead man's family also had no comment, and threatened me and this newspaper with legal action. "Justice is only for those who can afford it," Coraline told me. Freedom, it seems, also comes with a price.

INNOCENT CRIMINAL

There is no note. No explanation. Just a crumpled old newspaper article written by my wife several years ago. I remember the story and how much it upset Abby at the time. My wife was an amazing journalist. She found out all kinds of things about the dead man's wealthy family—things the legal team at the newspaper refused to let her print—including that they bribed Coraline Thatcher's defense lawyer to do a shoddy job and make sure she was convicted. But Abby always had to do the right thing, and she kept digging until she uncovered enough truth to get some justice for that poor woman. The creepy-looking antique doll I found in her car the night she disappeared had been sent to her at the newspaper. Her editor watched her open the box and was convinced that the doll with its mouth sewn up was a warning. The police tested the doll for fingerprints but found only Abby's.

I don't understand why someone is sending me this old article now. Or why they couldn't tell me to my face. Unless it is a clue about what happened to Abby? What else could it be?

Maybe I *didn't* imagine seeing my missing wife on the island.

I read the newspaper clipping again. The words seem to blur

and twist and move on the page, but I put on my reading glasses, and try to focus. Abby's article says that Coraline Thatcher was dressed all in green when they met. Like Cora at the corner shop. One of Cora's many badges said she was at least eighty years old, and the woman in the article would have been seventy-five seven years ago, so the age fits. Could Cora Christie be Coraline Thatcher? Even if she is, what is the connection to my wife if they barely met? Did Abby dig too deep into the rapist's family? Were they responsible for the threats she had been receiving before she disappeared? Did they send the doll? And who was the one-handed dead man who washed up on the beach last year around the same time Abby vanished?

If someone is trying to tell me something then I don't understand who or what or why. But someone knows something, and they came to the cabin to try to tell me. And it was someone on the island, which means there can be only twenty-five suspects.

It's late, it's been a long time since I got any real rest, and I'm so tired I feel as though I could fall asleep standing up. Columbo is already snoring at the foot of the bed and I think he has the right idea. Maybe this will all make more sense in the morning, though I doubt it. I replace the floorboards and the rug and pour myself another small glass of whiskey—just a little something to help me sleep.

It doesn't work.

It rarely does.

I lie awake thinking about Abby, as always.

What if she was scared that someone was going to hurt her, so she decided to disappear and find somewhere to hide? Somewhere remote like the Isle of Amberly, where she would be safe? Where nobody would think to look?

Hope can be just as devastating as despair.

I worry that not sleeping properly for months has done permanent damage to my mind. Nothing has been the same since that night. Even when I do sleep it is rarely for long. The first few doctors I saw about my insomnia were sympathetic but useless. Saying things like *pills are a last resort* and suggesting I make a list of my worries before bedtime. Another told me to try meditation. Surprisingly, to me, that worked for a while until it didn't. They all told me to cut down on screen time and avoid alcohol. Both of which are things I can't do, and besides, alcohol is the only thing that *does* sometimes quiet my mind when life is too loud.

I think there are just too many questions rattling around inside my broken brain:

What happened to my wife that night?

Where is she?

Is she alive?

Questions that nobody has answers for.

I remember showing our joint bank statements to Kitty, pointing out the large sums of money Abby had withdrawn in the months before she disappeared. Kitty was as baffled as I was about her goddaughter's behavior, and too polite to say out loud what so many others I'm sure were thinking: that Abby had staged her own disappearance. I didn't blame them because that's what I would have thought too. But they didn't know her like I did; she would never do something like that. And now, just like all those other nights, she is all I can think of. Wondering how well I really knew my wife and whether I'll ever know the truth.

The last doctor I saw took pity on my sorry story and reluctantly prescribed sleeping pills, but they don't really help. Not unless I double the recommended dose. Even if I manage to get a few hours rest, I'm so deeply tired after all these months that my head feels fuzzy. Like there is permanent white noise all around me. My memory is noticeably affected too, and some days I barely have enough energy to function. Sometimes I can't form proper sentences anymore; I literally can't find the words, which is a bit of a problem for a writer. I've read that long-term insomnia can cause hallucinations and paranoia, and I'm starting to wonder if that's what is happening to me now. But I find the newspaper article and it's real. I didn't imagine that. *Someone* is trying to tell me *something*.

Writing a book can mean long periods of isolation filled with intense self-doubt and sustained self-loathing. If the books are not well behaved it feels like doing daily battle with myself for months, and I fight dirty when cornered. Not all varieties of self-harm are possible to see. The people who tried to support me when Abby first disappeared soon stopped calling. I didn't have the energy to see or even talk to people and they didn't seem to understand. How could they? My whole world imploded the day she disappeared. I couldn't eat. I couldn't sleep. I couldn't write, and sometimes it felt like I couldn't breathe. I was too tired to see anyone, too tired to do anything much at all. I told everyone I was busy, that the best cure for heartbreak was hard work, but really all I was doing was staring at a blank page on a screen and drinking myself to oblivion. Lost inside myself. Reliving the night she disappeared over and over again, thinking she'd still be there if I had done something differently. It felt like the end of my world, but I soon learned that the rest of the world goes on spinning with or without you.

Abby made me happy. And writing used to make me happy too. It was something I truly loved; I lived to write and I wrote to live. But all of that has changed for me now. Writing is like being beaten to death by your own dream. It began with not being able to write, but these past few months I've been so tired I can't even read. When I try, the words seem to move sideways across the page, like the view out of a fast-moving train. I know I need to rest but I can't, not until I know what happened to the woman I loved.

I see her everywhere but I thought it was just my tired mind playing tricks on me. After what Midge and Sandy told me tonight about a mystery woman coming to Amberly last year, and the newspaper article slipped beneath the door, I'm not so sure.

What if my wife really was here on this island?

What if she still is?

Unable to switch off the thoughts and fears that are always too loud, I lie awake in the darkness. I long for sleep but it doesn't find me. I open my eyes and am grateful for the beautiful view at least. The glass doors at the back of the cabin really do bring the outside inside and I am living on the edge in more ways than one. From my bed, I can see the almost full moon reflected in the ocean beneath a star-stained sky. The sound of the sea in the distance, a sound Abby hated, calms me like a watery lullaby.

Until I see a face in the window.

SILENT SCREAM

A number of characters in my books have emitted a silent scream when something terrifying happens to them. In real life, I do not scream silently. In real life, the sound that comes out of my mouth when I see a face outside the window in the middle of the night is surprisingly high pitched and very loud.

The dog leaps off the bed looking terrified, but only because he has been woken from a deep sleep by a sound his owner has never made before. I jump up too, but when I look back at the window there is nobody there.

Fear is a shape-shifter. Mine soon turns into anger. *Someone* came in here and took those bones from beneath the floorboards, *someone* left an old article written by my wife for me to find, and *someone* was outside just now, in the middle of the night, watching me. I instinctively reach for my phone, forgetting that it doesn't work, but who would I call if it did? There are no police, only Sandy. There might not be any crime on this island but *someone* is up to no good.

I'm not imagining it.

I look around the cabin for something I can use as a weapon to defend myself should I need to, and settle on the iron poker next to the wood-burning stove. Then I unlock the huge glass doors, sliding them open, adrenaline pumping through me.

"I know you're out there. Show yourself!" I say, trying not to sound afraid.

I close the doors behind me to prevent Columbo from following, and step out onto the decked area, the roar of the sea suddenly loud in my ears. The temperature has dropped dramatically and the cool night air stops me in my tracks. Coming out here in just my pajamas wasn't terribly smart. I spin around, like some wild, untamed creature—careful not to get too close to the edge or the steep drop it hides in the dark—but I can't see anything. Or anyone. All I can see at first are clouds of my own breath. My eyes adjust to the light as I look up at the darkest of skies and then down at the unforgiving black ocean. The night sky here is so clear and the stars are so much brighter than I have ever seen them anywhere else. It's strange to think that this spectacular night sky is always above us, wherever we are. We're all just too busy looking down to remember to look up. The tide is in now and the sea, like my mind, is not calm tonight. I can hear the waves smashing into the cliff below, and a sentinel of trees swaying, creaking, and groaning in the distance behind me as though I have disturbed them. Woken them from their slumber.

I glimpse something move out of the corner of my eye.

A shadow darts through the trees to the side of the cabin.

I turn just in time to see that it is a large stag with huge antlers. It stops, then twists its head to look back at me from the safety of the forest, two enormous brown eyes staring in my direction. Maybe that is what I saw in the window?

Then I hear something else, something unfamiliar at first.

Somewhere deep inside the forest I hear what sounds like someone playing a harmonica.

I stand perfectly still and I listen and I'm sure I can hear someone playing "Feeling Good" by Nina Simone. It's faint, and when the wind rustles the leaves on the trees, I can't hear it at all. Am I imagining it? Am I hearing things? I remember the red harmonica that was on the writing desk when I first arrived and hurry back inside the cabin. I search everywhere, but the harmonica is gone.

BUSY DOING NOTHING

stand outside again, straining to hear the harmonica, but I don't hear anything except the wind in the trees and the sound of the ocean. Eventually, when I am so cold I can hear my teeth chattering, I go back inside. I don't know whether I imagined everything that just happened, but I lock the doors behind me and drag a chair over to lodge beneath the main handle so nobody can get in. Then I pull all the curtains and blinds so nobody can *see* in either.

I lie down and close my eyes and somehow I sleep, and when I do I dream of drowning.

When I next wake it is still the middle of the night, and I am still exhausted, but I am too scared and confused—of and about everything—to even try to close my eyes again. There's something very strange about this place. If I had anywhere else to go I would leave. Maybe I should leave anyway. But what if someone here does know something I don't about my wife? I'll never find out if I go now. I see the framed paper napkin on the desk again, the now familiar words scribbled on it in black Biro: *The only way out is to write.*

Whoever wrote it wasn't wrong.

I make myself a cup of black coffee and start working on the book. I plan to transcribe the whole thing onto my laptop and then edit it. Make it my own. The basic plot and the characters are great. It's about a writer trapped on a remote island, and it makes me wonder how happy Charles Whittaker really was living here if he came up with the idea. It's a story about finally having everything you thought you wanted in life, only to discover that it makes you exhausted, lonely, and sad. I can relate to that. I don't know how long it will take me to turn the idea into a Grady Green thriller, but I'm sure I can do it in three months. Possibly less time if I work really hard. And then, who knows? Maybe Kitty will find me a new publisher. Perhaps there will be an auction and I'll get a big advance, pay my debts, find a new home, start again. I am always filled with hope when I start a new project. I think all authors must be, otherwise they wouldn't spend days, weeks, months, sometimes years of their lives hiding away from the world desperately trying to write the perfect book. I've been doing this long enough to know that there is no such thing, but I'll keep trying, even if it kills me. You can only rearrange the furniture of your life a number of times before things look the same as they did.

I have to concentrate on the book, focus on the writing, do the work.

Nothing else matters and I can't afford to get distracted.

This might be my last chance.

I've managed to copy almost fifty pages by the time dawn arrives. My body feels stiff the way it always does when I sit at a desk for too long. I stretch and notice the wedding ring still on my left hand. It's never felt right to take it off, even after all this time, but I know that at some point I do need to move on. Or at least try to.

I stand up, roll my aching shoulders, walk over to the sliding doors, and remove the chair that was wedged under the door handle. When I pull back the curtains a truly breathtaking view of the sunrise over the ocean greets me, and I feel grateful and lucky to be here despite all the strange things that have happened since I arrived. I open the doors and step out onto the splintered, faded decking to enjoy the moment fully, staring up at a pink-stained sky. Nobody else will ever see this exact view from this precise place at this time. This incredible sight is unique for me, and it makes life feel worth living again.

I find it increasingly difficult to concentrate when I return to my desk—even without the distractions of the internet and social media—so I go to make myself another coffee. To my dismay, I discover that I am out of pods. I can't work without caffeine. I struggle to function at all without the right fuel. I should have bought coffee when I was at the shop yesterday; I can't believe I forgot. The sooner I can rewrite the novel and send it to my agent, the sooner I can get off this island. But I can't do that without coffee. And maybe a little chat with Cora Christie might help me understand the newspaper clipping that someone wanted me to read.

Once I am washed and dressed and horribly uncaffeinated, Columbo and I head out on what is starting to become a familiar walk. The trees seem to whisper when we wander beneath them and the whole place feels so *alive*. The stroll through the forest and along the coast feels magical in the daytime, whereas last night I couldn't wait to get inside the cabin and lock the doors. We amble along the twisting main road, slowly heading down into the valley. Rugged hills the color of rust rise up out of dark blue rivers, and there are grass fields speckled with sheep in the distance. The island—and the people who live here—might be a little strange, but nobody could fail to notice how beautiful it all is.

I can hear the sound of a bell ringing in the distance as we approach the village, but as soon as we turn in to the lane opposite the church, the sound abruptly stops. I see that the doors are wide open and my curiosity gets the better of me. I'm not religious but I have always liked visiting old churches. I find them calming. Saint Lucy's has a wooden lych-gate outside the entrance, which draws me closer. I love these old sheltered gates, a place to take refuge, and designed to mark the division between holy and unholy land. I look up as I walk beneath it and see an inscription carved into the wood: MORS JANUA VITAE. Latin, I presume. The church itself is small. It looks old and charming with plenty of character. There are stained glass windows in the gray stone walls, and there is a wooden shingled spire. As I approach the open doors I think I can hear voices inside, but I must have been mistaken because when I step into the church nobody is there.

I see that the floor is made from ancient-looking tombstones, the engraved names on them almost completely worn away from years of being walked on. There are two neat little rows of old wooden pews, a small stone altar, and the place has that unmistakable church aroma. I can smell candles too, and I spot a small display of them just inside the entrance. There are five lines of five short, thin white candles and I see they are all lit. All except for one. Twenty-five candles for the twenty-five residents on the island perhaps? I spot a poster saying CHURCH ROOF REPAIR FUND next to a little wooden donations box and I have an idea. It might not be a bad one. It is time I moved on—or at least tried to—so before I can overthink it and change my mind, I remove my wedding ring and post it through the slot.

The church doors slam closed as though a gust of wind has blown them shut, which is strange because today's weather is calm and still. The candles flicker, all twenty-four of them, and I spot movement in the corner of my eye. I spin around just in time to see someone leave the church through a small door at the back. Someone wearing a red coat.

"Can I help you?" says a female voice behind me.

I have never known how to behave around beautiful women.

I tend to get tongue-tied and find it hard to look directly at them without squinting, like when staring at the sun. If I had to guess I'd say the woman was in her early fifties, a few years older than me. Her long, natural-looking blond hair forms perfect waves framing her pretty face, she has porcelain skin and big brown eyes. She's almost too good-looking. So attractive that it could be considered rude. An aging supermodel dressed as a priest.

"I'm Grady," I say, then realize she didn't ask my name.

"Good to finally meet you, Grady," she replies. Her words sound like a cat purring and she smiles at me, revealing perfect white teeth. "I'm Reverend Melody Bates. You can call me Melody. I've heard a lot about you, welcome to Saint Lucy's—"

"Thank you," I say, staring over her shoulder. "Sorry, but was there someone else here a moment ago?"

She follows my gaze to the door then shakes her head. "No. We're quite alone."

"You're sure?"

The reverend raises a perfect eyebrow.

"I can swear on a Bible if you'd like?" she says, then picks up a copy. She places her hand on top and says, "Fuck." Then she smiles. "I swore on a Bible, get it? And there's no need to look so shocked. Swearing isn't a sin." I smile too—can't help it—but I also can't let it go. I take out my phone and scroll until I find a picture of Abby.

"Sorry, I believe you—of course—but have you ever seen this woman?"

She stares at the screen then shakes her head. "Who is she?"

My heavy heart sinks.

"Just someone I used to know. I thought I saw her on the island but I must have been mistaken."

She nods in understanding and smiles kindly. "People come here for all sorts of reasons. Saint Lucy is the patron saint of writers and the island has always been a haven for creative souls. This old church has been visited by a lot of struggling artists over the years, seeking inspiration, comfort, a sense of direction and purpose perhaps. After all, creativity is a gift which can't be given back. I like to think our Saint Lucy has helped to get writers who were lost back on the right path. Which was good for them. Good for us."

It feels as though she is talking to me about me.

"I get the impression you know who I am," I say.

She shakes her head. "I only know *what* you are, not who you are. News travels fast in a place where there's rarely any news."

"What do you mean?"

"You're the new author, aren't you?"

"It's starting to feel as though everyone is talking about me."

"They are, but don't let it go to your head, you'll be old news soon enough. This island, and the people who live here, have seen it all over the years. Take this old church, it's beautiful, but it was built on the wrong side of history. They used to burn witches here," she whispers, even though there is nobody around to overhear. "When the island decided they wanted to make a woman disappear, they called her a witch and with a puff of smoke—and a bonfire—she was gone. A murderous magic trick. First they got rid of all the birds, then they tried to get rid of the women." I think I pull a face because she raises an eyebrow. "I'm sorry, did you want the Disney version?" She smiles again then, and I do too, as though it is contagious. "Are you religious?" she asks.

"God, no," I say before realizing my mistake. "Sorry, Reverend."

"Please call me Melody," she says, touching my arm. "And there's no need to apologize. It's a very close but mixed community here on the island, and this is the only place of worship. People of all faiths—and those who haven't found faith yet—are welcome at Saint Lucy's. Everyone is welcome here. Even four-legged visitors," she says, looking down at Columbo. As soon as she gives him attention, he wags his tail and looks up at her adoringly. I realize that I am doing the same. I can't remember whether female priests are allowed to have relationships and I feel guilty just for wondering. I glance over at the donations box and my finger suddenly feels naked without my wedding ring.

"I heard the church bells a little earlier," I blurt out, oddly desperate to keep the conversation going. "It was a strange sound. A single bell, ringing very slowly, but repeatedly and echoing all around the valley."

Melody's smile vanishes and her body language changes. "The tolling of the death bell. It rings once for every year a person lived."

"Did someone die?"

She shrugs. "We're all dying from the day we are born. It was just a rehearsal, nothing for you to worry about. But if you want to be helpful, the best thing you could do is leave."

The stale air feels a little colder than it did a moment ago.

"Sorry?"

"The church," she says, smiling. "So that I can lock up," she adds, producing a giant set of keys.

"Right, of course," I reply, already heading out of the door. "What does the inscription mean? The one above the gate?" I ask, seeing it again.

"Mors janua vitae? It's Latin for 'death is the gate of life.' If you like that sort of thing you might want to visit the cemetery too before you go, it's always very popular with visitors. Good to meet you, Grady. You take care now."

The beautiful priest remembered my name.

She closes the large wooden door in my face before I can reply. Then I hear the jingle of keys and the unmistakable sound of heavy bolts sliding into place. Locking church doors seems like a strange thing to do on a tiny island that has no crime.

I do what I always do after meeting someone I like. I replay the conversation in my head, reliving all the moments I wish I could change, hoping I wasn't quite as awkward as I fear I might have been, and thinking of all the things I should and could have said better. I start to walk away from the church but then hear what is becoming a familiar sound on the other side of the locked door—the crackle of a walkie-talkie.

DEVOUT ATHEIST

Columbo wanders off toward the cemetery at the back of the church, and I follow like the obedient owner that I am. The corner shop doesn't open for a few more minutes so we have some time to kill. My tired mind is now preoccupied with my missing wife *and* the woman I just met. I feel as though I've been unfaithful for finding someone else attractive. I never cheated on my wife, but I sometimes worry that she didn't love me like she used to, that maybe I disappointed her in some way.

There were a lot of conspiracy theories at the time after Abby disappeared. Her colleagues at the newspaper were sure that it was something to do with her work because of the antique doll that was found in her abandoned car; they thought that she was investigating the wrong person and was silenced. I didn't agree with them at the time. I thought it sounded too far-fetched. But the newspaper article someone slipped under the cabin door must mean *something*. I need to talk to Cora and find out what she knows, if anything, but I don't know what to say to the woman. Abby was the one who always knew what questions to ask. People are a tricky landscape to navigate.

The cemetery is large for a place with such a small population. Some of the ancient headstones are too weathered to be able to read the names once engraved on them, while other old stone slabs covered in moss are leaning at precarious angles or have completely fallen down. There is a section of more recent-looking graves toward the back of the cemetery, and I wander over to take a look. I am not religious—more of a devout atheist—but I sometimes wish that I had faith. I believe that when we're gone, we're gone, but that doesn't mean I don't respect other people's beliefs. Whenever I wander through an old graveyard like this, I read all the headstones and make up stories for the people buried beneath them.

I don't have to make up a story for the next one I see. It stands out from all the others as it is bigger and made from black stone, and I instantly recognize the name. Charles Whittaker's headstone is impressive, though the epitaph isn't what I would have expected.

CHARLES WHITTAKER
"Go away. I'm still writing."

Loved by all.
Known by none.
Alone at last.

Close by I spot a mound of freshly dug earth and see an empty grave. The hole is dark, and dank, and so deep I struggle to see the bottom. I stumble backward, afraid of falling in—being buried alive is one of my all-time biggest fears. Maybe someone died recently and the islanders are getting ready for a funeral. That would explain why they were ringing the "death bell" and why only twenty-four of the twenty-five candles were lit in the church. My tiredness is catching up with me, but I walk a little farther and notice that there are a lot of children's graves. There are twelve that are almost identical, made in the same style and size. The only thing that is different about them are the names carved into the white marble. They all have the exact same date just over thirty years ago engraved on them, and I wonder if the children got sick with the same thing. Something which they might have survived had there been a doctor on the island.

"The Children of the Mist," says a voice behind me.

I turn so fast I'm surprised I don't have whiplash. An elderly woman carrying a walking stick is standing there. She has long gray hair that has been woven into a neat plait resting on her shoulder, and she's tall, so tall that she stoops a little, as though embarrassed by her own height. She's dressed head to toe in tweed, wearing a stylish coat with a matching tartan hat, and I wonder if she might be Sandy's mother.

"You shouldn't be here," she says.

"I'm sorry, I didn't mean to intrude—"

"You should *go*. Leave while you still can. Before it's too late," she whispers, staring intently at me before looking over my shoulder. I turn to see what she is looking at but there is nobody there, and when I turn back she is gone.

"Hello?" I call, wandering through some of the headstones, but there is no sign of her.

I start to wonder if I imagined her. Like I imagined seeing Abby. Then I wonder if I am losing my mind.

I think maybe I just very badly need to sleep.

Columbo and I hurry out of the cemetery and back toward the village green; the shop should be open by now. It's impossible not to notice how picturesque and quaint this little corner of Amberly is. Walking around it feels like stepping back in time. The pretty little gardens in front of the thatched cottages are neatly kept, hiding behind dainty white picket fencing. Immaculate window boxes explode with perfect blooms of colorful flowers. Everything is freshly painted and tidy, no sign of any litter or graffiti, unlike in London. Up close, I can see that the thatched cottages all have quirky names above their different colored front doors: Whit's End, Middle of Nowhere, and The Last Straw.

Someone on the island has a sense of humor.

It continues with the old-fashioned street signs: At one junction, a wooden crossroad sign points in three directions: ONE STREET. ANOTHER STREET. LANE WITH NO NAME.

There is a small row of shops, including a butcher's, a bakery, and what looks like a gift shop selling mainly candles, and everything looks perfect. A little too perfect, perhaps, until a large Highland cow walks down the lane and comes to stand in the middle of the green. I've never seen one before. Her distinctive horns look almost prehistoric, and her woolly coat is gray, with wavy strands that look silver in this light. Columbo barks, but the cow just stands and stares in our direction, one eye peeking out from her shaggy mane. Watching me. She turns and walks away, her tail swishing, and I cross the road and head toward Christie's Corner Shop.

"Back so soon?" Cora asks before I've even stepped inside. I guess the little bell above the door lets her know when someone comes in, but it's as though she knew it was me before she saw me. "Don't mind Daisy, our Highland cow. She's the island's unofficial mascot, a real sweetheart and ever so friendly, despite the horns."

"Good to know," I say, taking in today's all-green outfit. "I forgot to get coffee yesterday."

"If it's *real* coffee you're after, I can help. If it's those strange pods some people like for their machines, I'll need to order them from the mainland for you."

"Real coffee would be just fine." There was a *cafetière* in the cabin. Cora points me in the right direction and there is a surprisingly good selection.

"How's the book coming along?" she asks when I pay.

"You sound like my agent," I tell her.

The bell tinkles again and the door opens just enough to reveal a middle-aged woman. She is dressed as though there is a blizzard outside, even though it's pretty mild for the time of year, and is pushing a vintage-looking buggy, which she struggles to get inside the shop. I rush to help.

"No thank you," she says curtly, with a determined shake of her head. She heaves the buggy backward up the step, then pushes it past me. I suppose some mothers are very protective of their children. But when I look inside the stroller, there's no baby, just a pug dog wearing baby clothes. It stares back at me and growls.

Cora raises one of her barely there eyebrows. "And don't worry about our Ada," she whispers when the woman—and her buggy—have disappeared down an aisle. "She's a funny one. Comes in every day. Sometimes she steals a chocolate bar and hides it beneath the baby blankets. I pretend not to notice."

"Does she *have* a baby?" I whisper back, wondering if I imagined seeing a dressed-up dog.

Cora shakes her head, leans closer, whispers again, "No. She did have a child, but she lost it. Lost the plot too, when it happened. Ada is harmless, just a bit broken is all."

I know the feeling.

I need to find out what, if anything, Cora knows about my wife. And whether Cora Christie used to be Coraline Thatcher from the newspaper article. Looking at her now it seems like a bit of a stretch.

"Have you always lived on the island?" I ask, and the smile vanishes from her face.

"Why do you ask?"

"Just curious."

"Curiosity doesn't only kill cats," she says. "Amberly is the only place I've ever thought of as home."

If Cora is Coraline, if she killed a man who raped her daughter and went to prison for it, then I need to be sensitive about what I ask.

"Maybe I'll take a newspaper," I say, picking up a copy of yesterday's *Times*. "Have you ever been interviewed by a journalist?"

Cora laughs. "Why would a journalist want to speak to me?"

"I don't know . . . something you might have done in your past?"

Cora's face looks very serious all of a sudden. "Well now, let me see. I did do a *terrific* job of pricing up all the tinned food that was close to expiration date last week. I'm surprised that there wasn't a gang of press on my doorstep, desperate to get an exclusive interview and ask me all about it!" She laughs again. I don't.

"Do you have a daughter?" I ask, and the smile vanishes from her face.

"Are you okay, Grady? You're looking a little tired, if you don't mind me saying so."

I *do* mind. Patience comes with an expiration date too.

"I don't blame you," she continues. "I'd have trouble sleeping in an old haunted cabin in the woods, perched on the edge of a crumbling cliff, wondering if I'd ever wake up or whether I'd die in my sleep when the place fell into the sea. Which it will, it's only a matter of time. You do know Charles Whittaker died in that cabin?" Cora hands me my bag of shopping but doesn't let go when I try to take it. She has a surprisingly strong grip.

"I don't believe in ghosts," I say.

"Do you believe in tea?" she asks, still holding the bag. "Bog myrtle tea is wonderful for insomnia."

"I didn't say that I had—"

"The tea is made here on the island and it's *very* popular with visitors." She reaches beneath the counter and puts a small floral cardboard box inside my bag. "Try it. On the house. You can't write a bestseller if you're dead tired."

CLEARLY CONFUSED

start heading out of the village. Other than coffee, I feel like I didn't get anything out of that visit. Why couldn't Cora give me a straight answer? Is she hiding something? Maybe the sweet old lady running the corner shop *is* a killer. Or perhaps she is just a bit aloof in general? I don't know what to make of any of it. Abby was so much better at reading people and asking the right questions.

Columbo stops outside the butcher's, sniffs the air, and stares up at me.

"You're quite right. We could do with a decent dinner after Midge's cooking last night," I tell him, and the dog wags his tail as though he understands. Also, I figure meeting a few more of the twenty-five residents will surely help me to figure out what is really going on here. One of them has to know something.

The shop stands out from the others with its traditional red-and-white Victorian awnings and old-fashioned signage. The door and window frames have all been painted a bright red color, and there are glazed tiles depicting sheep. Bill's Butchers looks like something from an old film and also appears to be closed, so I'm surprised when I try the door and it opens. Another little bell tinkles to announce my arrival—bells are obviously popular on Amberly—and a small woman with jet-black hair and olive skin appears behind the counter. Almost as though she had been crouching down, hiding beneath it, hoping that I wouldn't come inside. She does not look like a Bill.

"Hello," I say, feeling unwelcome. But then she smiles, and her whole face lights up as though someone just switched her on. I see she is wearing a necklace spelling out the name Mary.

"Good morning," Mary replies with a Spanish accent I did not expect. She speaks as though on autopilot, smiling so much it is a tad unnerving. She's a neat and tidy–looking woman with minimal makeup and not a hair out of place. A little younger than me, I think. She's wearing a bright white, slightly bloody apron. I take in the steel rails on the walls and huge wooden chopping blocks, the oversize scales, and rows of large, shiny, extremely sharp-looking knives. "Is there anything I can help you with?" she asks, still smiling. The way she stares at me with her big eyes and bright white teeth makes me feel so uncomfortable I have to look away. I cast an eye over all the meat on display instead. There's a lot of it for a tiny island.

"There's so much to choose from," I say.

She nods enthusiastically. "We do our best. At the moment we've got leg of lamb, lamb chops, lamb shoulder, lamb rack, lamb burgers, lamb cutlets, minced lamb, lamb shanks, lamb loin, and some lovely lamb cheeks."

"That's . . . a lot of lamb."

She nods again. Beaming. "It is."

"You don't sell any other types of meat?"

The smile vanishes from her face. "No. We sell lamb."

My eyes are drawn to the very sharp-looking knives again.

"Well, in that case, I'll take some lamb chops please," I say.

The smile returns, and she starts adding the meat to the scales.

"Life on a small island like this isn't always easy," she says.

"Meat is best fresh but the ferry only sails once, sometimes twice a week, so we slaughter our own in the abattoir out back." She turns to look over her shoulder at a door behind the counter. I look too, and think I see someone standing there behind the frosted glass, but maybe it was just a trick of the light. "Everything you see here," she says, looking back down at the meat counter, "would have been alive and well only a day or so ago. Walking around, breathing the sea air, feeling the sun on its back. Now they're *dead*. Just like that, their life is over. Finished. Extinguished. Ended when it had barely begun. How is the writing coming along?" The unexpected question tacked on the end of her speech knocks the wind out of me a little. I didn't realize she knew who I was too. "Small island. Everyone knows everything about everyone here," she adds, as though reading my mind.

"I'm starting to realize that."

"Nobody has any secrets on the Isle of Amberly. I hope you left yours behind."

Her words somehow feel like a threat and a warning at the same time.

"Writers don't have secrets, and if we do we hide them inside our books," I tell her, but she just smiles. "You have a beautiful accent. Are you from Spain originally?"

"I always find that fascinating about the British. The way they don't ask what they really want to ask but still expect to find out what it is they want to know," she says.

"Sorry, you've lost me."

"Again, no. You are lost because of you, not me. You asked if I was from Spain, but what you really wanted to know is why I am here, on Amberly."

She's clearly confused. I was actually just trying to make polite conversation.

"Why *are* you here?" I ask, indulging her.

"Why does anyone do anything? There are only ever two

reasons: for money or for love. In my case, love. I was living in Barcelona when the love of my life walked into the café where I worked. That was five years ago. We've been together ever since, and being married to a butcher has plenty of advantages," she says, smiling again.

I stare at the BILL'S BUTCHERS sign on the tiled wall behind her. "Well, Bill is a lucky man."

"Bill is dead," she replies, still smiling.

"Oh, I'm sorry—"

"Don't be. I was talking about Alex. We took over Bill's Butchers when Bill had a heart attack. We were here on holiday—just visiting the island—but ended up running the business. It was a case of right time, right place."

Not for Bill, I can't help thinking.

The door behind the counter swings open. I catch a brief glimpse of the room it hides, filled with lots of shiny metal surfaces. There is what looks like an operating table in the middle, with a carcass on top. And a saw. The bloody limbs almost look . . . human—

"Gosh, sorry, didn't know we had a visitor," a skinny young woman says, quickly closing the door.

They kiss and I feel a little old and out of touch for assuming that Alex was a man.

Alex—the woman—has short blond hair, round rubber earrings that stretch holes in her lobes, and when she wipes her bloody hands on her otherwise crisp white apron, I see that she has tattoos on each of her fingers. A skull, a star, a sun, a moon, and a heart. She catches me staring and smiles in a way I find deeply unsettling.

"How delightful. A *visitor*. Out of season." She speaks the way someone does when they have known nothing but wealth. It catches me off guard because her posh British accent doesn't match her appearance; it's out of sync, like when the sound doesn't match the image on your TV and your brain can't immediately process what is wrong. "I hope you're not writing about us in your book."

"You and Mary?"

"The *island*. This is a quiet place. A peaceful place. A *private* place. We don't need authors or journalists coming here, writing about Amberly, attracting even more *visitors* and turning our home into some sort of Scottish island Disneyland. We like things the way they are." She says it all with a friendly smile but her words still sound menacing.

"Did a journalist come here?" I ask, wondering if she was referring to Abby.

"We get a lot of visitors during the tourist season—too many— it's impossible to remember them all," Mary interrupts.

"And they're all the same," Alex adds.

Mary smiles apologetically, then wraps the meat in paper before placing it inside a red-and-white stripy bag. "I've added some lamb sausages for the dog, my treat," she says, smiling at Columbo, who is sitting outside staring in through the window.

I thank her, pay, and then turn to leave. The little bell tinkles when I open the door.

"Thanks again," I say. Neither of them replies, but when I look over my shoulder their big white smiles are still firmly in place.

The people on this island are strange. All of them. I don't think I'm imagining it.

But maybe that's what happens when you're cut off from the real world for too long.

ONE-MAN BAND

The older I get, the less I understand the world and the terrible things that people do to one another. Being an author is like being in a one-man band and I like that aspect of my job. I enjoy the safety of solitude. Other people baffle me these days, and not in a good way. The horror inflicted by humans that Abby used to write about for the newspaper seems even more foreign and strange and disturbing to me now. I find it hard to comprehend that people capable of such things are the same species as us, and it makes me want to run away from the real world even more. I suppose, in so many ways, that is exactly what I have done.

As Columbo and I climb the hill and make our way through the forest, I feel a little bit jealous of my dog. He doesn't have to deal with a world that is frequently too loud and too awful. His days are almost always the same, and so long as he is fed, and walked, and loved, he is happy. I wish my life were so simple. Still, there is lots to be grateful for, I remind myself. Again. I look forward to retreating to the cabin, a safe place to seek shelter from the madness of the real world. Until I open the door.

Someone has slipped another envelope beneath it.

It has the words *Read Me* written on the outside again, and contains another newspaper article written by Abby.

8ᵗʰ January 2019   The Times   Page 7

PRIVATE FAMILY FUNERAL FOR VICTORIA SPENCER-SMITH RUINED BY PRESS INTRUSION

Abby Goldman

What should have been a private family funeral for Victoria Spencer-Smith resulted in violence and two arrests yesterday.

The wife of MP Alfie Spencer-Smith died last week, two weeks after her husband's affair with his secretary was front-page news for several tabloid newspapers.

According to friends of the family, Victoria was hounded by photographers once the news broke. She was followed everywhere, felt trapped in her own home by journalists camped outside, and withdrew into herself, shying away from the support she clearly needed.

She was convinced that her phone had been hacked and felt she couldn't talk to anyone about what had happened.

Victoria Spencer-Smith took her own life. The coroner's report said that there was a high risk of further deaths in similar cases if harassment by the British press was not stopped or at least tackled.

It is true that the whole family were pursued after the revelations about her husband's affair. Even the couple's teenaged daughter, Alexandra, was followed to school and photographed by the press

It was Alexandra who threw a brick at one journalist, breaking his nose, when she discovered him looking through the family's bins after the funeral service. The journalist and another photographer were arrested, but it didn't stop other press camping outside the family's home again overnight.

Victoria Spencer-Smith's sixteen-year-old daughter posted an emotional video of herself on social media after the funeral. In the video, which has since gone viral, she cut off her long blond hair in protest, blaming the press for her mother's death.

I confess I don't remember reading this newspaper article by Abby before. She always read my books cover to cover, but I didn't read every single story that she wrote; there were so many. Perhaps, in hindsight, I should have. Maybe then I would understand why someone wants me to see these articles now. They clearly have something to do with her disappearance, I just don't know what.

SWEET SORROW

—————

One Week Before She Disappeared

ABBY

"Sometimes I just want to disappear. I know I have a lot to be grateful for but I don't like my life. I want something else. Something different. Something *more*. And if I don't do something about it soon, it will be too late. I woke up one day and thought, *Is this it?* Is this really all I am going to amount to? All I am going to achieve? And I just can't get those thoughts out of my head. Maybe everyone feels like this. Maybe everyone reaches an age when they can't help thinking that they should have *done* more, *lived* more, *been* more than who they are. I'm not who I wanted to be."

The woman in black doesn't say anything, just listens.

Our time is almost up.

"And part of the problem is that I don't even know who *me* is any-more. I used to be so independent. I had ambitions and a life of my own, but it feels as though I've been fading since I met my husband. And falling. And I can no longer remember whether I jumped or was pushed. I feel as though I haven't been in charge of myself or my thoughts or my feelings for years. His thoughts about the world are now my thoughts, as though they were contagious."

I'm being more honest than I have ever been with anyone and I worry that I'm making a mistake. The woman's face is expressionless. It's impossible to tell what she is thinking.

"If you're going to tell me that I have a lot to be grateful for, a lot to be happy about, there's no need. I know that already," I say, hearing the defensive tone in my voice. "And while I am grateful for all the good things in my life, I'm not happy. And I have to do something to change that. Even if it means leaving my husband. Our lives are so tangled up in each other and that isn't an easy thing to unpick. I don't want to hurt him, but I need to fix me. The only way I can have a new life is to leave the old one behind."

"Do you still love him?" the woman in black asks, finally speaking.

"Yes."

"Do you think he still loves you?"

I think about that question before answering.

"He loves who I used to be. I don't think he's noticed that I'm not that person anymore."

We were at a friend's birthday party when the cracks in our relationship became a little too wide to ignore. One of *my* friends, not his. My husband has never liked parties, he prefers spending time with his characters and the dog. He complained the entire car journey, all the way to London, but when we arrived he turned on the charm. He drank and he danced and he became the person they all thought he was, the man I had fallen for when we first met. The author. The public persona he presented to the rest of the world and the person I knew had very little in common by then.

Seeing him like that—confident, fun, the life and soul of the party—made me feel strange. I worried that perhaps it was me making him miserable at home. He was often moody when it was just the two of us, especially if one of his precious books wasn't going well. I felt jealous of the women he was talking to and smiling at. I didn't like the way they looked at him, or how they laughed at his jokes, even the ones that weren't funny. One of them even asked him to sign their copy of his latest novel and he was like a pig in mud.

"Your other half is on good form, isn't he," said the friend who was hosting the party. It was a statement, not a question. We'd been friends since school and had always been close—she even named her daughter after me—but our lives had taken us in different directions. She had a child; I had a career. I was very fond of her daughter, having known her since she was born, and my friend thought my job was far more exciting and glamorous than it was. She owned this amazing town house in Notting Hill and was always hosting extravagant parties. There would be caterers with trays full of expensive-looking canapés, and endless champagne; she even hired a string quartet once. It was as though she needed the world to think she was happy, even though she wasn't. Looking back, maybe we were both a little jealous of what we thought the other had. I found myself irritated by the way she and all her mom friends stared at my husband that night. As though he were a genuine celebrity, like a film star, not an author. My opinion of writers changed a little after I married one.

I wanted to leave.

I followed him to the upstairs bathroom and waited for him to come out.

"I think we should go," I said as soon as he opened the door.

He looked genuinely concerned. "Why? What's wrong?"

"Nothing."

"Well, then I *am* in trouble. Whenever you say nothing is wrong it means that everything is. Did I do something to upset you?"

Yes.

"No. It's fine."

"Clearly it isn't. I give up. I didn't even want to come to this party, but you insisted, so here I am and you're still not happy."

"Would *you* be happy if you had to watch me flirt with other people all night?"

He laughed. "I haven't been *flirting*. I don't think I even remember how. I've been talking to people because that's what people do at parties. Would you rather I stood in the corner, stared at the wall, and didn't speak to anyone?"

"I'd rather you spoke to me."

The words rushed out of my mouth before I could stop them, and I hated how jealous I sounded.

"We talk all the time," he said, looking confused.

"No, we don't. We don't talk anymore. We don't laugh anymore. I can't remember the last time we had sex . . ."

"Is that what this is about?"

"Keep your voice down. Someone will hear us."

"I'm sorry if I've been a bit distant—"

"A bit distant? We're like two strangers sharing a house."

"Don't say that."

"It's true. You don't even touch me anymore. Not even to hold my hand."

"I'm sorry," he said, taking my hand in his. It felt warm and strong and nice. "You know I had a deadline and the book—"

I shrugged his hand away. "I don't care about your books. I'm sick to death of listening to you talk about your books as though that's all that matters. I care about us. I get that you love the way women look at you while you blather on about yourself and your stories, but—"

"So now I'm in trouble for the way other people look at me?"

"Don't think I haven't noticed how you're looking at them too."

"What does that mean? Should I walk around with my eyes closed? I only have eyes for you. You know that. You're always the most interesting woman in the room."

"*Interesting* is an interesting choice of word."

"It's true. You have an amazing career. A life. All the women downstairs talk about are endless stories about their children—"

"There's nothing wrong with being a mother. What if I wanted that too one day?"

He looked at me as though I had told a joke. Then, when there wasn't a punch line, he looked at me as though I had lost my mind. "But you don't want children. You never have. I think you've been working too hard, you're stressed, and you're taking it out on me. As usual."

Me working so hard benefited both of us, financially and in other ways. I was tired of his complaints about the long hours and late nights.

"I'm sure it's all very flattering and a nice little ego boost when they flutter their eyelids at you," I said. "But none of it is real. They think you're something you're not."

"And what am I?"

I bit my tongue. Until he met me, his writing career had hit a dead end. My connections were the reason he was a success. We both knew it; I didn't need to say it. But I didn't want to hurt him. I still don't.

"You used to look at me the way they do," he said then. "As though you believed in me. As though you were proud."

"You used to look at me as though you still found me attractive."

He frowned. "I do still find you attractive."

Then he kissed me in a way that he hadn't for so long.

"Stop that. Someone could come up here any moment," I said, pushing him away.

"I can't kiss my wife now?"

"It's been so long I'm surprised you remember how."

He pushed me up against the wall and kissed me again.

"I remember how," he whispered, and this time I kissed him back. We stumbled down the hallway like drunk teenagers, tugging at each other's clothes, until we found an empty bedroom. In the darkness he pulled the hem of my skirt up, my underwear down, and maneuvered me to a vintage armchair in the corner of the room. He fucked me on that chair. There is no other word for it. One of his hands bent me over from behind and held me in place, the other covered my mouth.

Despite what he'd said, I felt like I could have been anyone, and that something had changed between us.

Sex didn't feel like making love after that night. We took what we needed from each other, when we needed it, and intimacy became even more of a rare currency in our marriage. Then it stopped altogether. I could see in the mirror that I didn't look how I used to, but he looked better than ever. Some men get more handsome with age. Our jobs became our lives, and the women he worked with—publishers, publicists—all seemed to be getting younger and prettier. It's hard for a woman my age to compete with a twentysomething with stars in her eyes.

We started to unravel and I didn't know how to fix us or if I even wanted to. I was always working, he was always writing, and we muddled on. There is nothing sweet about sorrow. Sadness can consume a person if it is allowed to linger too long. It takes root and buries itself inside a person's soul, until every thought is too heavy, too painful to think. It felt like we had lost the version of us that knew how to be happy. We're still together but I have never felt so alone.

"He thinks he still loves me," I tell the woman in black, realizing that I have allowed myself to wander and get lost inside memories I would rather forget.

She waits for me to say more, but I don't.

I have forgotten how it feels not to feel lonely.

Sometimes at night, while he is sleeping right next to me but seems so far away, I remember how things used to be. Retired feelings of desire return and I can't sleep unless I do something to satisfy them. When I am sure he is sound asleep, my fingers creep beneath the sheets, silently slide down my tummy, and find their way between my legs. I've learned to be silent as I touch myself the way he used to touch me. Sometimes I pretend that it is his hand, his fingers, him, even though he is unconscious and uninterested. Other times I pretend that other hands are touching me. People I know, people I don't. I've never cheated on my husband in real life, only in my fantasies. I thought I could fix us. Find a way to make things work.

Wives think their husbands will change but they don't.

Husbands think their wives won't change but they do.

BIG BABY

GRADY

My past has been leaning hard on me lately. My mind keeps revisiting parts of it I would rather forget. Nobody wants to be constantly reminded of their mistakes or shortcomings, but I guess there are some we can't ever run from. My wife and I rarely argued—it sounds far-fetched compared with most married couples I know—but it is nevertheless true. She had a rather unfortunate habit of storing up all the things that I had done to annoy her, and then letting me have it with both barrels in a fit of rage that was otherwise quite out of character. There was seldom any warning for these outbursts, but I had learned over the years that there were some topics of conversation best avoided.

If we did disagree toward the end it was often about the same subject: children. She occasionally thought she wanted them; I always knew that I didn't. It was a topic that came up rarely because it always resulted in the sort of conflict neither of us wanted. I remember the last time we talked about it as though it were yesterday.

"You keep saying I should quit my job at the newspaper but then what would I do?" Abby said as we strolled along Brighton pier hand in hand. We'd had a night away in a posh hotel to celebrate our anniversary, and were walking off fish-and-chips. Seagulls danced in the blue sky above us, the sun was shining, Columbo was trotting along the boardwalk by our side, and I was holding hands with the love of my life. Life was good until it wasn't.

"Be at home. Be with me," I replied, pulling her closer and kissing her.

"You spend all day writing. What would *I* do?" Abby asked, pulling away.

"I'm sure you'd think of something. Something less dangerous than being an investigative journalist. Something that didn't mean us spending so much time apart."

"Oh look, a Zoltar Machine!" she said, dragging me toward the entrance to the arcades at the end of the pier. "Do you remember this, from that film? The one where the kid wished he was big?"

"It was called *Big*."

"Okay, genius. We should ask it to tell us our fortune, and then make a wish."

She found a coin in her purse and slotted it in the machine then closed her eyes.

"What are you wishing for?" I asked.

"Obviously I can't tell you that or it won't come true."

The animated fortune teller came to life and started speaking, it sounded mostly like gobbledygook to my ears. Abby—who was normally so mature and sensible—suddenly resembled a child. She had a mind mostly ruled by logic but a soft spot for anything related to fortune-telling. Zoltar stopped speaking and a paper ticket popped out of the bottom of the machine. She snatched it, her smile vanished, and then my brave and courageous wife cried.

"What's wrong? What did it say?" I asked.

"Nothing."

One person's nothing is sometimes a whole lot of something for someone else. I didn't believe her and I was right not to; we argued all the way home. The car journey was punctuated by awkward silences or my wife listing ways in which I'd disappointed her. The subjects were all the usual suspects: I was selfish; I didn't pull my weight around the house; I wasn't affectionate enough; I forgot our anniversary. I confess that I did forget. That's why I booked a last-minute night away, and I chose somewhere relatively close to home so I didn't have to take too much time off from editing.

"You care more about your books than you do about me," she said, and not for the first time. Then she talked about *maybe* wanting to have a baby. It wasn't the first time she'd said that either, but just like all the other times, she offered no explanation for how *us* having a child would work in reality. Abby's job took up almost all of her time, I needed quiet to write, neither of us had family who could help with childcare. So who was going to look after our baby if we had one?

"Unless you're going to take at least a year off—which you've always said you can't because of your career—and never work full-time again, I don't see how it is possible," I said gently, trying to concentrate on the road ahead.

Abby folded her arms across her chest. "If it was something *you* wanted we would find a way."

"But I *don't* want a child. I've been honest about that since we met, long before we got married. Think about the world we live in. Humanity is broken, you write about that fact every day, why would you want to bring a child into this world? Children are expensive and high-maintenance and they don't come with an off switch. None of our friends with kids are happy and they all look permanently exhausted."

"The real reason you don't want a child is that you still are one. I'm married to a big baby. You're so selfish."

"You're right. I am. I don't want to sign up for looking after some brat for twenty years who might not even love me. Who might not even love you. Who we might not love. Having a baby doesn't always mean unconditional love and happy families." She didn't answer straight away. She was quiet, which was always the most dangerous part of any argument we had, because it meant she was planning her next attack.

The Abby I knew could be cruel if she didn't get her way. The rest of the world only saw an award-winning journalist, but I had a front-row seat with the best view of the real Abby Goldman. The real Abby wasn't as tough as I think her colleagues believed. She spent Sundays in her PJs watching black-and-white films, wore fluffy bed socks, and slept with a water bottle because she always had cold feet. She couldn't walk past a homeless person without offering them a hot drink and some food, even if it meant giving them her own lunch. She secretly donated 10 percent of everything she ever earned to charity. Secretly because she believed people who shout about their good deeds are often only doing them for themselves. Even her job seemed like a variety of atonement. What I never understood was why she felt so bad in the first place.

My wife wasn't perfect, but she was perfect for me.

Even if she did sometimes say cruel things when she was upset.

"So because your parents didn't love you, I don't get to be a mother?" she said, and I had to grip the steering wheel.

They did love me, I just disappointed them.

"You didn't have a happy childhood either," I countered. "Look what your mother did to you: was that love?"

"So now you're saying you think I'll be a bad mother like my mother? You're saying that I'm like her?" Every question was a trick question when we argued. Everything she said was a trap. She made it seem impossible for me to say the right thing, but I still tried.

"No. I'm saying, if Kitty hadn't taken you in who knows what would have happened to you. We are not good parent material; we were never taught how to be. I don't want to hurt a child the way my parents hurt me, or the way your parents hurt you. You think a child will make you happy but it won't."

"What will make you happy, Grady?"

A New York Times *bestseller.*

Somewhere quiet to write without interruptions.

A wife who doesn't frequently make me feel like I'm letting her down.

"I am happy," I told her. I thought it was a lie but now I think it might have been true.

Abby stared out of the window and we didn't talk for the rest of the journey.

I found the Zoltar card torn in two inside her coat pocket that night.

Zoltar Speaks Your Fortune
The questions you ask and the answers you seek,
Will do nothing to help make you feel less bleak.
No man is an island, and love is rarely true,
We're born alone, we die alone; do what feels right for you.

I never talked to Abby about what that card said or why it upset her so much.

Back in the present, I sit in silence in the cabin. It's as though the residual guilt is dripping down the wooden walls. There are so many things I wish I could change; words I wish I could take back. But then I give myself a good talking to. I have to stop reliving the past and focus on my future. I waste so much time replaying old conversations, wondering if things might be different now if I had said something different then. But it's all a waste of time. Wishing you could change the script of your life when the scene is over is pointless.

This is my chance, maybe my only chance, to write a new book and get my life back. Newspaper clippings under the door don't change that.

I might not have always been the perfect husband, but I loved my wife.

I hope she knew that.

As much as it hurts, and I think it always will, Abby is gone.

Wherever she is now, I need to learn to move on.

STUPIDLY BRILLIANT

For six weeks, all I do is write, eat, occasionally sleep, repeat. I take Columbo for walks in the forest or along the coast, and I go to the village when we need supplies, but I don't stray too far from the cabin or my laptop and I rarely see another human being. There have been no more strange incidents *or* islanders—possibly because I've locked myself away so I haven't seen any—and I've settled into a routine. I'm finally writing again and it feels good. But I still can't sleep for more than a few hours—despite drinking gallons of Cora's bog myrtle tea, which is surprisingly delicious—and there are permanent dark shadows beneath my eyes. I write all day and almost all night, *every* night, and it feels stupidly brilliant. Sometimes I feel so exhausted I think I might fall over, so I sit back down at my desk and write some more.

Admittedly, the book started out as Charles Whittaker's story about an author on an island, but I have taken his idea and turned it into something of my own. Perhaps something even better, something that my readers will enjoy. I genuinely believe this might be the book that gets my career and my life back on track. I received a typed letter from Kitty a couple of weeks ago and she's excited too. There is no postman on the island; Cora gave it to me when I was last in the shop, and it's the only piece of correspondence I've had from the outside world since I arrived here. I confess life is much quieter without access to emails, WhatsApps, news websites, and social media. The cabin doesn't even have a TV. There is nobody and nothing to disturb me or distract me from the book, and I truly believe that this little Scottish island might be just what I needed. It makes me sad to think how few messages there might be if my phone did work. Kitty is the only person who knows I am here. The only person who still cares. I keep her letter in a little drawer in the desk, and I take it out again now.

Dear Grady,
The new book sounds wonderful and I can't wait to read. I knew you could do it!

I know you'll send it when you're ready but the sooner the better.

Hoping I'll have it in time for the London Book Fair.

Kitty

xx

I don't think I could do my job without someone else believing in me. That person is Kitty, and I am determined to repay her kindness. I don't feel guilty about Charles; the man is dead. I'm sure he could have published the book if he had wanted to, but instead he hid the manuscript beneath the floorboards, and to be honest, it has taken a lot of hard work, rewriting, and editing to turn it into the story it is now. *My* story.

At this stage in the process I would normally print the book out before starting a second draft, but I don't have a printer, just my laptop. I stand and feel dizzy. The edges of my vision blur a little and I have to lean on the desk to steady myself. I'm so tired but I can't sleep, I mustn't even try. And I mustn't let my mind wander to thoughts of other things. Like my wife. She isn't here. How could she be? Why would she be? I need to focus on my work and move on. I can't slow down until the book is ready.

I must keep writing.

Abby was always my first reader.

Mustn't get distracted.

This will be the first book of mine she hasn't read.

Need to focus on the work. Only the work.

Columbo is staring at me and I think I might have been talking out loud. It doesn't mean I'm crazy. Just tired. I think I always lose a few marbles when I spend this many hours at my desk. I haven't had a haircut for a couple of months, and I haven't shaved for weeks either. Being cut off from the real world for this long is liberating, but I'm not even sure what day it is anymore. In the hope that it is a weekday and the shops might be open, I head into the village.

"Hello, Grady," says Cora as I hurry into Christie's Corner Shop. She's one of the few people I have seen and spoken to lately, and I've seen her only because I need food and this is the only place to get it. I seem to bump into Sandy almost every time I leave the cabin too, but that has been a happy coincidence. I like Sandy. In another life I think we could have been friends. "How is the book?" Cora asks, interrupting my daydream. My mind has been drifting more than normal.

"That's why I'm here, actually. You said that if I ever needed anything that wasn't in the shop you could get it for me."

"Of course."

"Well, I need a printer."

"A printer?"

"Yes. So that I can—"

"I might be old but I'm not daft. I do know what a printer is." Her face lights up like a Christmas tree. "Does this mean the book is finished?"

"Yes and no. It's just a first draft."

Her smile fades. "How many drafts do you need to do before it is done?"

"Three, usually. If the book behaves itself."

She looks completely crestfallen. "How long do drafts two and three take?"

"That's a bit like asking how long a piece of string is." I laugh, she doesn't. "But they normally take less time than draft one. A few weeks at most."

"Then good for you." She beams as though she is genuinely happy for me. "And good for us," she says beneath her breath.

"What do you—?"

"Did you have a printer in mind?"

I do and I've already written it down for her. It's the same model I had back in London. It's basic but it will do the job and it's all I can afford. I grab some more food while I'm here, a few more lamb ready meals, some milk, and two boxes of bog myrtle tea. When I count out my cash I realize I don't have much left, but hopefully there's enough to feed myself and Columbo until the book is ready. Cora takes a KitKat from the chocolate stand by the checkout and adds it to my bag of groceries.

"That's on me," she says. "I know they're your favorite."

I don't know why she is being nice to me but I like it.

It almost makes me sad to be leaving the place, but that's exactly what I plan to do as soon as the book is ready to send to Kitty.

"I'll miss this little shop when I leave the island," I say.

Cora frowns. "Why would you leave the island?"

"Well, as fun as it's been, my work here is nearly done."

Her smile returns. "We'll see."

BACKSEAT DRIVER

T wo days later there is a loud knock on the cabin door.

"This came for you on the ferry today," Sandy says. "Thought I may as well bring it straight here, rather than watch you try to lug it up the hill all the way from the village." She stares at my new beard before pointing down at a large cardboard box. It must be the printer. Goodness knows how *she* carried it here.

"Thank you. Do you want to come in for a—?"

"No, don't want to disturb you. I hear you're close to finishing the new book. But if there's anything else you need don't hesitate to tell me," she says, already turning to leave.

"Actually . . . when is the next ferry to the mainland?"

"Grady, every time I see you, you talk about leaving the island. A woman can take these things personally, you know."

"It's just that I might be going back soon."

She frowns. "But you haven't finished the book."

"Well, I probably will before long, and then I'll be returning to London. I was never going to stay here forever." I smile but Sandy doesn't. "I know the ferry only sails once or twice a week and I still haven't seen a new timetable. Is there one?"

She huffs. "The ferry sails at the best times according to the sea, the tides, and the weather. When you live on a small island you learn to fit your life around things that are bigger than you. Things any smart person would understand they cannot control."

"What does that mean?"

"It means life here is different, that's all. It's a life some people fall in love with."

She seems offended that I don't want to stay and I have an idea.

"It might be easier to fall in love with the place if I had my car and could see more of the island."

"I've told you before, no nonresidents are permitted to bring vehicles onto Amberly. If I break the rules for you, I'd have to break the rules for everyone, and then where would we be? An island overrun with cars and pollution and litter and *visitors*. I'm sorry. I have to protect the island and the people who live here. Maybe if you were to move here permanently one day . . . but there are no rules about you driving someone *else's* car," she says.

"I doubt anyone wants to loan me their—"

"Charles had an old Land Rover. Didn't drive it much toward the end, but it must still be here. The battery is bound to be dead, but we could try and jump-start it. Did you ever look inside the big old shed?"

"No. I couldn't find the keys," I tell her.

"Well, they must be in there somewhere. Did you check all the drawers?"

Of course.

"Yes."

"Mind if I take a look?"

"Be my guest," I say, stepping aside so she can come in. I regret it instantly. The place is as much of a mess as I am after six weeks of writing all day and night.

She stands in the middle of the cabin, her hands on her hips, taking it all in. "It looks just like it did when Charlie was here," she says, and I wonder if she means the cabin, or whether Charles Whittaker was surrounded by dirty cups, plates, piles of books, and piles of laundry when he wrote too. The place has descended into untidy chaos, and I don't think I look or smell any better myself. Sandy takes in the views of the ocean from the sliding doors at the back of the cabin.

"You really are living life on the edge," she says, before walking over to the kitchen area and opening a couple of drawers. I don't mind the intrusion—this place isn't really mine—but it's a complete waste of time. I've already looked and there are no keys in there or anywhere . . .

"I think this might be it," she says, holding up an old key attached to a paper luggage tag that says *Cabin Shed*. I don't know how I could have missed it all this time.

I follow Sandy outside, where we walk through the trees to a large shed that nobody would ever find if they didn't know where to look. The key fits the rusty padlock on the door, which Sandy pulls open to reveal a very old car in excellent condition. The ancient dark green Land Rover looks like it belongs in a museum but it is also spotless, as though someone might have polished it this morning.

"There she is. The Land Rover Defender 1953 series. Fit for a queen. You know this was her majesty's vehicle of choice when she was alive? Old Charlie boy was a bit of a backseat driver whenever I gave him a lift in my truck; he much preferred being in the driving seat, so he got himself a Land Rover when his books were still selling," Sandy says.

"You didn't think to tell me this was here before now?"

She shrugs. "It's not up to me to tell a man he can take another man's things."

There is an edge to her voice and for a second I think Sandy knows I have stolen Charles Whittaker's manuscript. But I tell myself I am overthinking everything, and feeling paranoid due to lack of sleep. She just means the car.

The Land Rover isn't even locked and we find the keys for it in the glove compartment. Of course it doesn't start, but Sandy seems sure she can fix it. I guess if she can sail a ferry she knows a lot more than I do about mechanics. I head back inside to make us some tea and when I come back she's already managed to get the engine running.

"There you go, all yours," she says, giving me the car keys then taking the tea. She sniffs her mug. "What is this? Bog myrtle?" I nod. "Not for me, thanks," she says, handing it back. "I'd best be off anyway."

"One tiny thing before you go . . ." I point at the overgrown forest. "How do I get the Land Rover through the trees?"

Sandy laughs. "You drive it!"

When she has gone I head back inside the cabin and print the book. Then I spend the next twenty-four hours reading it. Other than some small changes, I'm pretty happy with what I have. I would normally do three drafts before sharing a new novel with my agent, but I suppose Charles did the early drafts for me. The only thing missing now is a title; Charles just called it "Book Ten" and that will never do. I'd hoped I would come up with something while I was writing, but didn't, nothing good anyway. I see the map of Amberly and look at it for inspiration. A lot of the buildings have quirky names: Whit's End, The Final Straw, The Stumble Inn to name a few, but none of them are quite right for a book title. Then I see something called Beautiful Ugly on the map. I've no idea what it is, but it's perfect.

I pick up the Magic 8 Ball, which I seem to use for all decision-making these days.

"Is the book ready to send to my agent?" I ask out loud, waiting impatiently for the answer.

WITHOUT A DOUBT.

I smile and the sensation feels strange. Smiles have been in short supply since my wife disappeared. I don't want to push my luck but I can't resist asking another question.

"Is it a good book?" I surprise myself with the importance I place on the next words to appear on the tiny screen.

AS I SEE IT, YES.

I check the time and see that the corner shop will be closed, meaning it's too late to post the manuscript today. "We should celebrate anyway," I tell Columbo. I mostly talk to myself or my dog lately and I find he is a better listener. "What would you like to do?" I ask and he wags his tail. "I quite agree. We should go for a big walk and then crack the seal on a bottle of something nice when we get home. Maybe we should go and see one of the highlights on the island? Would you like that? May as well see it now, since with any luck we'll be leaving soon."

I didn't want to sound rude in front of Sandy. She clearly loves Amberly and it's been her home all her life, but it isn't mine. This place has been good for me in lots of ways, but the people here are a bit strange and there are things I miss about London. Things I didn't think I would. And for reasons I don't understand, this island seems determined to make me think about my wife even more than I did before. As soon as Kitty tells me the book is good and that she can sell it, I'm out of here, and I have no intention of coming back.

UPWARD FALL

take Sandy's advice and drive the old Land Rover very slowly
and very carefully through the overgrown forest, until I reach
the clearing where she usually parks. It's obvious that nobody
has driven it out of the shed for years, and it's a slow and bumpy
ride, but the big sturdy jeep crushes any bracken blocking its
path with ease. Columbo is strapped into the passenger seat next
to me and seems pleased with our new set of wheels. I am too. If
I can get to grips with driving the damn thing it'll mean we can
explore the rest of the island before we leave.

I continue to take it slowly along the coast road, but it feels good
to be behind the wheel again. Changing gear is tough and there's
no power steering, but the Land Rover is incredible to drive. The
open windows allow the wind to blow my overgrown hair in all
directions. The smell of the sea is so strong I can almost taste it, and
I feel a strange sensation. Something like happy. Columbo has been
cooped up for days while I finished the book, so I want a fun walk
for him as well as for me. Having looked at the map, I think I've
found a good option not too far away.

The Orphans is the name of the iconic rocks that form a popular walk to one of the highest points on Amberly. It's one of the

few things that did come up online when I was researching the place. It's a distinctive standing formation of rocks that form a ridge, with views of the island and the sea, almost splitting the island in two like a broken heart. I've seen a lot of pictures and I want to see it with my own eyes. From what I can remember about what I read it's an easy enough walk. Nothing Columbo and I can't handle.

The sign in the car park suggests I might be wrong about that.

DANGER

THE ORPHANS FOOTPATH IS CURRENTLY CLOSED.

"Well, that's disappointing. What do you think, Columbo? Should we risk it anyway? I have plenty of water and Scooby snacks."

He barks which I interpret as, "Yes, we should definitely climb up this mountain. We'll be fine."

One of the many things I love about my dog is that he always agrees with me.

We walk around the sign and start to climb up the winding path. It's steep, but with every step the views become more and more impressive. I keep stopping to take in the majestic beauty of it all. And to catch my breath. The spiky pinnacles known as The Orphans rise up out of grassy hills, bathed in sun and casting a series of long dark shadows. Dirty white clouds drift by overhead, casting shadows of their own. It takes forty minutes to reach the top. There's no sign of danger—nothing too tricky to navigate at all—and I can't imagine why the path would be closed.

That's when I see her, sitting on the other side of the stones, reading a book.

"Hello again," I say.

She looks startled, but then her face softens into a smile. "Hello."

"I didn't expect to see you up here," I say.

"God is a fair boss. The pay is shite but I do get an occasional day off," says the Reverend. Melody Bates looks even more beautiful than I remember and she doesn't look much like a priest today. Her long blond hair is tied back in a perfect ponytail. The black uniform and white collar are gone too, and she is dressed in tight denim shorts and a simple white T-shirt. From where I am standing I can see her cleavage and am doing my best not to look directly at it. It's made more difficult by the ring she is wearing on a long, delicate chain around her neck. It's a silver thistle, just like the one Sandy and Midge wore, I'm starting to wonder if they're all part of a cult. Melody was reading a book when I walked over and snapped it closed when she heard me, as though embarrassed. Or as though she had been caught. She buries the paperback inside her backpack before I can see what it is.

"I meant that I'm surprised to see you because of the sign," I say and she looks confused. "It said that the footpath was closed."

"Did it? I didn't notice. I always climb up here when I have the time—it's a good place to get away from it all. Somewhere quiet to think."

I would have thought that the church was pretty quiet.

"If there is a more beautiful place on this earth I haven't found it, and yet so many ugly things have happened here. Do you know why they call them The Orphans?" she asks, holding the ring between her fingers and looking up at the peaks of the mountain.

"No. Can't say that I do."

"Rumor has it, in medieval times, a king from the mainland tried to capture the island. When the islanders saw the boats carrying his army approaching, they knew they would be outnumbered. So they sent their children up this mountain to hide, trying to keep them safe. It was the right thing to do. All the men who lived on the island were murdered straight away, the women were raped then killed, and the land was stained red with their blood. When the king's troops had eaten all the food that did not belong to them, drunk the wine that was not theirs, and taken anything of value, they sailed back to the mainland. The children were spared, but only because the king's army couldn't find them. They hid up here, on this mountain, until they saw the boats sail away. Their parents had told them not to come down until they came to collect them. But nobody came. Some stories say that the children starved to death, or died from the cold, that they were lost on the mountain and couldn't find their way down. Others say that those poor little orphans were turned into these rocks, and now they guard the island that their parents failed to protect."

"That's an interesting story," I say.

"It is, isn't it. All nonsense of course. Men have been causing problems on this island since forever, but these peaks were formed from volcanic activity millions of years ago, shaped by hot molten lava."

"You sound like quite the geologist!"

She smiles. "Not all religious people are incompatible with science, Grady. I'm glad we bumped into each other. I've been thinking about you since we met."

The beautiful priest has been thinking about me.

"You have?" I can feel my heart thudding in my chest.

"I found the wedding ring that you very kindly put in the church donations box and I wanted to talk to you about it."

For a second it feels as though my heart stops.

"Oh. That," is all I manage to say.

"It will be a big help and go a long way toward fixing the church roof, but are you sure? And are you okay? If you ever need someone to talk to—"

"I'm fine, honestly. My wife is gone. It's been difficult—when I first arrived here I thought I saw her everywhere—but I need to move on."

She nods. "I'm very sorry for your loss. Grief can do strange things to a person. I see a lot of loss in my job—the world is full of broken hearts—but I see a lot of survivors too. Sometimes when a person gets knocked down by life it can be an upward fall, even though it hurts so very badly at the time. If there's anything I can—"

She's doing the head tilt of sympathy and I can't bear it.

"I'm glad my old wedding ring is going to a good cause," I say.

"Okay. Well, you know where to find me if you change your mind. I'd best be off. Prayers to pray, sinners to absolve, people to bury." She stands up and dusts the dirt off her short shorts and now I feel bad.

"Please don't leave because of me. I'll be gone soon," I say.

She shakes her head. "I don't think that you will."

Then she heads off down the mountain.

I sit for a while and wonder if I'll ever be anyone other than the man whose wife disappeared. Someone people feel sorry for and awkward around. I am going to spend the rest of my life wondering if my wife is dead or alive. Maybe it simply isn't possible to move on from something like that, no matter how far you travel. Columbo sits next to me and I'm grateful to have a silent companion. We share an apple while taking in the view. The clouds start to roll in a little faster, hiding the sun for longer until the air is distinctly cooler than it was before. I decide we should probably start heading back. I normally find going down-hill much easier—my knees complain but the rest of me prefers it—but something doesn't seem quite right. The journey up was straightforward enough because I could see The Orphans and I knew what direction I was headed in. But on the way down, I soon start to feel lost. I find myself on a rocky mountain path that I do not recognize or remember. A blanket of low cloud has drifted across the valley while we've been hiking, making it difficult to see where we have been or where we are going. I can no longer see The Orphans behind me, and I can only see a few feet ahead of me.

I begin to retrace my steps and Columbo starts to bark. I turn to see what has bothered him but I can't see anything through the mist. Nothing at all. The wind has picked up too, and I think I hear someone calling my name in the distance.

"Grady."

At first, I think it is the priest, but the second time I hear my name I recognize the voice.

"Grady, are you there?"

An army of goose bumps line up on my skin.

I spin around, trying to identify which direction the voice came from, but I can't see a thing. Then I hear the voice again, a little closer this time, and there is no doubt in my mind. It's her. Abby. She's here. I can hear her.

"Grady, why won't you come and find me?"

"Where are you?" I shout into the mist, but there is no reply. Only the wind howls back.

I'm imagining it. I must be.

I can barely see my own hands when I hold them in front of my face, and I can't see the dog at all. I curse myself for not putting him on the lead, I can't lose him too. I spin around again but still can't see a thing. I call Columbo's name, then I start to run, tripping over on the path, bashing my knee on a rock and badly grazing the palms of my hands. I hear him bark in the distance and I'm up and running again. I don't care about me, but I do care about the dog. He's all I've got left. There were some steep drops on the way up to the viewpoint. Easy enough to spot and steer clear of when mist wasn't covering the mountain, but now I don't know if he's daft enough to run right off the edge. The idea of Columbo falling or being injured makes me feel sick. I run but I can't find him. The barking has stopped. Everything is silent.

"Columbo!"

I shout his name, over and over, but nothing.

I spin around but all I can see is a thick fog in every direction.

Then I see several sets of eyes in the mist, staring at me.

MINOR MIRACLE

have never liked sheep: I find them creepy, and these ones have horns. I call Columbo's name again but he doesn't come back. I think I'm dangerously close to the cliff edge and if something has happened to him, if he has disappeared from my life like Abby, I'll never forgive myself. Everyone I have ever loved leaves me; I can't lose him too.

Columbo barks. I call him and he runs through the dissipating mist toward me. I'm so relieved to see his face I could cry. The sheep scatter and I grab hold of him, then I take the belt from my jeans to fashion a lead, looping one end through his collar. I hold the other end tight in my hand. The worst thing about this situation is that it is all my own fault. The sign said DANGER and I carried on anyway. He's safe now, but my heart is still thudding in my chest and my hands are still shaking. Guilt is such a sticky emotion; you can't wash the damn thing off.

My mood spirals downward as the path leads us down the mountain. My head full of self-pity and self-loathing. I've never learned how to play the game when it comes to real life. I didn't have anyone to teach me. I was raised by my nana, who loved me, but let me live inside a world that wasn't real, reading books and dreaming of writing my own. My parents concluded that having a child didn't suit their lifestyle when I was nine years old. They dumped me on my nana—literally dropped me outside her flat in East London one day with a suitcase and a note. It's not something I talk about—I do my best not to think about it at all these days—but I don't know if it is possible to recover from that level of abandonment. It hurt me badly at the time—no child should be made to feel that unloved and unwanted by their own parents—but in hindsight, I'm glad things turned out the way they did. Nana was a librarian and her home always smelled of toast, Oil of Olay, and Marlboro Lights. She was a bookworm who smoked like a chimney. I used to steal cigarettes and books from her handbag and she used to pretend not to notice. I always put the books back. My nana died before I became a published author and it's one of my biggest regrets. I wish she could have seen my name in print, she would have been so proud. She took care of me when nobody else did and I still miss her every day. I wasn't an orphan, I just wished that I was.

I don't think she would be very proud of me now.

If she knew I had taken another writer's manuscript, stolen their story, and that I was going to pretend it was my own, she would be so disappointed. I thought that what I was doing with the book wasn't doing anyone any harm—Charles is dead after all—but now I'm not so sure. I just keep making mistakes and unfortunately I'm not the only one who gets hurt when I do. Like today, ignoring the DANGER sign. But Columbo is okay and that's all that matters, because I don't have anyone else in the world left to love.

It feels like a minor miracle when we arrive at the car park, having somehow safely made our way back down the mountain in the mist. We clamber into the Land Rover and I lock the doors without really knowing why. This island just gets stranger and stranger. I want to leave but I can't, not until my agent tells me the book is good. Not until I know she can sell it and I can find a place to live. I don't know what I'll do if she doesn't. The mist has disappeared just as quickly as it arrived but I still feel unsettled. Unsafe. When my heart rate has slowed and I've caught my breath, I start the engine and head back toward the cabin.

The door is wide open when I get there, and there is something on the desk.

Something that wasn't there before.

It's another newspaper article, and the red harmonica that went missing weeks ago is sitting on top of it like a paperweight.

18ᵗʰ March 2021   **The Times**   Page 10

WOMEN HAVE HAD ENOUGH

By Abby Goldman

The recent demonstrations in London started as a peaceful vigil for a woman raped and murdered while walking home. It isn't the first time that women have taken to the streets in the hope of being heard, but something does feel different this time.

One group of women were dressed as suffragettes, and carried banners with the words "Same Shit, Different Century." A sentiment shared by many.

Although it might feel like we have been here before, there is a definite change of tone. Women aren't just scared anymore, they're angry.

Since the #MeToo movement there has been a global determination to change things.

The prime minister, along with the minister for domestic violence (who, despite several interview requests, refused to comment), are meeting with heads of women's charities this week, but a spokesperson said it was too little, too late.

"Women have had enough," was the headline of a joint statement issued by those charities today. They gave several examples of women who have been let down by a system they say is broken.

One was a victim of domestic abuse who called the police for help when she was badly beaten by her husband. In a recorded call she was told by a senior officer (who has since been suspended as a result of this article) that the police were too busy to deal with "silly rows" between husbands and wives. She called a second time later that night and explained in a calm and coherent voice that she thought her husband was going to kill her. The woman was told all the shelters were full and offered a tent in the middle of winter. Listening to the recording of that call, to a vulnerable woman begging for help and in fear of her life, is even more harrowing when you see photos of what happened next.

That night, her husband beat her unconscious. He broke her arm in two places and she lost several teeth. Her head injuries were so severe, doctors put her in an induced coma and she was in the hospital for six weeks. She has since relocated to the (*continued page 11*)

I read the article twice. I don't know who the woman Abby wrote about was, but I do know that my wife often campaigned for victims of domestic abuse. As we all should. I don't understand any man who could hit a woman, but then most acts of violence baffle and appall me. This is the third article that someone has left for me to find inside the cabin. I have a rule about the number three, one that cannot be ignored. Something happened to Abby. She had a habit of upsetting the wrong kind of people. She put herself in danger and I can't help thinking I might be in danger now too.

OLD NEWS

First thing in the morning, I grab the manuscript and the dog and jump in the Land Rover. Nothing spooky or strange happened while I was writing. Everything was fine. Good. Great even. Nothing but peace and quiet; the perfect writing conditions. But now I keep hearing things, seeing things, finding things again. The latest newspaper clipping wasn't slipped beneath the cabin door, someone let themselves in. I don't know why someone wants me to see old articles Abby wrote before she disappeared—it's a cruel thing to do to a man who lost their wife—but I no longer care. My plan today is to send the manuscript, then find out when the ferry is next sailing back to the mainland. I thought this island was the perfect place for a writer. It all seemed so *nice*. But places, like people, can often seem nice at first, until you get to know the real them and see them for what they are. My books mean everything to me but nothing is worth living in fear. I'll head back toward London, find another dirt-cheap hotel if I have to. It's only until Kitty can sell the new novel and I can get a new place of my own to call home. I just hope she likes the book. My whole future depends on it.

We drive out of the forest and onto the coast road and everything is blue. The cloudless sky and the calm sea are almost exactly
the same shade, making it hard to tell them apart. As though there
is no horizon. The weather feels like a good sign, or at least that's
what I'm telling myself. Sending the book to my agent has always
been the most stressful part of the process for me. I don't talk about
the books—with anyone—until I have finished them. It's just how
I have always worked. I'm fine with collaborating, and I always
listen to my agent, my first readers, and my editors, because there
are always ways to make any book better, and of course I want my
books to be as good as they can possibly be. But this stage, before
I send the book, it is all mine. And this one is perfect.

I wish I had someone to celebrate with.

Women used to flirt with me a lot more than they do now.
They flirted with me when I was young, because everyone flirts
when they are young. Then they flirted with me when I was bor-
derline old because they thought I was successful. Now that I am
neither young nor successful, flirting is an endangered species in
my world. Even if I think a woman is flirting with me, I daren't
do anything about it in case I've misread the situation. Beautiful
women have always made me make poor choices. I remember one
publication day when I somehow made the right one.

Even when you've had a smidgen of success, publishing doesn't
always go according to plan. Kitty sold one of my favorite books
to a lovely editor, who unfortunately got fired two weeks after I
had signed a contract. As a result, the publishers dumped me on
another editor who made it very clear from our first meeting that
she didn't like me (fair enough) or my books (slightly more problematic). The months leading up to publication were filled with
anxiety and unanswered emails, and when I dared to ask about
publicity, I was informed I'd be working with someone "whose

skill set matches our ambitions for the book." She was the office intern.

On publication day I was asked to come to London for an "organized" book signing. On the train to the city I saw endless posters for other authors who were being published that week, billboards in every station displaying their work, tables containing teetering piles of their books at the front of every store. I struggled to find a single copy of my own novel anywhere, which might have been less soul destroying if it hadn't been my favorite. The publicist was an hour late, and most of the bookshops we visited—on the book signing she'd organized—didn't even have the book in stock. I had to spell my name repeatedly while they tapped it into their computers and shook their heads, and the whole experience was as excruciating and uncomfortable for the booksellers as it was for me. The publicist was too busy looking at her Instagram account to notice.

There were no events for the book, no interviews, nothing much of anything. Crickets could have made more noise to promote it. I felt like old news, a has-been who never was, and at the end of what was a horrible day, I went back to my hotel room and lay in the dark for a while wondering if my career was over. It wasn't the first time my dwindling confidence as a writer had been torn to shreds. You can't do this job without confidence, so when people stamp on it, or steal it, you have to learn to protect yourself. I needed a drink. I always needed a drink. I also needed to call my wife. Abby was the only person who might have been able to make me feel better. I'd already texted her to say what a complete disaster the day had been, but she was too busy working to properly talk. As always.

I'd received a rare piece of physical fan mail via my agent the previous day. The reader had been incredibly kind and complimentary about my work, said she was my biggest fan, and had even written her number at the bottom of the note. She wrote that she was sure I was too busy, but invited me to meet her for a drink if I was ever in London. I normally told my wife everything, but confess I didn't tell her about this. I looked the mystery fan up online; she had a quirky surname and it wasn't too difficult to find photos of her on social media. In one heavily filtered picture she was even posing with my book, and she was stunning. It was the sort of thing that never happened to me and I admit it did make me feel better about myself; having a young woman flirt with me and tell me I was good at something. Especially when the rest of the world was making it very clear that I wasn't. I sat in the hotel room, stared at her number, and thought about what I would say if I called her. She was so kind and lovely, and I was feeling so sad and lonely. I'm the first to admit that men can be very stupid.

I was relieving the hotel mini bar of its contents when she knocked on my bedroom door.

My wife, not my biggest fan, and I was very happy to see her.

Abby was holding a bottle of champagne and I was so shocked by the surprise visit that at first I didn't know what to say.

She pretended to walk away. "Well, if you don't want me to come in . . ."

I grabbed her hand and pulled her inside the room. "This is a nice surprise."

"Is it?" Abby said. "Oh, good. I was worried you had another woman in here for a moment. You sounded so down in your messages; I didn't like the idea of you being alone and sad on publication day. Here, open this." She handed me the bottle while she hunted for two glasses. "Was today really so bad?" she asked.

"It wasn't great. Only one of the bookshops knew who I was and had the books in stock." I popped the cork and poured the champagne.

"Well, one is better than none isn't it?"

"They sat me down at a table with a pile of fifty books and put up a sign that said QUEUE HERE. Do you know how many people queued up to meet me and get a signed copy?"

"Oh dear," she said. "I'm scared to guess."

"One. I sat there for over an hour and only one woman came up to me with a book to sign. It wasn't even my book. It was a copy of *The Edge*. She thought I was Charles Whittaker. In some ways I was flattered, but the guy was twice my age when he died. Do I really look that old?" Abby pulled a face, but not the one I was expecting. "Oh my god, you think I look like him too—"

"No! Of course not, I'm sorry. What did you do?"

"What could I do? I signed it. 'Happy reading, best wishes, Charles.'"

She laughed then, but it wasn't her real laugh and I could tell she was distracted by something. Work probably. There was an awkward moment where neither of us seemed to know what to say and it felt like I'd missed something.

"Well, cheers," she said, raising her glass.

"Yes. Cheers to Charles." I took a big gulp of my drink.

"No! Cheers to you and your book. May it fly off the shelves!"

"It would have to be *on* the shelves in order to fly off them—"

"Come on, cheer up. Publication day is supposed to be a happy occasion isn't it?" she said, taking a tiny sip before putting down her glass and refilling mine. "Have you talked to Kitty?"

I took another gulp of champagne. "Yes. She agreed publicity in the UK has been a shit show, but said the numbers still looked good."

"Well, there you go. Just because a few bookshops in London didn't stock it doesn't mean it isn't selling elsewhere. It's your best book yet."

"Thanks. Could you tell the publishers?"

"The book will find readers, you'll see. Against all odds."

She was right. It was an instant bestseller. But we didn't know that until the official sales figures were published a week later.

Abby's phone buzzed, as it so often did, and when she looked at it her whole face changed.

"What is it? What's wrong?" I asked.

"Probably nothing."

"Tell me."

"Someone has been emailing my boss, making anonymous complaints about me and what I've written. Now they're bombarding me with messages on social media, accusing me of all sorts. Some of the messages are quite disturbing. Threatening even—"

"Show me."

"No. Not tonight," she said, but her phone buzzed again.

"If that's one of these messages then I—"

"It's just Kitty," Abby said. "We've had a bit of a falling-out."

"That's not like you—"

"I know, but I did something that she disapproves of and now she's worried about me."

"Should I be worried too?"

"Let's not do this now. You know what she's like, always thinks she knows best. I'll call her back tomorrow. Tonight is about you and me and us and your wonderful new book. I don't want anything to spoil it. You're an amazing writer," she said. "You've still got publication in America to look forward to, with a publisher who *does* believe in your books, and I'm sure everything will be okay in the end—"

"Can you say that again?"

"It will all be okay—"

"No, the other thing."

She smiled. "You're an amazing writer."

"What are you doing?" I asked as she put her full glass down again and walked over to the main light switch by the door.

"Turning off all the lights."

"I can see that. Why?"

"Because look at this view," she said, pulling back the curtains.

"I think sometimes things have to get really dark for us to see what we have. The world always looks more beautiful at night, when the darkness hides everything that is ugly." She was right, the view was amazing. It was as though we could see all of London down below. She stood there smiling at me, then started unbuttoning her blouse. Everything started to feel right again when I kissed her, and I forgot about everything that was wrong when I was inside her. We made love in the dark. The sex was slow and gentle and instinctive, the variety that can only be had with someone you know better than you know yourself. Afterward we lay in a tangle of sheets wrapped in each other's arms, watching the sun rise over London.

"Are we okay?" she whispered.

"Of course. Always and forever," I replied, kissing her on the forehead. "Don't confuse problems with work with problems at home." My wife was the most beautiful, clever, hardworking woman I have ever met, despite a childhood that was just as difficult and lonely as my own. At the age of ten she was abandoned and alone in the world, a bit like me. But Kitty took her in and loved her as though she were her own daughter. Abby was always so strong—I think a hard life made her that way—and I hated seeing her career slowly destroy her.

"Yes, maybe it's just the job getting me down. People can be so terrible to each other. I thought I could help people. Fix things. I thought I could change the world if I became a journalist," she said sadly.

"You are changing the world. One story at a time."

"Am I?"

"Yes. I believe in you," I said, but she still looked so unhappy. I didn't understand it then and I still don't know why. I kissed her again then whispered, "I hope you die in your sleep."

She smiled. "I love you too, Grady Green. Always and forever."

A week later she disappeared.

LEAD BALLOON

———◆———

try to leave my past where it belongs and focus on the future. Things are going to be different with this book. Things are going to be great. That's what I keep telling myself because that's what I need to believe or I won't be able to go through with it. I park outside Christie's Corner Shop then head inside before I can change my mind.

"What's this then?" Cora asks, as I meander over to the cash register.

"A parcel I'd like to send to London."

"Right you are," she says, and I can tell the nosy old bat is desperate to know what it is.

"It's my new book," I say to save her asking, and she beams at me. "Do you have a copy of the ferry timetable?" Her face falls, she looks away and shakes her head.

"No."

"Who does?"

She shrugs. "I'm sure someone else in the village must have one, but I haven't left the island for years. Sorry, can't help. But I can get this sent off for you. How about a KitKat to celebrate?" she asks while I search inside my wallet for something to pay with.

"I've popped it in this paper bag along with a little something else," she says when I look up. "My treat."

I feel good when I step back out onto the street. Optimistic. *Happy* even. It feels strange. Cora said the parcel should leave on the mail boat today, which means that Kitty could, in theory, have the new book on her desk in London as soon as tomorrow. I'm excited and I want to celebrate with someone, and with more than a chocolate bar, but I can't use my phone to call anyone and, even if I could, I can't think of anyone I would call. The pub catches my eye. It's been a long time since I had a decent pint and I could really do with one.

I let Columbo out of the Land Rover and we amble over to The Stumble Inn. My heart starts to sink when I read the sign: OPEN THURSDAY TO SUNDAY. I've been working so hard that I still don't know what day of the week it is. The days tend to bend and blur into one another when I am writing. There is a sign above the door too, stating the landlords' names. It used to be a legal requirement, but I haven't seen one for a while, and I've never seen one quite like this. It's a brass plate with black letters:

SIDNEY AND ARABELLA KING
Licensed to serve intoxicating liquor, wine, and beer.
With the intention of getting you horribly drunk.

I try the pub door and find myself overwhelmed with joy when it opens.

The pub is rather lovely inside. A traditional old inn with low ceilings, wooden beams, and a surprisingly large selection of beer on tap. There is an eclectic collection of tables as well as wooden booths on one side of the pub. There is also a row of rickety-looking stools in front of the ancient bar. Everything is cozy and low lit, the kind of place you want to spend time with people. Except that, just like on all the other occasions when I have visited the village, there is no one here. Nobody. Not a single person. I'm considering helping myself to a drink when a woman I'm guessing must be Arabella walks out behind the bar. She's in her thirties, and is wearing a pretty dress and a friendly smile.

"What can I get you?" she asks in a London accent.

"A pint please. Is there something on tap you can recommend?"

She smiles and I see a shiny gold tooth. "I'm rather partial to Dark Island myself."

"Sounds . . . perfect." I notice a big old scar on her arm as she starts to pull me a pint. "Interesting sign outside, and in here too," I say, nodding toward the chalkboard behind the bar. It says drinks are half price during "sad hour."

"Thank you. It started as a bit of fun, swapping happy hour for sad hour, but then I thought it made more sense. Not everyone likes to drown their sorrows, some people like to swim in them."

"Though not today it seems," I say, looking around the empty pub.

"It's always like this when the tourist season ends. We open up the island for visitors for a few months each summer, and we make most of our money then. Same with almost all of the businesses on the island—the Highland Cow Candles sell all year long, but most places rely on the tourists once a year to get by. I'm glad of all the money the visitors generate, but I'm even more glad when they all leave! I prefer it when things are quiet."

"Me too. You don't happen to have a timetable for the ferry, do you?" I ask and she shakes her head. "Not to worry. Do you do food?"

She puts the pint glass down in front of me and shakes her head again. "Only the variety that comes in packets."

"Then I'll have some cheese and onion crisps."

"Right you are, my love. Is that all for now?" she asks, nodding toward my drink. It's the color of honey and my mouth waters just looking at it. She clasps her hands together and I notice the silver thistle ring on her finger.

"Your ring. I think I've seen a few people on the island wearing the same one—"

"Yes, we're all part of a cult," she says, and when I don't respond she laughs. "Just pulling your leg. It means we're part of the Isle of Amberly Trust, that's all. Part of a group who care passionately about this island and will do anything to protect it. The thistle is a symbol of resilience, strength, and protection."

I think it sounds a bit like a cult but keep my thoughts to myself.

A short while later I am sipping my pint in a cozy corner of the pub, and Columbo has a bowl of water and a dog biscuit. Life is good for the first time in a long time. There are little vases of fresh flowers on each table and they remind me of something. It takes me a moment to figure out what, but they look exactly like the ones that were in the cabin when I first arrived.

"How are you finding island life?" Arabella asks from behind the bar.

"Okay so far," I lie. "These vases of flowers . . ."

"Pretty aren't they? The vases are from Beautiful Ugly." I frown. "The pottery on the island," she explains. "The flowers are from Meera at Highland Cow Candles. Meera uses the wildflowers native to Amberly to make her scented candles, which are sold next door. Her slogan is 'Nature Knows Best,' and we like to reuse things here. There's a bit of a make do and mend mentality. Meera used to be a chemist but she was the victim of a violent armed robbery—two bastards in ski masks—and she wanted a quieter life after that. She found one here, making luxury candles. She makes these little bouquets from anything left over. The bog myrtle is good for keeping the midges away and other things. She even blends her own teas! The corner shop sells one of them made from bog myrtle. I like the taste, but it's a hallucinogenic; it can make you see things that aren't there."

Her words shock me but I do my best not to overreact or mention how much of the stuff I've been drinking. Maybe that's why Sandy wouldn't touch the cup of tea I made her.

"Right, well, I'll try to remember that. This is a great pub by the way."

"Thank you, we do our best. The place was in need of some TLC when we took over, but I think all the hard work was worth it."

"You're not from here originally?"

"What gave it away?" she asks in her thick London accent. "Sid and I are from London originally, but we've been living here for four years now. I haven't set foot off the island since."

"You haven't left Amberly for four years?"

She shakes her head, smiles as though I've asked a silly question. "Not once."

"Not even to visit friends or family, the people you left behind?"

"I left everything I left behind for a reason. Sid is the only person I couldn't live without. If you stay long enough, you'll soon discover that everybody on this island has a story. All of them. Some of them might come in handy for one of your books." *So she does know who I am.* "This is a place for people who have spent their lives living in the margins, never feeling like they really belonged anywhere. They come here to find that sense of community they've been craving, a surrogate family made up from people who were once strangers, a place they can finally call home. Then they never leave."

"I plan to leave," I say, taking another sip of my pint.

"Do you not like old Charlie's writing cabin?" she asks.

"I like it fine. There are things I miss, that's all."

"Like what?"

"Like . . ." I struggle to think of anything at first. It's been so long since I lived anything resembling a normal life I've forgotten what one looks like. "I miss going to the theater, or an art gallery, or going to the cinema to see a movie. I miss walking around London. People watching. Going out for a nice meal."

"We serve food here in the evenings and at weekends!" she says. "Charlie used to come here every Sunday for a roast beef dinner and a pint. Creature of habit, that one. Sat there in the corner every weekend with his dog."

"Charles Whittaker had a dog?"

"Always. The last one, Dickens, was very old but Charlie didn't go anywhere without him. Sandy used to join them here most Sundays too. I can still picture the three of them now, the dog sleeping under the table . . ."

"I didn't know Charles and Sandy were such good friends."

I wonder why Sandy never mentioned it.

"Oh yes, thick as thieves those two. Charlie didn't really engage with anyone else on Amberly. Only Sandy. He kept himself to himself, didn't get involved in community matters, but I think maybe he was just shy. Charlie didn't behave that way with Sandy. They went walking together, fishing together, drinking together. But they had a big falling-out before he died. The news of his death went down like a lead balloon, everyone was devastated. We didn't see Charles in his final months, nobody did. He locked himself away in that cabin, stopped coming to the pub, rarely came to the village at all. It was hard on Sandy. I don't know what they fell out about, but before then Charles—who struck me as a man who didn't trust anyone—trusted Sandy. So much so, she was his first reader. Read all of Charles's books before he even let his agent read them, apparently. Including first drafts."

I put my beer back down on the table. My hands are shaking too much to hold it without spilling.

"Really?" I say, and my voice sounds strange. Strangled.

"Oh yes. Sandy read all of Charlie's early drafts, she was the only person who did. I think he shared all of his stories with Sandy, even the ones he never published, before they stopped speaking that is. Sandy was heartbroken when Charlie killed himself."

What?

"Charles Whittaker committed suicide?" The words stammer out of me.

"Yes," she says. "Sorry, I presumed you knew. I think that's why the place was empty for so long. He did it in the cabin where you are staying, hung himself from one of the wooden beams in the ceiling, and it was a while before they found him because, like I said, he preferred to keep himself to himself. Sorry, I'm such a blabbermouth. I shouldn't have mentioned it."

My head is spinning. My chest hurts. I feel sick.

"And Sandy read all of Charlie's first drafts?" I ask.

"Every single one. Are you all right, my love? You're looking a bit peaky."

"Yes. Fine. Thank you. I've just remembered that I need to be somewhere," I tell her, standing up so fast I accidentally knock the table.

"What about your pint? You haven't finished it—"

"Another time. Sorry."

"Well, we look forward to seeing you again sometime soon," she says.

I'm out the door and across the road in less than a minute, Columbo trotting beside me as though he thinks this is a game. It's not. I am sweating and it has nothing to do with how fast I am running. Why did nobody tell me that Charles Whittaker killed himself? Stealing his last novel, which despite the changes I've made is exactly what I've done, now seems so much worse than before. And if Sandy read the first draft she'll know what I did, then everyone will know. There won't be a new book deal, or a new home, or a new anything. Kitty will dump me as a client, my career will be over, and I'll be finished.

I *have* to get the manuscript back.

The sign says CLOSED and the door to the corner shop is locked but I knock on it anyway. When nobody answers I knock a little louder until I can see Cora through the glass coming toward me. She opens the door, but only wide enough to stick her head through the gap.

"We're closed for the rest of the day, out of respect. Did you forget something?" she asks.

"The parcel, I've changed my mind. I don't want to send it."

"You're too late. It was collected just after you left the shop. It'll be on the mail boat by now." I feel sick and I'm shaking. "Are you always like this when you send a new book to your agent?" Cora asks, looking mildly concerned.

"Yes," I say, because it is the truth and I am.

But I've never been this worried before. Because, despite all the editing, I know that the book I have just sent to Kitty isn't really mine.

But what if Sandy *didn't* read Charles Whittaker's first draft of this book?

Then nobody would know what I've done and everything might still be okay.

I need to find her.

DULL ROAR

remember the way to Sandy's house without checking the map, but I find it hard to concentrate on the road ahead. My worries bleed into all other thoughts, soaking them in anxiety. The old Land Rover now feels like a disobedient beast to drive, it's too slow, but Columbo seems to enjoy sitting up front and sticking his head out of the window. At least someone is having a good time.

It doesn't take long to get to the House on the Hill. The dark gray exterior looks even more forlorn than the last time I was here, and despite the turrets on either side, this is no fairy-tale castle. I'm dismayed not to see Sandy's pickup truck parked outside but knock on the door anyway. It takes Midge a long time to answer, so long that I was about to give up and walk away, but then the door finally opens. She looks very different from the smiling, bubbly woman I met a few weeks ago. Smaller, as though she has been deflated. Midge is wearing a tatty old pink dressing gown even though it is early afternoon, and no makeup. Her hair looks unwashed and her eyes are red as though she has been crying. She doesn't speak, just stares at me. I remember Cora saying that the shop was closed out of respect, but I didn't think to ask out of respect for what. There is obviously something going on that I am not aware of.

"I was looking for Sandy. Are you okay?" I ask.

"My sister isn't here."

"Do you know where she is?"

"This isn't a good time, Grady."

I can see that.

"I'm sorry. It's important."

"I can't contact her. She's turned off her walkie-talkie. Always does on the anniversary . . ." Her words trail away and she appears to be staring at something in the distance behind me, as though she has forgotten I am here.

"Midge?"

Her eyes find mine again. "I expect she'll be at Darkside Cave. With *her*." Midge's eyes fill with fresh tears that soon spill over, streaming down her cheeks. "If whatever it is can wait until tomorrow, then you should probably do that," she says, closing the door before I can even say thank you.

I climb back into the Land Rover and look inside the glove compartment for my map of Amberly. I find something else in there, too, and stare at the newspaper clipping in my hand. I have no idea how it got there or when.

10th April 2019   The Times   Page 48

BESTSELLING AUTHOR
CHARLES WHITTAKER DIES AGED 82

By Abby Goldman

Charles Whittaker, the author of nine global bestsellers, has died at the age of eighty-two fol- lowing a short illness. He passed away peacefully at his London home, surrounded by family.

Beloved by readers around the world, Whittaker was a shy man and exceptionally private. He was seldom seen in public, rarely attended events, or awards, or even film premieres celebrating his work—several of his books were adapted for the big screen. With over 50 million books in print worldwide, he was a man who lived to write, and wrote to live. Charles Whittaker will be remembered for his stories, which those closest to him say is exactly what he wanted. He will be buried in a private ceremony.

I don't understand what I am reading. Abby was an investigative journalist, she didn't write obituaries. And so many things about this one are wrong. Charles Whittaker did not die in London surrounded by family. He died here, alone, on this island. And it had nothing to do with a short illness, he killed himself. By all accounts, he lived on Amberly for over thirty years, never left, and is buried here. I've seen his headstone. And yet, there is no mention of the island at all. As though he were never here. Why would Abby, who believed in truth above all other things, write so many lies?

I don't have time to get distracted by this. I need to find Sandy and find out if she read the book I have basically stolen. I shove the obituary back in the glove compartment and find what I was looking for. Darkside Cave is clearly marked on the map on the other side of the island next to something called the Bay of Singing Sands. It's somewhere I haven't been before and would have struggled to get to without a car. I haven't slept properly for weeks and I wouldn't normally drive when I'm *this* exhausted—I know how many road accidents are a direct result of tiredness—but I have to find out the truth. If Sandy didn't read a first draft of Charlie's last novel then everything is okay. But if she did . . . then I don't know what happens next. If anyone finds out what I've done my career, my life, my everything will be over.

My map-reading skills must be improving, because ten min-

utes later I see a sign. I pull off the road into a small car park
where I find Sandy's pickup truck. It is parked next to a large
wooden noticeboard, just like the one I saw the day I arrived on
the island, with BAY OF SINGING SANDS & DARKSIDE CAVE carved
into the top. Behind the glass, I see the now familiar hand-drawn
map of Amberly. Next to Darkside Cave on the map is the bright
red triangle reading YOU ARE NOT HERE. It's strange, but so are
many things about the island, so I pay no attention.

There is a track from the car park leading through a field of
heather, a vast sea of purple stretching all the way from the road
to the cliffs, and I can hear the dull roar of the ocean in the distance. If I want to find Sandy I guess I'll have to follow the track.
It looks unsafe—there doesn't appear to be anything between the
path and the cliff edge—so I leave Columbo in the car. It's not
something I like to do, but it's a cool day and the roof and windows on the old jeep are all open.

The sound of crashing waves gets increasingly louder the
closer I get to the cliffs, and then I hear something else. It's like a
ghostly choir singing in a language I have never heard, their quiet
voices sometimes completely stolen by the wind. I look around,
but I am quite alone, and I start to wonder whether I am losing
my remaining marbles. Then I remember what the pub landlady
said about bog myrtle tea being a hallucinogenic. I've been drinking a lot of the stuff, and I wonder if that might be why I keep
seeing and hearing things. The track splits in two directions a
little farther ahead, one leading to the cave and the other leading
to the bay. There is another sign that I stop to read.

In the right conditions, you may hear
the sound of singing as you approach the bay.
There are many tales about who or what makes the sound.
But it is a natural phenomenon created by the wind
in this particular cove.

It might be a natural phenomenon, but the sound is unlike anything I have ever heard before. It no longer sounds like singing; it sounds like sobbing coming from the sea. There is a voice in my head telling me to turn back, drive away, and get off this island for good. But then I'll never know if Sandy read the book. And then all hope of a better future will be lost. I follow the sign that says DARKSIDE CAVE—where Midge said I would find Sandy—and that's when I see her in the distance. A woman in a red coat, just like the one Abby used to own. She is too far away for me to recognize her face, which is hidden by her hood. As soon as she sees me she turns and runs in the opposite direction.

I'm not imagining this.

"Abby?" I call.

Is it really her?

Whoever she is doesn't answer, just keeps running. I don't want to scare a woman who is clearly running away from me, but I have to know the truth. I chase after her toward Darkside Cave, and slow down only when I reach some stone steps carved out of the cliffs. They're steep, leading downward and curving around the cliff edge. There is another DANGER sign and I can see why. But then I see a flash of red again in the distance and I hurry on. The steps have crumbled away altogether in some places, and the ones that still exist are wet and slippery with seawater. It's easy to see why when the waves crash into the rocks down below causing a large cloud of spray. I try to take each step carefully, but I'm desperate to catch up with her. My trainers slip more than once as the path leads around the edge of the cliff, and I cling to the rocks for dear life. I can no longer see the car park and I'm starting to wonder if this was a good idea. But then I turn another corner and find myself standing in the mouth of a large dark cave. The woman in the red coat is nowhere to be seen, but Sandy is here. She is leaning against a glistening granite wall, and she does not look happy to see me.

"Where did she go?" I ask, catching my breath.

"Who? You shouldn't be here," Sandy says, wearing a look of discomfort.

"The woman in the red coat."

"What woman? I don't have time for this today, Grady."

Did I imagine her?

"Sorry, Midge told me where I could find you—"

"Is it an emergency?" she asks, looking up at me.

Yes.

"No."

"Then this isn't a good time." I can see that. She looks as though she has been crying and she's holding a bottle of whiskey. "This cave isn't safe. Did you not see the sign?"

"I'm sorry, I'll—" She squints in my direction and cups her hand over her ear as though she cannot hear me. I realize I'll have to shout to be heard over the sound of the sea and take a step farther into the cave. "I was just apologizing, I shouldn't have come. It can wait—"

"That's what *I* thought," Sandy says, interrupting me. "I thought things could wait, but they can't. Life doesn't wait for anyone, and death is always too soon or too late, never on time."

I don't know what to say to that. She takes a sip of whiskey.

"Are you . . . okay?" I ask, even though it's obvious that she isn't.

Sandy shakes her head. "Can you hear them?"

"Who?"

"The children. I thought I heard her once, on the anniversary, calling for me. I've been coming here every year since. Midge won't come anymore, she doesn't believe in that sort of thing, but she's wrong. Can *you* hear them? I thought I saw her once too. Just there, behind where you're standing." I look over my shoulder and move away, even though there is nobody there.

"*Who?*"

"Do you believe that we can sometimes see the dead?" Sandy asks.

I think of my wife but don't answer. I'm not sure how to. I don't know if my wife is dead but I think I see her all the time. I still sometimes forget that she's gone, and when I remember, it's like being swallowed by my grief all over again.

Sandy glances over to the back of the cave where it is too dark to see. "I only come here to let her know that she is not forgotten. This island used to be such a safe place, for everyone, but especially for children. There was never any need to lock your door or to say 'don't talk to strangers' because there weren't any. Everyone knew everyone and everything about them. Warts and all. Until they started letting *visitors* come to Amberly. Can you really not hear them?"

"Visitors?" I can only hear the sound of the sea.

"No. The children. Crying. We put that sign up on the coast path about the 'Bay of Singing Sands' so as not to scare the tourists away, but that's no *natural phenomenon*. How on earth would *sand* sing? It's not logical. I've lived here all my life and I never heard that sound until *after* it happened. Some people don't hear anything. Did you? And did it sound like *singing* to you? Or did it sound like crying? What you heard is the ghosts of dead children." The cave seems to get smaller and darker and colder. "You might have noticed there's no school on the island. No children at all apart from Holly at The Croft. Well, there used to be. There were thirteen children living on Amberly back then, including my daughter, all of them under the age of ten. One of the oldest little girls led all of the children here one day. Old Mrs. Marchant—the only teacher on the island—was seriously ill, so the person left in charge of the school that day was a last-minute stand-in, a substitute teacher from the mainland. He didn't know our children, and he didn't even know that they had disappeared until it was too late. He'd been in the pub for hours, drinking when he should have been watching the children, and he was a *liar*. The whole island stopped what they were doing to help with the search, but by the time we knew where they were it was too late. You see, this cave fills with water at high tide. They didn't stand a chance. The seawater flooded in, trapping them and blocking their only path to safety. Then it flooded back out and took the children with it. All of them."

"I'm so sorry." My words come out as a whisper.

She waves me away, tears in her eyes, and I can see she is a woman doing battle with herself. I know what it's like to keep all your hurt bottled up inside.

"There was a strange mist that night," Sandy says, her voice so quiet now I can barely hear her above the sound of the waves, which seem to be getting louder. "The likes of which I'd never seen before but I've seen plenty of times since. It was like a fog settled over the island. Whenever the mist rolls in I hear them everywhere." She stares at me. "You can hear them now, can't you?" she asks and I nod, because I can hear *something* and it does sound like children crying. "And here comes the mist, right on cue," Sandy says, with tears in her eyes.

I look out toward the opening of the cave and sure enough, something cloudlike has settled on the ground outside. I feel like I have stepped into a horror movie.

"They are the children of the mist and they don't want to be forgotten. Some of their broken little bodies were found in this cave, some were found washed up on the bay, *some* were never found and the island was never the same afterward. Whole families left, people who had been born here just packed their bags and moved to the mainland, leaving everything behind. The population dwindled, houses were empty. *Everything* changed after that day because of one man not doing his job. We lost everything because of one selfish, dishonest, despicable man. Things had to change after that and they did. Nothing like that could ever be allowed to happen again, so I set up the Isle of Amberly Trust and vowed to protect this island and the people who live here. I've made that my life's work, but I'll never forget my daughter. She was such a happy soul. She loved playing in the woods and she had this red harmonica that—"

"A harmonica?"

"Yes. The sound used to drive me nuts, but I missed it so much when she was gone. The world was too quiet without her in it. She would have been forty if she was still alive, but in my heart she's a little girl forever. No parent should have to bury their child. Especially when all you get to bury is an empty coffin because the sea took everything that was left of them away. There's no vaccination for heartbreak and there's no cure. Children born on the island are cursed, that's what people here believe—me included—so we knocked the school down and no child has been born here since. Probably sounds crazy to someone like you. The worst part is not really knowing what happened to them in those final moments, do you know what I mean?"

I do. I think about my wife and the night she disappeared.

"I'm . . . so sorry for your loss," I say.

"No, I'm sorry. You didn't come here to listen to all of this."

"It's fine, honestly. I know what it is like to lose someone."

Her face darkens again, as though I have insulted her. "*You* do not know what *this* is like. Grief is like a fingerprint, different every time. Mine is not like yours and you are not like me, but I doubt that is within your spectrum of understanding," she says, slurring her words.

"Can I maybe give you a ride home?" I offer.

"You think I've had too much to drink?" I nod and she does too, as though agreeing with me. "You're not looking so hot yourself, Grady. You look like you haven't slept for weeks. I'll be all right. I just want to stay a little longer," she says, sliding down the wall of the cave to sit on the ground. I look out at the sea and the water seems higher than it was before.

"You said the cave floods at high tide. Maybe we should—"

"Why were you looking for me? It must have been something urgent for you to have driven all the way out here."

"It can wait. Another time—"

"No, tell me. I could do with something to take my mind off of all of this."

My problems seem so trivial now that I have heard what she has been through. But I do still need to know.

"It's nothing, really. Just that I heard that you were Charles Whittaker's first reader—"

"Do you want me to read your book? I'm flattered—"

"No!" I say and she frowns. "I mean, maybe. I wondered if you had read any of Charles's unpublished work?"

Sandy nods and closes her eyes. "The man was a writing machine until something inside him got broken. Charlie was like a father to me when my little girl died and we became close after that. He lost someone too at around the same time and we bonded over grief. He let me read everything he wrote, all of it. There were some books he decided never to publish, and one which I'm sure he should have. The famous Book Ten. I read a first draft and it was brilliant but nobody could find the manuscript after he died."

"Why didn't he let anyone else read it?"

"He was scared his agent wouldn't like it."

His agent is my agent.

"Why did he think Kitty wouldn't like it?"

Sandy shrugs. "I don't know. I searched the cabin after he died—his agent wrote and asked me to—but I couldn't find it. Maybe he burned the thing. It wouldn't have been the first time that the crazy old fool did something like that. I confess we had a falling-out before he died, but I still respected the man. He never wanted to publish a bad book; that was his number one rule, but sometimes I don't think he knew how good they were. Book Ten was the best, but I'm the only person in the world who was lucky enough to read it."

GUILTY PLEASURE

Columbo is overjoyed to see me when I climb back into the Land Rover. I feel drunk with tiredness but I'm grateful for the affection. A thick mist has now settled over the island, and I close all the windows to stop any more of it getting inside. My hands are trembling and I don't know whether it's a result of extreme exhaustion or because of something else.

I haven't eaten at all today except for the crisps I had at the pub, and I suspect my blood sugar must be low. I'm not sure I should be driving given the state I am in, and although I don't care much about myself in this moment I do care about my dog. I remember the KitKat in the paper bag that Cora gave me in the corner shop—chocolate has always been one of my guilty pleasures—and despite having no appetite now, one bite might help boost my energy level. Enough to get us safely back to the cabin at least. I open the bag and see something unexpected inside. I remember Cora saying it now, though it didn't make sense at the time. *I've popped it in the bag along with a little something else.* If she had mentioned it was a letter from the mainland I would have read it straightaway. I recognize Kitty's handwriting and tear open the envelope. According to the postmark it was sent a week ago.

Dear Grady,

I'm sorry not to be telling you this in person, I've tried calling but your phone just goes to voicemail. I hired a private investigator when Abby disappeared. I never told you about it then because there was nothing to tell. But now they've uncovered something rather unpleasant. I think it best not to go into detail in a letter, but I fear not everyone on the island is who they say they are. Please call me as soon as you can.

Kitty

xx

I can't call her. I can't call anyone.

The uncomfortable feeling I've had since I arrived on Amberly now feels a bit too real. Why couldn't she share whatever the private investigator discovered? Am I in danger? From who? I already wanted to leave but now I have to find a way to get off this island to speak to Kitty and find out what she knows.

The engine rumbles to life and I try to turn on the car radio. After listening to Sandy's story, even I think I can hear children crying on the wind now. I'm desperate to drown out the sound, but the radio signal is patchy. I suppose it is to be expected given where I am and the strange weather conditions. I pull away with the radio barely working, preferring to listen to the crackle of poor reception than the sound of ghosts.

I drive very slowly along the cliff road even though I've never been in more of a hurry. Thick fog is everywhere I look and visibility is almost zero. It probably isn't safe to drive but I have to get out of here for so many reasons. I just want to get back to the cabin, pack up my things, and find a way to leave. If the ferry isn't an option there must still be a way off the island. I'm sure I've seen a rowboat attached to a wooden jetty on one of the southern beaches. Perhaps I could borrow it. We're only ten miles from the mainland, maybe I could row that far. I'll drive around the entire coastline if I have to until I find a way to get out of here, that's what I'll do.

I'm so tired and my thoughts are too loud and the radio keeps going berserk. Occasionally I hear old-fashioned music I don't recognize, but most of the time all I can hear is static or interference, despite constantly twisting the dial. When I hear what sounds like children whispering I get goose bumps and reach down to turn the damn thing off.

That's when it happens.

There is a loud bang and a blur of color in front of the windshield.

I hit the brakes and instinctively put my left arm out to protect the dog as the Land Rover screeches to a halt.

I took my eyes away from the road for only a second, but I think I've hit something.

Or someone.

I don't move. I peer out through the windscreen into the fog, but I can't see anything. I'm already spooked by Kitty's letter and everything that happened in the cave, and I try to tell myself that I imagined whatever my brain thinks I just saw. But then a patch of mist right ahead clears enough for me to see it. The shape of a person lying in the road. A woman.

I have the strangest feeling of déjà vu, which makes no sense because I didn't see someone lying in the road the night my wife went missing. *She* did.

Instinct tells me not to get out of the car. Guilt makes me do it anyway.

I should call someone, get help, but I can't without a phone.

It looks like the woman was riding an old-fashioned bike. I can see it, twisted on its side a short distance from her. Why would anyone ride a bike on a cliff road that has no crash barriers in thick fog? It's such a dangerous thing to do. I can understand if she didn't *see* me, but surely she must have *heard* me. The ancient Land Rover is so loud it sounds like a tank. I still haven't moved and neither has she, whoever she is.

The person lying there has their back to me.

I take a step toward her.

I can't see her face, but I can see she is wearing a red coat.

The coat makes me think of Abby again. A year feels like a lifetime when you lose someone you love, but now, in this moment, it feels like it could have been yesterday. I know it isn't her. I've thought that I've seen her so many times now that I've learned not to trust my own eyes. I gave up hoping she would come back to me a long time ago. But there is no denying that the red coat this woman is wearing looks a lot like the one Abby was wearing that night. I remind myself that it was from a high street shop; there must be hundreds just like it, maybe thousands. Besides, the police found Abby's coat soon after she disappeared.

The woman in the road remains perfectly still.

"Hello?" I call.

There's no reply. No movement. Nothing.

I take another small step closer, afraid of something I still can't see.

"Are you hurt?" I ask when I am only a few steps away, but she still doesn't move.

The mist starts to clear and then, just as fast as it arrived, it is almost completely gone.

When I see her face I start to tremble. I can't move, can't

speak, it feels like I can't breathe, because this time there is no denying it.

I'm not seeing things.

I'm not imagining it.

The woman lying in the road *is* my missing wife.

FOUND MISSING

She's alive.

But now I'm worried I might have killed her.

I lean down toward Abby, still feeling dizzy and unsteady on my feet. I'm exhausted but suddenly feel wide awake, my heart thudding so loudly I can hear it in my ears. I stare at her and wonder if this is my fault, whether I might have fallen asleep at the wheel. I *think* I was reaching for the radio when it happened, but I'm so tired I'm not sure. Either way, I'm to blame for this. My mind is already editing the moment, rewriting what happened, trying to relieve the overwhelming stress of what I think I am seeing.

People are found missing all the time, but missing people are rarely found.

I reach out a hand to touch her face; I need to know if she is real. Her eyes fly open before my fingers make contact and she slaps my hand away. Then she sits up and glares at me.

"Who the fuck are you?" she asks, leaning away.

"It's *me*," I reply, but she stares at me with wild eyes.

Her eyes are the only thing that doesn't look right about her. They're brown, which is wrong. My wife's eyes were the bluest

I've ever seen. Her hair is longer than it was before too, but it would be after all these months. Her face looks *exactly* the same, except for a small cut on her forehead that is bleeding. I can't process what I am seeing. Or hearing.

"Stay the fuck away from me," says my wife who never swore.

"I can't believe it's you," I tell her. Abby stares at me as though I might be crazy.

She might be right.

Long-term insomnia can cause permanent damage to a person's brain, and in extreme cases, death. Confusion and paranoia are early warning signs of the mind starting to unravel. My doctor said he'd had insomniac patients who had seen the faces of dead relatives. Some had entire conversations with people who were not there. They even heard the other person talking, insisted that they were there in the room. What if that's what this is? A hallucination as a result of grief, stress, and extreme exhaustion?

I reach to touch her, again. She slaps my hand away, again. I think she's real.

Abby tries to sit up and is clearly in pain. I should help her but I am still frozen to the spot. I have so many questions but she beats me to it with one of her own.

"Who are you?" she demands again.

Another trickle of bright red blood starts to crawl out of the cut on her forehead and run down the side of her face. Someone needs to put some pressure on the wound and in the absence of anyone else I guess that's me. I take a clean hankie from my pocket and lean toward her, but she jerks away.

"It's *me*, Grady," I say.

"Okay, *Grady*. Why are you driving Whitty's old car, and why did you run me over?"

"Whoa! I didn't run you over!"

"The only reason I'm not dead is because I dodged you. You drove the car straight at me and knocked me off my bike."

"No. I didn't see you. The mist . . ."

"What mist?" she asks.

I look around and of course the mist has completely cleared now. But she must have seen it before she came off her bike; it was almost impossible to see anything else. She takes a tissue from the sleeve of her red coat and holds it to her head. Then she looks at all the blood on it and turns an even paler shade of white.

"Maybe you're right," she says. "Maybe *I* imagined you knocking me over. Oh, hang on, I'm lying in the middle of the road and bleeding. Are you off your meds?"

My wife used to say that too.

This is too much to process. *She* is too much.

"I don't understand what is happening. You're *alive*," I say.

"No thanks to you."

I stare at her. "Do you really not know who I am? You've been gone for over a year, have you been here all this time?"

"Gone? What are you talking about?"

Maybe *I am* losing my mind.

"Why are you acting as though we know each other? I don't know you," she says.

I feel like someone just turned my world upside down and shook it.

"*Know* each other?" I say. "I'm your—"

"Look, I don't wish to sound rude," she interrupts. "But I have somewhere I need to be and, thanks to you, I don't think I can ride my bike." The bike is on the side of the road. It has a large wicker basket on the front and is clearly very old. It belongs in a museum—like most things on this island—but otherwise I can't see anything wrong with it. Not even a scratch. "Given you almost killed me, do you think you could give me a lift?" she asks and I hesitate. "If it's too much trouble—"

"No, of course I can give you a lift. I just . . . maybe we should call a doctor."

"The doctor only visits on Tuesdays," she says, attempting to stand. I try to help her up but she makes it clear that she can do it on her own.

She looks like my wife.

She sounds like my wife.

She *is* my wife.

My mind scrambles to come up with possible explanations for what is happening.

Maybe she has a concussion from what just happened.

Maybe when she disappeared a year ago she lost her memory?

Maybe she's lying.

I don't understand what is going on but I have to know the truth.

I lift the bike into the boot of the Land Rover, then tell Columbo to get in the back seat before Abby and I climb inside the front. She even smells like my wife; she's wearing Abby's favorite perfume. I thought Columbo might jog her memory but it's as though she's never seen him before. He is very happy to see her, but he's happy to see everyone.

"Cute dog," she says, barely looking at him.

My mind is too full of questions. I decide to start with an easy one.

"Have you lived on the island long?" I ask, turning on the engine.

"Long enough," she replies. She fastens her seat belt, checks it twice. "If you head toward the village I'll guide you from there," she adds, as though not wanting to tell me her address. As if she is scared of me. As though I am a stranger. Her hands are neatly folded in her lap and I take my eyes off the road just for a moment to look at them. They look like my wife's hands except that she isn't wearing her wedding ring, and instead of varnish, her nails seem to be covered in splatters of blue-green paint.

"You don't sound like you were born here," I say.

"How observant. *You* don't sound like a hit-and-run driver."

"I didn't see you until your bike collided with the car, and I didn't run."

"I've lived here for as long as I can remember," she says. Which doesn't mean anything given I don't know how much she can remember. There might be no ring on her finger, but I think I can see a slight indentation on her skin where she used to wear it. I notice that she picks the paint off her nails, the same way Abby used to pick off her polish. It was something she did when things were stressful for her at work. A coping mechanism. A nervous tic.

I remember the newspaper articles that were left in the cabin and the car, maybe that's why someone wanted me to see them, because they knew she was here. My mind is now filling with all sorts of explanations for how and why Abby might have ended up on the Isle of Amberly. My wife's obsession with her work was one of the only subjects we ever argued about, and there were things I said before she vanished that I longed to take back after she was gone. I'd tell her that now but she doesn't seem to know who I am. Abby looks up as we approach a junction.

"Ignore the turning for the village and turn right instead, along the cliff road."

I'm on the cliff road.

That's what she told me the night she disappeared. It's one of the last things she said before she vanished. This feels like a total head fuck. I go along with it, with *her*, and I take the turning, but I can't seem to stop myself asking the question again.

"Do you really not know who I am?"

She stares at my face while I stare at the road, and I feel her eyes boring into me.

After an almost unbearable silence, all she says is, "Should I?"

I shake my head. Silence resumes.

"Wait, are you *the author*?" she asks then.

"*Yes.* Yes, I'm an author. Do you remember now?"

"I don't get out much, but I do remember Cora Christie telling everyone who came into the corner shop that another writer had come to Amberly. So that's you, is it? The author?"

"That's me," I say, trying to hide my disappointment. Either my wife has become an amazing actress or she really doesn't remember me.

"It's just down this lane here," she says.

I turn down a bumpy track and soon I see the sea. "This is where you live?"

"No, this is where I work. I like being close to the ocean. I find it calming."

But she hates the ocean.

There is a small white wooden building in the distance, in front of a vast white sandy beach. There is nothing else here. No other buildings. No other people.

"What is this place?" I ask. "It's beautiful."

"If you mean this part of the island, it's called Dead End Bay. If you mean the building, it's the island pottery."

I try my best to keep the conversation going. To find out as much as I can.

"Looks like a lovely spot. How long have you worked here?"

"I've owned the place for almost a year."

It couldn't be any longer because she was still with me before that.

My mind is a mess of thoughts I don't know how to untangle. Feelings I know I should have but can't quite reach. I don't understand what is happening or whether this is real.

But she *looks* real.

And she *sounds* real.

We park up and I stare at the sign above the building. It seems the name of my missing wife's new business is the name I just borrowed for my book: Beautiful Ugly.

GENUINE IMITATION

Are you okay?" she asks.

I can't answer. My brain feels like it is made of wool and I think the situation has overwhelmed me. I feel like I might cry, which is something I haven't done since the night she disappeared. How can she not know who I am? Concern clouds her face and distorts her features. I stare at her, this woman wearing a red coat who looks and sounds just like my missing wife. But then her face blurs and twists into something different, someone I do not know or recognize. She's staring at me, waiting for an answer, but I can't speak. It feels like waking up from a nightmare only to discover it wasn't a dream.

A year is a long time but it *is* her. There is no other explanation. Unless she had a secret twin? I study her again and survey the changes in the face I once knew so well. If it isn't her—and I'm almost certain it is—it's like looking at a genuine imitation. Her skin is more tanned—Abby was always so careful to wear sunscreen—her dark hair is longer, and it looks wavy and natural instead of heavily styled. She's thinner too; her cheekbones are more prominent than they used to be. She looks well, apart from the cut on her head. She's wearing clothes Abby wouldn't have been seen dead—or alive—in. Casual was never her style, and I definitely never saw her wearing dungarees. I remember the newspaper articles again. Someone on the island wanted me to know that Abby was here. If it really is her. It's her eyes that make her look unfamiliar. They should be blue, not brown. I can't help staring at them, but doing so clearly makes her uncomfortable.

"Thank you for the lift," she says, reaching for the door of the Land Rover.

"Wait, I didn't catch your name."

"My name is Aubrey."

No it isn't.

But Aubrey does sound a lot like Abby.

Maybe she doesn't know she's lying.

It doesn't make sense. How could she possibly have forgotten her old life, her job, the house we renovated? We thought it would be our forever home but I guess nothing lasts forever. How could she forget our dog, our marriage, us, me?

She opens the door and starts to climb out. "*Are* you okay?" she asks again. "I'm the one who was just run off the road but you're looking a bit pale and clammy. If you're in shock I don't want you driving into someone else. Do you want to come in for a glass of water?"

I am in shock and I do want to go inside because I don't believe a word she is saying.

"There are a lot of breakable things in the pottery. Maybe leave Columbo here for now so his tail doesn't knock them all over."

"Of course. Thank you."

Columbo jumps into the driver's seat—always his favorite spot—as soon as I walk away.

"I'm surprised they let you drive Whitty's old Land Rover," Abby says as we head toward the pottery.

"They?"

"The Amberly Island Trust has *a lot* of rules. Including that *visitors* aren't allowed cars on the island. Plus an old car like that isn't remotely environmentally friendly. The island is tiny. I don't know why everyone can't get around on a bike like me."

"You don't drive?"

She shakes her head. "Why would I? Amberly is only six miles long and five miles wide, I never even bothered to learn."

Abby loved to drive and she loved her car.

There is a large, prominent logo on the wall depicting a Highland cow. I remember seeing the same thing on the side of the black van on the ferry the day I arrived. Maybe it was Abby that I saw then. Maybe she's been here the whole time, right under my nose. When she reaches inside her pocket and takes out a set of keys, I see something on her wrist. A tattoo. My wife didn't have any tattoos; she hated them.

"What does that mean?" I ask, staring at the unfamiliar swirls staining her skin.

She holds up her hand, the way someone would if they were looking at a watch, and instead reads the ink-stained words.

"La'kesh," she says, as though I should know what that is. "It means my other self. I'm sorry, now that we're standing face-to-face you *do* look familiar. Have we met before?"

ABSOLUTE CHAOS

She opens the door and we step inside a small but impressive building. It's a modern timber-framed structure, with a lot of glass and a lot of light. Huge windows offer incredible views of the ocean and an endless stretch of white sand. There are tables and shelves everywhere displaying vases, pots, jugs, mugs, and bowls, and I notice that almost all of them are stained turquoise, with hints of blue and green. They look hand-painted and the colors remind me of the sea.

"I make everything myself," she says, pride shining in her eyes. She takes off her red coat and hangs it on a stand near the door. "Sorry the place is a bit of a mess. There aren't normally any visitors at this time of year and life has been absolute chaos recently. Take a look around if you like. I'm just going to patch this up." She points to the cut on her forehead. "Then I'll get you that glass of water, unless you'd prefer tea?"

"Tea would be great, thank you."

It will take longer for her to make tea, which gives me more time to think. And more time to snoop. She disappears out the back and I head straight over to the desk in the corner. It's a little too neat and tidy, but there is something of interest. A report from the Isle of Amberly Trust about their annual meeting. I start to read the first page listing the members present:

Sandy MacIntyre, Island Sheriff.
Midge MacIntyre, Island Secretary and Island Treasurer.
Cora Christie, of Christie's Corner Shop and Head of Island Retail.

I quickly scan the rest of the page and see that there are twenty-five names, which means twenty-five possible suspects, one of whom must know what is really going on here because someone does. I take the report and hide it in my pocket to read later, then I wander around the rest of the pottery, being careful not to bump into or break anything. I pick up a pamphlet from one of the display tables and see that it has the same logo as the sign outside—a Highland cow. There is a description of the pottery and a picture of my wife. Sure enough, it says her name is Aubrey. Aubrey Fairlight.

BEAUTIFUL UGLY
Unique yet functional pottery, inspired by the sea.

Abby hates the sea.
"Here you are," she says, holding two ceramic turquoise mugs. They are just like the ones on display but contain steaming hot liquid. She stares at the pamphlet in my hand.

"Don't mind if I keep this do you?" I ask.

"Not at all. I've got boxes of them and can always print more."

"Thank you," I say as she hands one of the mugs to me. She has cleaned her face and has a small Band-Aid on her forehead.

It looks like one designed for children, with a colorful picture of a unicorn. I have so many questions, but I don't know where to start or what to say. She clearly doesn't know who I am, or can't remember me, and it feels like I need to tread carefully. I take a sip of the not-altogether unpleasant tea.

"So . . ." she says, and I realize that she wants me to go.

I can't leave yet.

I take another sip and she smiles politely—exactly the way Abby did when she didn't want to hurt someone's feelings. How can she not know me? How can she not remember us?

"Your work, everything on display, is beautiful," I say in an attempt to keep her talking.

She beams at me and it hurts a little; I have missed that smile so much.

"Thank you. Do you want the ten-cent tour while you finish your tea?" I nod and follow her through the pottery. "It all started out as a hobby, really. A form of escapism I suppose, to take my mind off what a terrible world we live in. I use a traditional wheel, and I glaze every piece of pottery myself. But the best bit is outside." She opens the back door, which leads directly to the beach, and I follow her, the volume of the sea so loud now she has to raise her voice. "When the pieces are ready each one is fired in this ancient wood-fired kiln," she says, standing next to a tiny stone structure behind the pottery. It looks like an old mausoleum. She heaves open a heavy-looking metal door to reveal something resembling a medieval prison cell.

"*This* was all that was here when I bought the land," she explains, looking bewilderingly proud. "I put all the pieces I make on these shelves beneath the chimney, then seal the whole thing up. In the old days they used to brick it up, then open it one brick at a time three days later, but I added this removable fireproof door to speed up the process. I light small fires through these little holes around the bottom, and keep shoving in kindling and

wood until it gets nice and hot, like an oven. Then I keep it burn-
ing for two days and two nights. This kiln would have been built
hundreds of years ago to fire pottery, and now it's where I make
mine. Unlike mass-produced factory products, every single thing
I make is individual. Unique. Just like the people who will own
them. Some people think that something being a different shade
makes it imperfect. They even use the term 'different' as though
it were an ugly word. I choose to see the world differently, and
I think there is much beauty to be found in imperfection. And I
love that something beautiful can come out of something so ugly."

"Is that why you called the place Beautiful Ugly?" I ask as we
step back inside.

She stops and stares at me.

"We live in a world filled with hate and hurt, these are dark
times, but there is still love and light if you look for it. Everyone
you know is capable of being both good and bad. And one man's
right is another man's wrong. We have built a society that places
far too much importance on a phony idea of beauty and perfection.
The world is full of people behaving like clones, all trying to look,
sound, and be the same. Too busy constantly comparing themselves
to each other on tiny screens to see the bigger picture. I've accepted
that I can't change the world, but I do believe that uniqueness is
something to be celebrated, not feared or frowned upon. Life is
beautiful and life is ugly and we have to learn to live with both
sides of that same coin and see the light in the darkness. The world
is Beautiful Ugly, relationships are Beautiful Ugly, love is Beautiful
Ugly. Understanding that makes life easier to live with."

Abby disappears behind the desk I saw earlier then says,
"Beautiful Ugly was the only name that felt right because I believe that's what life is, and my work is my life. Anyway, I don't
want to keep you too long when Columbo is waiting in the car."

*That's the second time she mentioned him. I don't remember tell-
ing her his name.*

She starts looking inside the drawers then holds up a ring. "There it is, found it, thank goodness. For obvious reasons I always take my jewelry off when I'm working." She nods in the direction of the pottery wheel. "But doing so sometimes gets me into trouble. Especially when people accuse me of losing my wedding ring."

Her words dismantle me.

I stare open-mouthed as she slides the white gold band onto her finger.

"You're *married*?" I say, feeling as though I've been punched in the chest.

"No need to sound so surprised! Gosh, look at the time. I don't wish to sound rude, but I need to be getting home or my better half will be wondering where I am."

BITTERSWEET

—— ～ ——

One Week Before She Disappeared

ABBY

"Have you told anyone else that you want to leave your husband?" Hearing the woman in black say those words out loud makes the concept more real. Which makes the idea more frightening. I shake my head. I haven't said a word to anyone about it because it's nobody else's business. "Do you think he knows?" she asks.

That is a difficult question to answer.

"I think he knows I am unhappy. But I've been unhappy for such a long time, maybe he doesn't notice anymore. Maybe, like me, he finds it hard to imagine us being apart when we've been together for so long. So it doesn't occur to him that I might actually leave."

"You sound as though you have already made up your mind."

"I know."

"But then why talk to me about it if you have already decided?"

It's a good question and there are a lot of answers. I only give her one.

"Because I'm scared."

When I spend too long thinking about how and why our marriage unraveled, my memory tends to wander to happier times. We weren't always the us we are now. Which is probably why I am so afraid of walking away. What if I never meet someone who can make me that happy again? Because we were happy, before. Nobody has ever made me happier than he did. But nobody has ever made me feel this sad either. Is being with someone who used to love you better than being alone?

A few months ago, he said he had found the perfect property for sale. *Fixer-upper* was an understatement. The location was great—for him, not so much for me—but being a little farther out meant we got more for our money. Unlike where we were living, this place had a view, and he was excited about the idea of renovating something, making it our own. I think we both thought that fixing that broken old building would fix whatever was broken in our marriage. For a while, I think it did. But there were problems with the project—just as there always are with these things—and the builders kept asking for more money. Money we didn't have. There comes a point with everything in life where there is no turning back. We had spent an extortionate amount on architect fees and jumped through seemingly endless hoops to get planning permission, the builders made constant noise, and dust, and complaints, and demands, and the months that followed were not happy ones. Renovating an old property only sounds romantic if you've never done it. When the builders discovered something unexpected I wished we never had.

"The builders found something today," I said one night as soon as he walked in the door. He'd been away for a few days at a book festival, and I confess I had enjoyed myself while he was gone. Because he works from home he was always there, and I never got to spend any time alone, even on the rare occasions when I did have a day off. While he was away, I watched old movies, ate food he didn't like, and danced around the house listening to Nina Simone while drinking white wine—he prefers red—and it was bliss. Until the builders knocked on the door.

"The builders finding something doesn't sound good," he said, hanging his coat on a hook. "What is it this time and how much will it cost to fix it?" he asked, pouring himself a glass of wine from the bottle that was already open. The project had cost more than double the original quote by then, and things were tight. He hadn't sold a new book for a while—mainly due to the fact he hadn't written one—and he always had a head-in-the-sand approach to finances. I often worried that he might lose everything—including the house—if I wasn't around to keep on top of things.

"No dead bodies or bones or anything like that," I said. "But they did find something when they were digging the new foundations . . ."

"Keeping people in suspense is my job."

"You have to promise not to freak out."

"I never freak out."

He always freaked out.

"The builders found two sets of clothes, two pairs of very old shoes, jewelry, including two rings, some pots, glass bottles, and some coins."

"Were the coins gold?" he asked.

"Sadly no. But the builders think they are about two hundred years old; they found similar-looking ones on a project not far from here last year. The clothes were laid out flat like two people were wearing them and holding hands. So I called the Heritage Committee and—"

"You did what? Do you want them to stop us from building? This project has already cost everything that we have, *more* than that—"

"I had a very interesting chat with them actually."

"Great. How much did that cost?"

"The woman I spoke to said what we found was evidence of a two-hundred-year-old ritual. If a married couple thought they were going to be separated forever, perhaps because of illness or war, they would bury a set of their clothes together under the floor of their home. They would leave money, sentimental objects, and something to eat and drink. Then they would put linens over the top, like a protective blanket to sleep under, before covering the plot with earth and stones and replacing the flooring. Which was likely to have been wooden boards back then. The husband and wife thought it was a way to guarantee they would find each other in the afterlife. Apparently it's an ancient custom called 'the buried lovers.' I think you should see it for yourself."

We had to use a torch to see the site where the builders had been working. I aimed the light at the spot where the items had been found, illuminating two sets of old muddy clothes and shoes.

"Okaaay," he said, looking as unimpressed as he sounded. "Now I've seen it, can we throw it all away?"

"No! That's the important part. There is a superstition."

"Oh good. A superstition. Love those—"

"The woman from the Heritage Committee said that if you discover a pair of buried lovers—remember that's what *she* called them—you have to leave them *exactly* as they were or put them back as best you can. If you separate them on earth, you will separate them in the afterlife. And if you steal their true love from them for all eternity, they will come to steal yours and curse you with eternal loneliness."

He stared at me as though waiting for the punch line.

"You aren't seriously considering this, are you?" he said then. "The builders need to dig down much further for the foundations. We can't leave some old clothes and pots in the dirt because of some silly superstition."

"They said they could work around the items and then insert some extra steel beams and it would be okay."

"And how much extra will *that* cost?"

"Not much. But it will take a little longer." He closed his eyes. "What are you doing?"

"I'm trying to disassociate from my body so I don't have to listen to this anymore."

"Surely you don't want to risk eternal loneliness?"

As soon as I asked the question I remembered how much my husband enjoyed his own company. He's only happy when he is writing and he does that best alone. I think loneliness is his preferred way of life. But then he opened his eyes again and put his arms around me.

"Darling, the ghosts of people who buried some clothes hundreds of years ago are not going to haunt us or make one of us disappear if we move their things. How about we just bury them nearby?" he said, and I wrapped my arms around his neck and pulled his face closer to mine.

"Please, I don't want anything bad to happen to us."

"It won't."

"I missed you while you were away," I told him and realized that it was true. I enjoyed some time on my own, but I did miss him. I didn't like sleeping in our big old bed without him by my side. "Promise we don't have to move the buried lovers and you can make love to me right here."

"I promise," he said, then he kissed me.

A week later I overheard the builders laughing about how he had told them to throw everything they found in the trash and not tell me. My husband didn't believe in curses, but I did. I still do.

The woman in black speaks again, pulling me from my thoughts.

"A lot of people fantasize about what their life might be like if they hadn't married their partner, or if they were to start a new life without them. It's actually perfectly normal and nothing to feel guilty about," she says, but I'm not sure that I believe her. "I'm curious to know whether that's all this is. Just a fantasy because your marriage is going through a rough patch—again, perfectly normal—or whether a separation or a clean break is something that you are serious about. A lot of people don't know the answer to the next question, and that's fine too, but *if* you were to leave your husband, where would you go? What would you do?"

The answer was bittersweet.

"There is only one place I've ever thought of as home."

"Where?" she asked.

"The Isle of Amberly."

CLEARLY MISUNDERSTOOD

GRADY

"It was nice meeting you, Grady. Apart from the bit where you knocked me off my bike. But I need to lock up and head home to my better half," Abby says.

My wife needs to get home to her new husband.

I can tell I have outstayed my welcome but I can't leave. I've only just found her. The walkie-talkie on the counter crackles to life and we both stare at it.

"*Has anyone seen them?*" asks an unfamiliar female voice.

I'm probably being paranoid, but for a moment I wonder if they're talking about us.

"I hate these bloody things," Abby adds, interrupting my suspicious thoughts and snatching the contraption. "Aubrey here. I'm at the pottery with *the author*," she says, winking in my direction. "Is everything okay?" She hits a button and turns back to me. "The people on this island campaigned and voted not to have a mobile phone mast, but they're obsessed with these bloody things instead."

The walkie-talkie crackles again and the ghostly voice of a different woman speaks.

"*Has anyone seen Sandy? I'm worried something might have happened to her.*"

Abby's body language changes and she answers instantly. "I'm on my way."

"Thank you," she says when we are back in the Land Rover and on the road.

"Not a problem. It sounds like an emergency and me driving you there will be much quicker than you cycling up that hill."

"I'm sure Sandy is fine," Abby says, to herself as much as to me. "I hope she is—she's the beating heart of the island, our unofficial leader I suppose. Sandy is like family to me."

Like family? The only family my wife has is her godmother.

"How do you know Sandy and Midge?" I ask.

"Everyone knows everyone on the island. You must have figured that out by now."

I don't ask her any more about that. I have other more important questions. Like, "Does your *better half* live on the island too?"

She hesitates. "Of course. Life would be a little lonely if they didn't."

"Have you been married long?"

"Long enough," she says, sounding wary. At first I feel clearly misunderstood, but my questions probably do sound a bit strange if she doesn't remember who I am. I try to rein in my jealousy but it's running around my head at full speed. "I'm surprised you haven't met Travers already," she says, and now I know his name. *Travers.* It sounds familiar. I think Midge must have mentioned him that night at dinner, but that was over a month ago and she talked about a lot of people. I can't remember them all.

"Why is it a surprise that we haven't met?" I ask.

"Well, Travers is often hanging around in the forest, not too far from Whitty's old writing cabin where I believe you're staying."

I remember the face I saw in the window and all the other weird things that have happened. "Why does Travers hang around in the forest?"

"It would be strange if the island's tree doctor didn't visit the redwoods; monitoring and taking care of them is the biggest part of the job. Protecting those ancient trees is so important to the whole community. You need to take the next left-hand turning."

I pull into Sandy and Midge's driveway, wishing I'd driven more slowly. I'm running out of time. None of this makes sense. Perhaps Abby has a brain injury and that is why she can't remember who I am or who she was a year ago, or some form of amnesia maybe. She opens the car door, and I clamber out to help her get the bike from the trunk.

"I could come in? If there is anything I can do to—"

"No, no. You've already done more than enough," she says. "If we don't meet again, good luck with the book!"

If we don't meet again.

She offers her hand and I stare at it.

Then, for lack of a better idea, I shake hands with my wife as though we are strangers. Midge appears in the doorway and looks as though she hasn't stopped crying since the last time I saw her. She's still wearing an old pink dressing gown. "Is that you, Grady?" she calls.

"Hi, Midge."

"Did you go to Darkside Cave earlier? Did you see Sandy? Her truck is still parked near there on the other side of the island, but there is no sign of her. The tide is in and I'm so worried that . . ." Midge starts to cry and Abby rushes over to her.

"*Did* you see Sandy?" my wife asks, and they both stare at me.

I shake my head.

"No. I was on my way there when I bumped into you. I haven't seen Sandy since yesterday," I lie.

The walkie-talkie Abby left on the car seat crackles.

WISE FOOL

idge is a mess. I help get her back inside and then stand there like a spare part while my wife rushes around knowing exactly what to do. Just like old times. Abby is clearly very at home in Sandy and Midge's house. She puts the kettle on, doesn't need to ask where the mugs are kept—mugs she made from the look of it—and doesn't need to ask how Midge likes her tea. She listens patiently to the older woman about how long Sandy has been gone and how worried she is.

I do my best not to get in the way, and pretend to be distracted by looking at some framed photographs on the wall. I don't remember them being here when I was invited to dinner a few weeks ago, but maybe I just didn't notice them. I see them now, and can't stop staring. Some are very old—black-and-white images of relatives I presume, and a faded picture of Sandy and Midge holding a baby outside Saint Lucy's Church. A christening perhaps. But my attention is focused on a photo of Abby as a child. I'm almost certain that is what I am looking at. The picture shows a birthday cake with the number ten written on it in icing. Abby is sitting next to a blond little girl who looks the same age, and their cheeks are filled with air, preparing to blow out the candles. A younger Sandy and Midge are standing behind them with big smiles on their faces. I wonder if the blond girl is the daughter Sandy lost, which would make her Midge's niece. I'm *sure* the dark-haired child is Abby. I gawp at the photo, trying to put together pieces of a puzzle I didn't know I had to solve, my brain working overtime.

I never met Abby's parents—they were both dead when we got together. I only met Kitty, her godmother. Abby lived in London with Kitty since she was . . . ten or eleven, I think? She never mentioned the Isle of Amberly, not once, I would have remembered. I didn't know she'd even *been* to Scotland, let alone lived here. I'd suggested us visiting the Highlands so many times, but she always said it was somewhere she had never been and never wanted to go. So why is there a picture of her here as a child with Sandy and Midge?

There is another picture of Abby on the wall, a more recent one.

It's of my wife on her wedding day.

Not ours.

She is standing with a group of women I recognize from the island: Sandy, Midge, Cora Christie from the corner shop, Mary and Alex the butchers, Arabella from The Stumble Inn, and the Reverend Melody Bates. There are a few faces I don't recognize, but it looks as though they were all there when Abby married someone else last year. The whole *community*. She's still married to me; how can she have married someone else? Confusion and anger pollute every thought inside my head. I could wait, or I could confront them both now. Ask the questions that I want to ask and demand the answers I need. But then Midge starts to cry again and I decide this isn't the time or place. I feel like an outsider intruding on their grief.

"Sandy is a wise fool. I suspect she knew better than to drive back from the cave when she'd had too much to drink and is walk-

ing home. She'll probably come through the front door any minute. Try not to worry," Abby says to Midge.

"Would you mind if I used the bathroom?" I ask.

Both women stare at me as though they had forgotten I was
here, but it's Midge who answers. "Of course, you know where
it is."

I leave the kitchen, pass the downstairs bathroom, and creep
up the staircase to the first floor instead. I don't know what I'm
looking for, but I hurry down the corridor anyway, quietly opening doors and seeing what is behind them. Bedrooms mostly, until
I reach what looks like an office. The thing that makes me stop
and stare is that one of the walls is covered in newspaper clippings. There are hundreds of them.

I don't understand what this means.

Before I get a chance to see if the articles were written by
Abby, I hear a quiet but unfamiliar sound on the other side of
the wall.

Bang, rattle, whoosh. Bang, rattle, whoosh. Bang, rattle, whoosh.

I creep back out onto the landing and follow the sound to a
closed door. I slowly lean down until I can peer through the keyhole, and then I see her. The woman I met in the cemetery dressed
head to toe in tweed. The one who said I should leave before it
was too late. She must be Morag, Sandy's mother, the woman who
kept banging her walking stick on the ceiling when I was here for
dinner. She is sitting behind some kind of enormous loom; I think
she's weaving. I stand and try the door handle but it's locked.
Morag knows something, I'm sure she does. If only I could speak
to her I might be able to find out what. I lean down again, and
this time when I peer through the keyhole there is an eye staring
right at me. I leap back.

"You shouldn't be here. You must *leave*," she hisses. Then she
starts banging her walking stick against the back of the door.

I quietly hurry down the stairs and to the kitchen.

"I think your mother might need something—"

"When doesn't she?" Midge interrupts.

"I couldn't quite understand what she was saying—"

"My mother wasn't *saying* anything. She hasn't spoken a word or left the house since my father died."

I heard her speaking. Twice. And I saw her in the graveyard.

"These days she just bangs her stick when she wants something. Sorry, Grady. I didn't mean to snap at you, but today has been a lot. I'll go and see to her."

"Don't feel as though you need to stay, I've got this," Abby says when Midge has gone.

It's a relief to get out of the house for all of the reasons, but it feels strange to leave Abby behind when I've only just found her. I can't think of an excuse to stay any longer, and I don't know whether telling her the truth would be the right thing to do right now. She seems to have a whole new life here. As I walk across the driveway, I glance at the upstairs window and see Morag. She's frantically waving, almost as though she wants to warn me about something, but maybe she's just confused. She stands so close to the glass that it starts to mist, then she holds up a crooked finger and writes backward in the condensation. Even from here I can read the letters: *leave*. She shakes her head sadly then backs away until I can no longer see her. As if she was never there.

I can still smell Abby's perfume in the car as I drive back toward the cabin. It makes it hard to think about anything else. My mind is blown by the afternoon's events, and the Land Rover almost swerves off the road twice because I'm too tired to see straight. Too tired to properly process anything that has happened. What I *need* is sleep, but what I *want* is whiskey. My wife is alive but she doesn't remember me, and now she's married to someone else. If that doesn't justify a drink in the afternoon I don't know what does.

As soon as I get inside the cabin I pour myself a glass of scotch—just a small one, since I need to focus or at least try to—then I sit and stare at the ocean while trying to come up with a new plan. The old plan was to get off the island as soon as possible, find out what Kitty meant in her letter, and hope that she liked the new book well enough to sell it and help get my life back on track. There was nothing left to stay here for until I ran into Abby.

Now I don't know what to do.

So I do what I always do when I don't know what to do and pour another drink.

One minute I want to know *everything* about the man she has married, then I want to know nothing. Nothing at all. "The tree doctor," she called him, as though that was supposed to mean something. As if that might make all of this okay. None of this makes sense. How does someone disappear from the south of England and end up on a remote Scottish island? How can she have no memory of us? Of me? Should I tell her? Once again I find myself facing a moral dilemma with no right answer.

Now that I know she is here I can't just walk away.

Abby is the only person I have ever truly loved. What if she does remember us one day?

I keep thinking I can hear someone creeping around outside the cabin, so I check that all of the doors and windows are locked. I think about what my doctor said the last time I bothered to go see him, about long-term lack of sleep leading to paranoia, confusion, hallucinations, and all the other great stuff he predicted if I didn't find a way to switch off, learn to make my mind rest. I take a couple of sleeping pills he prescribed and wash them down with more whiskey.

I start to wonder if I imagined everything that happened today, if it was all just a dream, but then I take the Beautiful Ugly pamphlet from the pottery out of my pocket and there she is, my wife's familiar face staring right back at me. I pour myself another drink. Then I leave the pamphlet on the desk and take out the walkie-talkie instead.

It isn't mine, obviously.

I'm just "borrowing" it.

I'm hoping it might help me figure out what is really going on.

GROWING SMALLER

fall asleep—pass out—on the bed with the walkie-talkie still in my hand. My wife always said that it was impossible to wake me when I drank too much. But she was wrong because *something* does wake me and it isn't the walkie-talkie. It starts as a small sound at first. The variety that infiltrates your dreams so that it becomes part of them. Hiding, unnoticed, until the sound is too out of place to fit within whatever you were dreaming about. Like an itch you have to scratch. It distracts me from the imaginary scenes my subconscious mind has conjured, pulling me from the no-man's-land between sleep and wakefulness where dreams and reality blur. I hear the noise again and struggle to identify it.

It sounds like breathing.

And it sounds like it is coming from beneath my bed.

I wake up drenched in sweat. I don't move but I do open my eyes, blinking into the shadows, adjusting to the dark. I keep perfectly still and listen.

At first, I think that it was just a dream within a dream, but then I hear it again.

Someone is slowly coming out from under the bed.

I am lying on my side and I daren't move.

All I can see at first is a shadow, and again I think I must be imagining it, unable to believe my own eyes. But the shadow is shaped like a hand. Someone really is crawling out from beneath the bed very, very slowly. They must have been down there the whole time I was sleeping.

I should get up, defend myself, say something, *do* something.

But I do none of those things.

I am paralyzed with fear as the dark shape of a person finishes crawling and starts to slowly stand. My heart is thudding so fast and so loud inside my chest I am sure they must be able to hear it. I close my eyes when they turn to face me. Like a child who thinks they can't be seen by a monster if *they* can't see *it*. I have never been a brave man. When it comes to fight or flight I guess I am a coward; I'll choose to run every time. But I can't even move.

I hear them lean down then, looming over me until their face is so close to mine I can feel their breath. For a brief moment I think it is Abby because I can smell her perfume. But when I open my eyes, all I see is the shadow of a person with branches instead of arms and twisted twigs instead of fingers. Part man, part tree, some sort of *tree man*.

I scream.

Columbo barks and I open my eyes for real this time, and nobody except my dog is sitting on the bed beside me. His hot breath in my face, his eyes filled with inexplicable joy, his tail wagging and thumping loudly on the duvet. It *was* just a dream. There was nobody hiding beneath my bed—except maybe for the dog—and I feel like an idiot. My racing heart starts to calm down and I wipe the sweat from my brow with the back of my hand.

I am trapped on this island in so many ways: I can't leave un- less a boat will take me, I don't have any money to stay anywhere else for long if I do, and now my missing wife is here and I need to understand how and why. My options seem to be growing smaller every day and it feels like the walls of my world are closing in. I remind myself that what happened was only a dream. Nobody was really hiding under the bed. And nobody knows about Charles Whittaker's book, or what I've done. Nobody knows except me.

It's only when I sit up that I feel the cool breeze on my skin. I look over toward the door I remember locking, and see that it has been left slightly open.

HONEST THIEF

S omeone was here in the cabin while I was sleeping. It isn't the first time that someone has let themselves in, but it never happened while I was here before. In bed. Unconscious. Someone has been spying on me since I arrived on the island. I'm sure of it now, and for some reason I am convinced it was *him*—Travers, the so-called tree doctor who Abby married—and I think that's what my subconscious was trying to tell me in my dream. My wife's new husband has been watching her old one. Which means he knows who I am even if she doesn't. But who is he? And how has he tricked her into forgetting her old life with me?

I find the Isle of Amberly Trust report that I swiped from Abby's desk and scan the list of attendees until I see what I'm looking for. "Travers Fairlight, of The Croft. Island Ranger." *Island Ranger.* Hardly an impressive job title. But then *Has-Been Author* doesn't sound very attractive either. I need to stop comparing myself to a man I have never met and do something to fix this. I find the map of Amberly and see that The Croft is at the top of the island. Now that I have a car it's not so far away. Maybe Travers knows what really happened and what is going on here. He's stolen my wife so let's see if he's at least an honest thief. Because he must know whether the woman he married has lost her memory, and whether she has always lived here. I grab the keys for the Land Rover and head out early, taking Columbo with me in case whoever let themselves in last night decides to come back.

My fragile ego can't stop obsessing about why Abby might choose this man over me. Success is as subjective as history. I might not have been as successful as I'd hoped, but I'm still proud of the books I have written. My whole career was a series of self-portraits, even though I didn't know it at the time. In all of my previous novels I have written about the things I am most afraid of. I think it is my way of processing what scares me most about the world: the terrible things human beings are capable of doing to each other. We are a peculiar species.

The three basic fundamental fears that all humans experience are:

Fear of death.

Fear of abandonment.

Fear of failure.

I experience all three on a daily basis. I fear death because I don't think I have achieved much with my life, and I fear I will be forgotten. I've already been abandoned by the people who were supposed to love me the most—my parents—so it's no wonder that fear of abandonment is something that haunts me. It's also why I find it so difficult to trust people. Fear of failure, well, I don't know what it is like not to live in perpetual fear of not living up to your own expectations. I should be a better person but there are some things it is too late for me to succeed at. I have always hidden my fears and myself inside my books rather than face facts or confront reality. Well, not this time. I'm going to find out the truth and nothing is going to slow me down or get in my way.

Until the walkie-talkie crackles as I drive along the main road.

I hit the brakes of the Land Rover, stop and listen, but hear nothing.

When I drive on it crackles again, but nobody speaks. Maybe it's broken.

With the help of the map it doesn't take too long to find The Croft. It's a modern wooden house at the end of a private lane. Hidden away. Secluded. I feel a strange sense of excitement tinged with dread as I park outside. This is where my wife has been living all this time. I've dressed myself up a bit for the occasion, I do not know why. My hair is still a tad wild-looking—I haven't had it cut since I arrived on the island—but I've had a shave and I'm wearing my best shirt. I came here to see the new husband for myself, ask him a question or two, but I notice that Abby's old-fashioned bike—with its wicker basket and childish bells—is leaning against the porch. So I know I'm in the right place. And I know she is at home. Which is good, because I am going to confront her about a past she may or may not remember too. Our past. I need to know what happened after she disappeared, and how she ended up here. She is the only person who can tell me.

I knock on the door but there is no answer. I feel like I'm trespassing when I walk around the back but I do it anyway. When I still can't see or hear any signs of life, I peer through the windows. It's a modern open-plan layout with industrial furnishings lacking in personality. The kind of place Abby would hate. I raise my hands to the sides of my head to shield my eyes from the sunlight, trying to get a better view inside the house. Then I hear a voice behind me.

"Can I help you?"

It's one of my top three favorite passive-aggressive terms, along with, *No offense, but* . . . and *Correct me if I'm wrong* . . . I can tell from their tone that this person does not want to *help* me.

I turn to see a ridiculously attractive woman with long dark hair. She's in her thirties, looks like a film star, and for a moment I am rendered speechless by her beauty.

"I'm looking for Travers," I say.

"Then I guess you found her."

Her?

My mind is properly blown.

"*You're* Travers?"

"Last time I checked," she says. "And you are?"

Meeting the man my wife had married was something I struggled to prepare myself for.

Finding out that she married a *woman* is too much to process.

I replay the conversation with Abby in my mind and realize that she never used the word *husband* when she told me she was married. When she said Travers was the island's "tree doctor" I had pictured a big tall lumberjack of a guy, maybe with a beard. I was secretly hoping my rival would have a beer belly, bad breath, problematic body odor, and a touch of baldness perhaps—I still have a full head of hair. I knew I would compare myself to him—how could I not—but I didn't imagine this. It seems she has married a beautiful woman who is ten years younger than me. Somehow that feels like an even bigger insult to my manhood. Travers is wearing jeans and a simple white shirt and looks effortlessly stunning. Her perfect face is makeup-free—she's not even trying—and yet I can't take my eyes off her. Her extremely green eyes are taking me in too, and I wonder if she knows who I am. I have never truly understood the term *devastatingly beautiful* until now, but that's exactly what this woman is. And having met my wife's new *wife*, I do feel devastated.

"Is Abby here?" I ask and she frowns. "I mean *Aubrey*." My voice sounds peculiar and I cough to clear my throat. Whatever first impression I am making it is not good.

"She's not home," Travers says.

"I saw her bike outside—"

She tilts her head and folds her arms. "I'm sorry, *who* are you?"

"I'm staying at Charles Whittaker's cabin for a while." Her face stays exactly the same. "While I write," I add, and her expression shifts.

"Oh, *the author*. Why are you looking for my wife?" Her words feel like a slap.

She used to be married to me.

"I wonder if I could ask how the two of you met? And when? And if she lived here as a child?" As soon as I say the words out loud I can hear what strange questions those are.

"You could ask, but if you did I'd probably tell you to mind your own business. I don't mean to sound rude," she says, sounding rude. "But this is not a great time."

In desperation, I take the Beautiful Ugly pamphlet from the pottery out of my pocket. I unfold it to reveal the photo of Abby and hold it out for Travers to see. "The woman in this picture, your wife, looks a lot like someone I used to know."

"Is that so?" she says, frowning down at the photo then back at me.

I look at it too and a second later I start to feel dizzy with confusion. The photo of the woman who owns Beautiful Ugly is not of Abby.

They share the same hair color, style, and length but she is not my wife. I don't understand. When I picked this pamphlet up in the pottery yesterday the photo was of her. I saw her with my own eyes. I watched her, I listened to her; it *was* her. But then how do I explain this? Who is this woman in the photo? According to the pamphlet, she is Aubrey Fairlight, the owner of the pottery, but this is not who I met yesterday. I think about my wife, who I could never imagine living somewhere like this and making pots all day. Abby who would never wear dungarees, or ride a bike, or live in a big modern house with no features or personality. She was a self-confessed workaholic. She spent more time in the newsroom than she ever did at home, always chasing the next story. Always trying to uncover the truth. Of course the woman I met yesterday isn't Abby. How could she be?

I *am* losing my mind. This confirms it.

I feel so unsteady I have to lean against the house to prop myself up.

"Are you okay?" the devastatingly beautiful woman asks.

No.

MAN-CHILD

—————————

One week before she disappeared

ABBY

I always wanted children, but he didn't, and I guess I let him talk me out of it during the first few years we were together. He made it seem as though what we had was enough. But then—maybe because so many people we knew had started having families—it began to feel as though something was missing. At least it did for me. He had his books and in many ways they were his children. I only had him and only when he was present, which he often wasn't even if sitting right beside me. I missed the child I never had.

I've been accused of being a workaholic all my life, but I think when you find something that you believe in and are passionate about, it does sometimes take over. I tend to beat myself up when I don't get things quite right. I so badly want to be good at what I do, but that determination to do better, *be* better, is sometimes overwhelming. It makes me withdraw into myself, pull away from the people who have chosen to love me. I know I can be distant and difficult to be around when I am working. And I'm always working.

But he did know that about me from the start.

I'm trying to do the right thing for us, not just me.

The woman in black shifts in her seat. Our time is almost up. She has other people to see and other problems to solve.

"I hope this conversation has been useful?" she says.

"It has. Thank you. The thing is, he doesn't want children and that makes us incompatible. I married a man-child and I can see that now. He is selfish and stubborn and he doesn't support me in my career the way I have supported him. He chooses his books over me, every single time."

She stares at me as though those are not terrible things.

It sometimes feels as though life has passed me by and I wonder if other people feel that way too. Surely it can't only be me. I don't remember when the years started to speed up, but they did. Seasons tumbling into each other, days disappearing into weeks, weeks into months. I can't seem to slow life down but I can't keep up with it either. The markers that are so familiar to me: New Year, family birthdays, Halloween, Christmas, all come around too fast. No matter how hard I try to stay one step ahead I am always behind schedule in the story of my life. I feel old, even though I'm not, and I constantly feel like I'm running out of time.

"I have to make a change before it really is too late."

"It sounds to me as though you have made up your mind," the woman in black replies.

"I think so. Yes."

"When will you tell him?"

"I don't know. He hasn't been himself lately. I do keep asking what is wrong, but he doesn't talk to me. Not like he used to. I was wondering if it might be depression. He has trouble sleeping and he's permanently anxious about his books and his career, no matter what I say to try to reassure him. He's become distracted and distant, a little more forgetful than he used to be. It's funny really; he worries far more about his work than he does about his marriage. I honestly don't know whether he is expecting this or whether it will come as a complete surprise."

"Are you scared of telling him?"

"*Scared* of him? No, of course not," I tell her.

"So you are going to tell him before you leave?"

"I'm not going to just disappear in the night if that's what you mean. He deserves to know the truth. I plan to tell him face-to-face; I'm just scared of hurting him. Nobody wants to hurt someone they love."

"So you do still love him?" she asks, and the weight of her question feels too heavy, as does her stare. I look away. Then the woman in black who has spent the last hour listening to me, watching me, judging me, says something that I already know is going to haunt me. "Nobody said it was easy, but love is always worth fighting for, isn't it? I think maybe it's the only thing worth fighting for."

WORKING HOLIDAY

GRADY

I'm about to leave The Croft when I hear the sound of a baby cry-ing. Travers looks up at an open window and nods, but when I turn to look I don't see anyone there.

"I am sorry to have disturbed you," I say, and make a hasty retreat.

I drive until I am far enough away to be out of sight, then I pull over onto the side of the road and cry like a baby myself. The sound that comes out of my mouth is so animal-like that the dog starts to whimper too. Columbo licks my face and I appreciate his concern and affection, but it doesn't make the tears stop. I feel broken and confused and scared. Am I so tired that I'm losing my mind? Or am I just so sad because I lost the love of my life that I simply cannot function? Maybe I need to talk to someone, get some professional help, but I don't know anyone and even if I did, what would I say? My sorrow is a ledge nobody can talk me down from and I prefer to fall alone.

I wish I'd never come to this island.

This working holiday isn't working and I have to get out of here. Things are getting worse for me, not better. I was in a bad place before, but since I arrived I seem to have completely lost my grip on reality.

I think I can still hear a child crying in the distance and the sound makes me shiver. Abby wanted to have a baby but I didn't. I made excuses, told her I didn't want them or that I didn't feel ready, and I think she had finally realized that I never would be. It became a taboo subject in our marriage, one that always resurfaced when we disagreed about something. She seemed convinced I would see things from her point of view one day, and I thought she'd give up trying to persuade me. We were both wrong. Her biological clock only ticked more loudly, and the parenthood debate clearly wasn't going to go away.

Which was why I had a vasectomy and didn't tell her.

It was such a simple procedure she didn't even know I'd been in the hospital.

If there was something my wife wanted she always found a way to make it happen. No matter what, and regardless of how I felt. *Against all odds* were three of her favorite words. She'd talked about wanting to try to get pregnant before she was forty, before it was too late. Said it might be her last chance, which made me realize it might be mine. So I made sure this was one thing that couldn't happen without my say-so. Not because she wouldn't have been a wonderful mother—I knew she would be; Abby was good at everything—but because I didn't come from a happy family and I think children sometimes inherit their parents' mistakes. I didn't want my child to inherit mine. I don't think I'm very good at loving people—I genuinely prefer dogs—and I was scared of not feeling what a father is supposed to feel. I know what it feels like to have parents who do not love you, and I didn't want to risk inflicting that all-consuming hurt on a child of my own.

I wonder if my life would have unfolded differently if Abby and I had a child.

I wonder where she is, if she's even alive.

I wonder if I'm going to imagine seeing her everywhere forever.

My head is too full of muddled thoughts but the loudest one
is also the clearest.

I take the pamphlet out of my pocket one last time and stare at
the owner of Beautiful Ugly. I blink through my tears, but there
is no denying it.

The woman I met yesterday is not my missing wife.

CLOSE DISTANCE

find myself parking in the village without really knowing how I got there. I remember leaving The Croft, then pulling over for a few minutes to try to compose myself. It clearly didn't work because then I just drove along the coast road, looking for fishing boats or anything I could beg to borrow, or steal, to get myself off this island. I think being here might be making me crazy. The walkie-talkie on the passenger seat crackles when I open the car door but I don't hear any voices. Trust me to take a broken one.

I head straight for Christie's Corner Shop and my heart sinks when I see the CLOSED sign. Cora was the only person I could think of to ask. It might be days until the next ferry now that Sandy is missing, but Cora will know when the next mail boat is due to arrive. I have to find out when that is so I can make sure I am on it. I'll bribe them if I have to. We're only ten miles from the mainland, it's such a close distance, and yet it seems impossible to make the journey. I don't care how I get off this island, I just know that I need to.

As soon as I start to turn away the shop door opens.

"You okay, Grady?" Cora asks, dressed in green as always. A tartan ensemble today.

She invites me inside and listens patiently while I explain that there has been a family emergency and that I need to get to the mainland as soon as possible.

"There's no boats at all for a couple of days I'm afraid," she says.

"Why not? Is there a storm coming?"

"No, it's just the weekend."

That means I'm stuck here for at least another forty-eight hours.

"Do you know why I always wear green, Grady?" Cora asks. "It isn't about luck, there's no such thing. I wear this color because green is made of blue and yellow." She stares at me as though waiting for a reaction I do not know how to give. "Blue and yellow are very different, wouldn't you agree? Like the sea and the sun. I like that *one* thing can be made from *two* such different things, because none of us are just one thing. Once you understand that, it's so much easier to know yourself and make peace with who you are. *Green* being your surname, I thought you might like to know. You're looking tired, Grady. Do you want some more bog myrtle tea to help you sleep?" she says, sounding genuinely concerned.

"No. Thank you." If I sound a little rude, it's because I suspect it might have been the tea she gave me that made me see things that weren't there.

"Okey doke," she replies with a crooked smile. Perhaps my paranoia is getting the better of me. "It's such a shame you want to leave."

"I didn't say I *wanted* to leave . . ." The lie sounds like what it is so I add a little truth. "But I'm afraid I need to."

"Well, I'll be sad to see you go. You've been much friendlier than the last one."

"The last one?"

"The last author. After Charles Whittaker, but before you. We hardly saw much of that one at all to be honest, he didn't last long. Very unfriendly. Cocky fellow too, but the book he wrote while he was here was terrible. More of a page burner than a page turner if you know what I mean. So I'm glad he's gone. We all were."

"There was another author living in the cabin after Charles Whittaker but before me?"

"Of course. It's nice to have a resident writer, but some live longer than others."

I stare at her. "Pardon?"

"I said some last longer than others. Are you feeling okay, Grady?"

Her walkie-talkie begins to crackle and she turns it off.

"Not really, no." I head for the door and the little bell above it tinkles.

Cora calls after me. "I know you *want* to leave but it might be best, for you, if you stayed awhile longer."

"I told you, it's not that I *want* to leave—"

"I wasn't born yesterday, Grady. How could you possibly know that there's a family emergency on the mainland when there are no phones on the island and no internet? I'd know if you'd received anything in the post and you haven't, nothing for weeks except a couple of letters from your agent. Nobody misses you, nobody cares, nobody even knows that you're here. There is no family emergency because you don't have any family."

I stare at her. "What did you just say?"

She frowns. "I said I'm sorry to hear about the trouble with your family."

My mind is determined to break me. I'm seeing things, I'm hearing things, I no longer trust my own senses. I no longer trust myself.

"It's okay," I tell her. "I'll just get the next ferry—"

"There might not be one for a while. Could be weeks, maybe even longer until you or anyone else can leave the island again."

"Why won't there be a ferry?"

"There's nobody to sail it."

"Because Sandy is still missing?"

"Sandy isn't missing. They found her. She's dead."

ILL HEALTH

climb into the Land Rover next to Columbo and lock the doors. My hands are trembling and I can't make them stop. I wonder if anyone knows I was with Sandy before she died? How could they? There was nobody else out by the cave; it's on the other side of the island. The relief that now nobody will know that I stole Charles Whittaker's book is far outweighed by the guilt, which is so heavy it is almost unbearable. Cora said she didn't know how Sandy died, but I'm guessing she must have drowned. I could have prevented it. No one must ever know I was there.

I don't understand how I didn't hear about Sandy when I have a walkie-talkie now. I pick up the one I borrowed from the woman I thought was my wife and stare at it. I'm useless with anything remotely technical, always have been, so I tentatively twist a dial, hoping not to break the damn thing. To my surprise, it crackles to life and I hear voices straight away.

"He looked surprised when I told him about Sandy," says one I recognize immediately. "All of the color completely drained from his face," Cora adds.

"So are we sure he isn't listening in since we changed the frequency?" asks a female voice I don't recognize.

"Certain. We can say what we like again," says Travers, the beautiful woman from The Croft. "I don't think he's a well man."

"I thought that as soon as I read his books," says someone else. "They were very disturbing."

"Someone needs to do something about him soon. It's not just a case of ill health anymore, I think he's losing it," Cora adds.

They're talking about *me*.

The voices continue their conversation and once again I think I might be losing my mind. They clearly think I am too.

"Does he know?"

"No. He hasn't got a clue."

"Where is he now?" asks another female voice, this time a London accent. I think it's the pub landlady.

"He's sitting in his car parked outside the shop staring at The Stumble Inn," Cora replies.

I *am* staring at the pub. There are no other cars. They really *are* talking about me.

That's it. I'm driving to the ferry, maybe I can figure out how to sail it myself. I start the Land Rover and it splutters to life, but after a few seconds it stutters and stops.

No, no, no.

There is a red warning light on the dashboard suggesting I am out of fuel.

I don't understand it. I could have sworn the tank was still over half full on the way here. I rest my head on the steering wheel and swear under my breath. I don't remember seeing a petrol station anywhere on the island, but there must be one. I climb out of the car, then see Cora Christie standing outside her shop and looking in my direction. Her head is tilted to one side and she's holding a walkie-talkie in her bony little hand.

"Car trouble?" she asks.

"I seem to have run out of petrol."

"Oh dear."

"I don't suppose there is somewhere nearby where I can get some?"

She shakes her head. "There are no petrol stations on Amberly. Living on an island like this isn't like living anywhere else; you have to plan ahead. Be prepared. You have to do what is best for the community. It's the only way to survive."

The strangest thing about her odd little speech, the thing that unsettles me the most, is that she is smiling the whole time. As though she already knew I had run out of petrol and is extremely happy about it.

CHEERFUL PESSIMIST

like to think of myself as a cheerful pessimist. Life is less depressing if you accept that people will always disappoint you. I don't think I ran out of petrol; I'm convinced I had half a tank when I arrived in the village. *Someone* did this to me, I'm sure of it. But as soon as I have the thought I feel less certain. I don't know how someone could have, unless they siphoned the fuel while I was in the shop. But why would anyone do that?

To stop me from leaving the island.

Delusions and paranoia can be common with insomnia. Confusion and memory loss can contribute to untrue beliefs, not grounded in reality, but which feel entirely real. I *know* this. I just don't know if that is what is happening to me. Can everything that has occurred since I arrived on Amberly really be due to lack of sleep? Or even bog myrtle tea? I don't think so anymore. I just heard them speaking about me on the walkie-talkie, I didn't imagine that.

I get Columbo out of the car and grab the walkie-talkie in case I catch them talking about me again. It's a shame I can't use it to contact someone on the mainland. As we start to leave the village the old red phone box catches my eye, the one that has been converted into a library. What if it *does* work? What if the islanders just told me it didn't for reasons I don't yet understand? What if it isn't really "a library" at all?

I run to it and when I pull the door open I feel dizzy and unsteady on my feet.

It is still full of books, but they are all mine.

Every single book on every shelf has the name Grady Green on the spine.

There are multiple copies of every book I've ever written, as though the whole island has been reading them. This is too much. This island, these people, everything about this place feels wrong. I'm not crazy, *they* are. I pick up the handset with trembling fingers and almost cry tears of joy when I hear a dial tone. It *does* work. I only know two mobile numbers off by heart: my wife and my agent. So I call Kitty. I keep looking over my shoulder in case someone comes to try to stop me, but the village is as deserted as always.

The phone rings once . . .

Twice . . .

Three times . . .

"Hello?" says a voice.

"Kitty, it's me. Grady. I really need to—"

"Hello? Is anyone there? This is a very bad line," she says, sounding impatient.

The phone crackles and I speak a little louder.

"Kitty, it's Grady. Can you hear me?"

"Grady, is that you?"

"Yes! I need your help—"

"Grady, this is a terrible line. Can you call me back? I am glad that you've called though, I really need to talk to you. I'm so sorry I sent you to the island, you need to leave as soon as you can. I don't think it is safe for you to be there. Since you left London I found out that—"

The line goes dead.

"Kitty?"

I stab the buttons, all of them, but nothing works. There isn't even a dial tone anymore. It's almost as though someone has cut the phone line.

Maybe they have.

I don't think I'm being paranoid anymore.

Kitty just said that I was in danger so I *haven't* been imagining it.

I grab Columbo's lead and we start to run.

RUNNING SCARED

W e run out of the village and toward the main road, then take the turning that leads to the south of the island. I have never sailed a ferry, but this is a very small one, it has to be worth a go. At the very least, there might be some equipment on board that I could use to contact the mainland. Try to reach Kitty again. We don't have to run too much farther to see where the ferry is docked, I remember the wooden pier well.

But there is no ferry there.

I can't see any boats at all.

There is nothing but the sea.

The frustration I feel is overwhelming. I want to scream at someone but there is nobody to scream at. Then I remember the walkie-talkie, take it from my pocket, and scream into that. Nobody replies. The damn thing doesn't even crackle. I turn back and start running in the direction we came from.

A lot of the journey is uphill but I don't stop, even when the steeper parts steal my breath from me. The sun is starting to set and the views on the coast road are spectacular. There is an ever-changing display of pink clouds drifting across a patchy purple sky above the ocean. The first stars have started to appear at the edge of the sky, impatient for the sun to leave, but I don't stop to enjoy the spectacle. I breathe the sea air, focus on the path, and keep running. Just before we reach the road that leads to the forest, I see a sign for the Standing Stones. I remember something Sandy said about it being the only place on the island where someone once had a mobile phone signal. Given the situation, I think it's worth a try. We carry on, only stopping when I finally see them: the Standing Stones. The twelve giant stones look like a smaller version of Stonehenge, forming a circle on the top of a grassy hill. They are eerily lit by the setting sun casting long shadows on the ground beneath them. I stop to catch my breath, and read an information board while I do.

The Standing Stones of Amberly are over 5,000 years old. There is much mystery over how and why they are here. Some believe the standing stones are the result of dark magic, and are the remains of twelve witches who were turned to rock. Others insist that standing in the center of the circle can transport people to another time and place.

We invite you to uncover the mystery for yourself.

I would love to be transported to another time and place—ideally the mainland—but I've never believed in nonsense. I climb the hill and walk to the center of the circle anyway, just in case, then take out my mobile. I don't have much battery left but I *do* have a single bar of signal.

I call Kitty but it goes straight to voicemail.

I hang up and try again but the same thing happens. I start cursing myself for not charging the phone, but there has been no point in doing so for weeks. It's getting dark, and it's already very cold, and I'm about to give up when the phone starts to ring in my hand.

When I look at the display it isn't Kitty calling.

It says THE WIFE.

I accept the call and hold the phone to my ear but I don't hear Abby's voice.

All I hear is the sound of the sea before my phone dies.

IMPOSSIBLE SOLUTION

t's completely dark by the time we reach the forest, and as we hurry toward the cabin I keep thinking that I can hear footsteps behind us. Twigs snap in the distance beyond the trees, the unmistakable sound of something, or someone, moving over fallen leaves. There are no birds on the island but there are plenty of other creatures. I tell myself that's all it is and carry on. Regardless of my mind's feeble attempt at being rational, I still rush through the giant redwoods, trying not to trip on moss-covered roots, the sound of my own labored breaths drowning out the other things I think I can hear. Even the soundtrack of the ocean in the distance isn't as comforting as it used to be; it sounds like the end of something.

It is a huge relief when I see the log cabin.

I no longer care what is going on or why. I have to plan. I need to get the Land Rover back, then I'll sit in it down by the dock until a boat comes. Any boat. I hurry inside, lock the door behind me, and reach for the light switch. It doesn't work. I try again, but the cabin remains in darkness. For some reason there's no power. I find the matchbox with the robin on the front that was here when I arrived and light a couple of candles so I can see what I'm doing. Then I open the curtains covering the huge windows at the back of the cabin, revealing a full moon that is bright enough to dampen the gloom. I spot low clouds on the horizon, like a slow-moving blanket starting to cover the sea, and I hurry. I grab a torch then go out to the shed where the Land Rover was kept, and for once, my memory is not playing tricks on me. Inside, among all the well-organized tools and cubby holes, I find exactly what I am looking for: a small red fuel can. I pick it up and am happy to hear it is full. I breathe a sigh of relief and tell myself there is no such thing as an impossible solution. I return to the cabin, pack up everything I can't leave without. Then I do something that is very difficult for me.

"It will be quicker if you stay here," I say to Columbo. He doesn't look convinced. "I'm going to run to the village and then I'll drive straight back to get you. I really won't be long and then we'll leave this place for good. Okay?"

I do run. Not just because I'm scared and want to get out of here but because I don't want to leave my dog for any longer than I have to. I locked all the windows and doors in the cabin, and tell myself that if someone wanted to hurt Columbo they would have already. It's *me* the people on this island seem to have a problem with. I'll run to the village, I'll top up the tank, drive back, load up the car and go. It's a simple plan, a good plan, the *only* plan. What can possibly go wrong?

The temperature drops dramatically on the island as soon as the sun sets. The icy air slaps and pinches my skin, and my legs feel heavy as I try to propel myself forward. When I leave the forest to join the coast road, I see that what I thought was low cloud seems to have completely spread across the ocean. I can still hear and smell the waves crashing on the rocks below, but I can't see them. Every time I look over my shoulder the mist seems closer. A few steps later I can't see anything at all in any direction; the mist seems to have completely enveloped the island.

Then I hear the sound of children crying in the distance.

I wish I *didn't* remember the story Sandy told me about the Children of the Mist.

But I do, so I remind myself what my nana always told me when I was scared as a child: there's no need to be afraid of the dead, it's the living you have to watch out for.

I force my feet to run a little faster anyway.

My heart is racing by the time I reach the village. The petrol canister is heavy and difficult to run with, so I feel a surge of relief when I see the lights in the distance. All of the windows in the thatched cottages appear to be glowing, as are the ones in the other houses and buildings, including The Stumble Inn. It seems I'm the only one with a power cut. Lights are shining all over the village and I can smell open fires, and see wisps of smoke snaking out of chimneys. It *looks* so welcoming, even in the dark. Picture-postcard perfect. The mist is thinner here away from the coast, and nothing feels as sinister or as threatening as it did a moment ago. Almost as though I imagined it.

I'm not imagining that the Land Rover has gone.

I spin around but it isn't parked where I left it or anywhere else.

As usual I can't see any signs of life in the village, but I can *hear* something: the sound of raised voices coming from inside the church.

I have never been in the village at night before. In the dark. The stained glass windows are illuminated from the light within, and as I get closer, I can see that they are not as traditional as I had presumed. They do not display religious icons. Instead, each one is made from glass images of faceless children. And every window has one word carved into the stone above it.

WE. WILL. NEVER. FORGET. OR. FORGIVE.

I don't know how I didn't notice this in the daytime, I guess sometimes we only see what we expect to see. I hear raised voices inside the church again. It's a Friday night—not a typical time for a service—and there is a voice inside my head screaming at me to walk away. But everything about this island now feels slightly off-kilter, and I have to know what is happening.

The metal gate that leads to the graveyard has been left open and swings back and forth in the wind, squeaking on its hinges as though trying to break free. I leave the petrol can next to it, and creep a little closer to the main entrance of the church, putting my ear against the huge ancient wooden doors. I can hear multiple voices now, but I can't make out who is speaking or what they are saying. After a great deal of deliberation I try to quietly push one of the doors. It swings wide open surprisingly fast, making a comically loud creaking sound. The chatter inside abruptly hushes. Everything stops.

They're all here. Almost everyone I've met so far on the island, and from the size of the congregation, everyone I haven't. I'm no great mathematician, but I'm fairly sure this is what roughly twenty-five people looks like. Most of them are sitting in the wooden church pews and have turned to stare at me. I can see Midge in the front row, sitting next to Arabella from The Stumble Inn and Cora from the corner shop. Alex the butcher grins at me while Mary just stares open-mouthed. Behind them I can see Travers with a baby. She holds the child as though she weighs nothing and looks at her as though she means everything.

They're all women. Every single one. *All* of them.

That can't be right, can it? An island with no men?

Nobody says anything, including me, because I'm staring at the person standing in front of the stone altar. It isn't Reverend Melody Bates; she's sitting in the back row.

Seeing the person standing at the front of the church is like seeing a ghost.

"Hello, Grady."

LIVING DEAD

S andy is standing there. The same Sandy they said was dead. She is very much alive.

"You look surprised to see me," she says.

I am. I feel like I'm in a scene from *Night of the Living Dead*.

"I'm relieved," I say. "I thought—"

"We all know what you thought," she interrupts, and there are murmurs from the rest of the women.

"I'm so glad you're okay," I say.

"Are you?"

"Of course. And I know you said there's no crime on the island but there have been some very strange things happening that, as the sheriff, you may want to know about—"

"Oh, there's not much that goes on on this island that I don't know," Sandy says. "For example, I know that Charlie had written a tenth novel because I had read it. And I know that you have sent a very similar-sounding novel to your agent. You do know that it's wrong to steal things don't you, Grady? I presume that's why you left me to drown? You didn't want to get caught stealing something that wasn't yours."

"I didn't—"

"I'm also aware that we had a theft on the island recently. Are you ready to hand over your walkie-talkie?"

I pull it out of my pocket but hang on to it. "The things that have happened since I arrived here aren't my fault. I heard you all talking about me," I say shakily.

The congregation rustles and murmurs again. It sounds a bit like the sea.

"Why would we all be talking about you, Grady? Sounds to me like you've become a bit paranoid since moving into Charlie's cabin. *Seeing* things and *hearing* things. Maybe you should see the doctor when she visits the island next week. Perhaps she could give you a little something to calm you down."

"I don't need anything to calm me down and I'm not imagining it. Someone on this island knows something about my missing wife. They've been slipping newspaper clippings, stories that she wrote under the door." Sandy looks surprised then frowns. "If someone here knows what happened to her I deserve to know the truth."

"People rarely know what they deserve. They almost always think they deserve more or less than they do."

"What is this place? Why are there no men on the island?"

She doesn't answer at first, just stares.

"I'm going to need you to hand over your mobile phone too," Sandy says.

"To hell with this, and all of you. I'm leaving."

Sandy shakes her head. "I don't think you are."

"Perhaps we should give them some space and some privacy," says the Reverend Melody Bates, dressed in her black clothes and white collar. She flicks her long blond hair over her shoulder, then stands and steps out of the pew she was sitting in. The others do the same, and soon they are filing out of the wooden doors I just stumbled inside. Each one of them glaring in my direction when they pass me. The doors creak as the last person closes them and I am left alone with Sandy.

But then the church doors swing open again.

I hear footsteps on the stone floor but I'm afraid to look. They're getting closer and Sandy smiles and nods at whoever it is. When I can't stand the suspense any longer I spin around, unable to process what I am seeing at first.

It's Abby.

I'm not imagining it.

I'm not hallucinating.

"I'll leave you two to it," says Sandy. She takes the walkie-talkie and my mobile from me before heading for the doors. The sound of them closing behind her echoes around the church and the place feels a little colder than it did before. This is not a dream, or a symptom of my insomnia, or a side effect of drinking too much whiskey. It's really her and she's standing right in front of me, staring at me with the bluest eyes I've ever seen.

Finally, she speaks.

"Hi, Grady. I think we need to talk."

HAPPILY MARRIED

———— ⌒ ————

After she disappeared

ABBY

"Tell me again what happened that night."

"My mobile rang when I was driving home. It was attached to the dashboard displaying my fastest route, and my heart sank when I saw Grady's name; I was running a little late and I knew he'd be disappointed. It was as though my husband thought my life revolved around his. He's like a child in that way, always needing attention. So I answered the call and put him on speaker, even though I hate doing that when I'm driving. Especially at night on dark country roads.

"I'm on my way, almost there," I told him.

"You said you would be here," he replied, sounding like a whining little boy. "This is important to me."

I didn't mention all the things that had been important to *me* over the years, things which he made it very clear he couldn't care less about. Someone had to be the grown-up in our relationship.

"I'll be there soon, promise. I've got fish-and-chips," I said.

Fish-and-chips had become a bit of a tradition. It's what we ate on our first official date, and when Grady proposed a few years later. When we moved into the cottage we ate fish-and-chips sitting on a sofa surrounded by cardboard boxes, and it was what he bought me for dinner to celebrate when I got promoted at the newspaper. A job

I used to love but he always hated. Here's the thing, I don't even like fish-and-chips. I often found myself just going along with his choices to keep him happy. But that's my fault, not his.

It was the night he was going to find out if his new book was a *New York Times* bestseller. News that he thought would make him happy and I thought would make it easier to tell him the truth.

"Heard anything?" I asked.

"Not yet."

"Well, get off the phone or they won't be able to get through."

I hung up, concentrated on the road.

Grady always resented how hard I worked, but even when I was at home he rarely seemed to notice me. His mind was always elsewhere, normally inside his novels. When we first got together he couldn't keep his hands off me, but things had changed in that department too. I think there are several varieties of lonely and I have known them all. I actually wondered if he was having an affair at one point—his emotional Morse code wasn't always easy to interpret—but his love affairs were only ever with his books. He was obsessed with them.

It was his idea to move out of the city and live somewhere more rural. He thought it would help his writing and I didn't want to get in the way of that. But I missed my friends, so sometimes I met up with them in London after work. Grady got jealous if I came home late. He seemed to think that me wanting to spend time with other people meant I didn't love him enough. It was as though he thought I only had enough love for one person, and he needed it to always be him. I get that he has abandonment issues because of his mum and dad, but everyone gets fucked up by their parents. It's almost a rite of passage, and at his age I do think it's probably time he got over it.

Sometimes he made me feel as though I was invisible.

And I started to wonder what that might be like.

To just vanish.

I was still driving home when he called again.

"Well?" I asked.

"You are speaking to the author of a *New York Times* bestseller," he said, and I could hear the pure joy in his voice. He'd worked so hard and I was genuinely happy for him in that moment, regardless of everything else going on and what I knew I had to tell him. I started to cry.

"I am so proud of you!" I said, trying to keep my emotions in check and the car on the right side of the road. "I love you," I added without thinking. The words sounded strange out loud. Foreign. I couldn't remember the last time we had said that we loved each other. When he didn't say anything in response I wiped my tears away with the back of my hand. "I'm almost home. Not far at all now. Take the champagne out and—"

I hit the brakes.

"Oh my god. What's happened?" Grady asked. My heart was thudding inside my chest and I wasn't able to answer at first. "Are you okay? Can you hear me?"

"I'm fine, but . . . there is a woman lying in the road."

"What? Did you hit her?"

"No! Of course not. She was already there, that's why I stopped."

"Where are you now?" he asked.

"I'm on the cliff road. I'm going to get out and see if—"

"No!" he shouted.

"What do you mean, *no*? I can't leave her lying in the lane, she might be hurt."

"Then call the police. You're almost home. Do not get out of the car."

I have never taken orders from a man and I wasn't about to start.

"If you're worried about the fish-and-chips getting cold—"

"I'm worried about *you*," he said.

When I started receiving threats at work I actually wondered if it was Grady at first. Whether he was trying to scare me into leaving my job. It wasn't him. I knew who was responsible for that by then. I'd started recording all of my incoming calls, and with the help of a police contact, I had a good idea who was behind the anonymous messages and hate mail. I only continued to record the calls to gather evidence. Earlier that day, a white box addressed to me was delivered to the newspaper. My editor was with me and more concerned than I was when I opened the box and saw an antique doll with its mouth stitched shut. I wasn't scared of the people who were trying to silence me, but looking back, I wish that maybe I had been. Perhaps then I might have stayed in the car.

Grady was still concerned that something was going to happen to me because of my chosen career. He even put an app on my phone so that he could see where I was at all times and know that I was safe. It made me realize that he still loved me—even if he'd forgotten how to show it—and that there was a way to fix us.

The woman lying in the road was wearing a red jacket, just like the one I owned. It seemed like a strange coincidence at the time but it was a common enough coat with a hood and large buttons, lots of women wore a similar style and color. I couldn't see the face under the hood, but I was worried there had been an accident—a hit-and-run perhaps—and that she was hurt. I unfastened my seat belt and opened the car door.

"Please *don't* get out of the car," Grady said.

"I have to. What if it were me lying in the road, wouldn't you want someone to stop and help?"

"Wait, don't hang up!"

"Fine, if it makes you feel better. I love you," I said again, then I quickly got out of the car so I didn't have to hear him not say it back.

It was cold, and dark, and it had started to rain. We weren't as happily married as Grady thought we were, but all I wanted was to go home and be with my husband. I was tired after a long day at work, and several sleepless nights spent worrying about what I needed to tell him. I had planned to tell Grady the following day and let him enjoy the success of his book that night. I didn't want to spoil his big moment. I'd been lying to him for some time by then and there were things I knew I needed to say. But because of what happened next I never got to tell him at all.

The noise of the waves crashing against the cliff down below sounded like a warning. Something instinctive was silently screaming at me to turn back, get in the car, lock the doors, and drive home. But I didn't do that. My conscience wouldn't allow me to walk away from someone in trouble. I suppose they knew me well enough to know that about me.

When I finally saw who was lying in the road I felt confused.

Then I felt afraid.

But it was too late.

CRASH LANDING

GRADY

"Hi, Grady. I think we need to talk," Abby says.

"Is it really you?" I ask.

She nods, takes a step closer, and I take a step back.

"Yes, it's really me," she says, then stares at me waiting for a response I don't know how to give. I'm not *imagining* this. Abby is alive and she is here on the island. At least I can be certain of that now, even if nothing else makes sense.

"What the fuck is going on?" I blurt out.

But I don't sound angry. I sound afraid.

"You don't look too good, Grady. Do you want to sit down?"

"I thought you were *dead*."

"This must feel like a lot."

"A lot? You *disappeared* over a year ago. I *knew* it was you at the pottery yesterday. I don't understand what is happening." The words tumble out of my mouth, tripping over themselves. "Why would you *trick* me like this? Why pretend not to know who I am?"

"Because I *don't* know you," she says, undoing my sanity slowly, like a zip.

"What do you mean?" I stare at her, unsure whether I can

believe a word she is saying. "I don't understand. Do you not remember us? Do you have amnesia?"

"Why don't you sit down? This must feel like some kind of crash landing—"

"Kitty, your godmother, she'll know what to do."

"I think you're in shock."

"We should call her. Call Kitty."

"There are no phones on the island, Grady."

"Yes, there are. But you're right, we can't stay here, we should leave. Call her as soon as we reach the mainland."

"You can't leave this island, Grady. They won't let you."

"What are you talking about? What *is* this place? Why are there only women living on the island and what are you doing here? Is it some kind of cult? Have these women brainwashed you? We could go home, pretend like none of this ever—"

"This *is* my home. Come on, I want to show you something," she says, walking toward the doors without waiting to see whether I will follow, which I do, but I feel as though I'm in some sort of trance.

The air feels strangely warmer outside and the mist has completely cleared. The night sky is coal-black and it feels close and solid, as though the darkness here is something I can touch. There is a full moon and a thick blanket of stars above us, and everything is still and silent, except for our footsteps. We cross the village green and carry on walking until we reach the pretty thatched cottages with quirky names. Abby stops outside the last one, called Whit's End, takes out a set of keys, and unlocks the bright red front door. She flicks on the lights and I'm scared of what I might see, but it's just a cozy-looking cottage. The place is quirky with low ceilings and wooden beams. The front door leads straight into a small sitting room, where there is a fireplace with bookcases on either side, a sofa with a knitted throw, and a sheepskin rug on the floor.

"Nice piano," I say when I see an old upright in the corner of the room. It's covered in painted birds and there is a metronome sitting on top of it. I'm surprised because Abby is gifted in many ways, but not musically. She always used to joke that she couldn't play a triangle.

"Take a seat," she says, nodding toward the sofa.

"I'd rather stand."

"Suit yourself. I need a drink, can I get you one?" I shake my head and she raises an eyebrow. "Well, that's a first."

She disappears through another door and I decide to perch on the edge of the sofa. I notice the turquoise vase on the mantelpiece above the fireplace. It's just like all the pottery at Beautiful Ugly and I wonder if Abby made it herself, and whether that part of her story was true. I no longer know what to believe, or think, or feel. She reappears with two glasses of whiskey and puts them on the table.

"In case you change your mind. Gosh, it's cold in here," she says, then lights the fire.

I am not cold. I feel as though every part of me is sweating.

"I spent some of my childhood in this house," Abby says. "Almost sold it a few years ago, but I'm glad we didn't in the end. I can't imagine anyone else ever living here, it would feel like letting someone trespass in our history."

"*Our* history?"

"Not *ours*. I had a life before you, Grady."

"Apparently you had a life *after* me too."

She stares at me and when I look into her blue eyes all I see is a ghost.

"There's a lot you don't know about me," Abby says.

"I know that your eyes were brown yesterday and now they are blue—"

She smiles. "They were just contact lenses. I fancied a change. Something different. Something to make you question whether it was really me."

"I don't understand—"

"You will." She finishes her drink and looks serious again. "But first I need to tell you a story about the Children of the Mist."

"I've heard that one. Sandy told me before—"

"Before you left her in Darkside Cave hoping she would drown? None of the islanders thought you would go through with it, but they don't know you like I do. They don't know that your books mean more to you than anyone or anything else."

"That's not fair. *You* meant more to me."

"Some of the islanders didn't like what we were doing to you. They thought you were a nice guy—including Sandy's mother, Morag, who I gather was slipping my old newspaper cuttings that Midge liked to collect beneath your door. I needed to show them what you were capable of in order to convince them that what we were going to do to you was fair. Everyone was on board after you left Sandy to drown." I start to stand. "Sit down, Grady. I told you I have things I need to say." I do as she asks because it feels as though I don't have a choice.

"The story Sandy told you was true," Abby begins, staring into the fire, which has begun to crackle and spit. "Nobody can remember every moment of their own history. Our overburdened minds choose which highlights to hold on to, and which files from our past to delete. But I know the story about the Children of the Mist better than anyone, because I was there that day at Darkside Cave, and what happened to those children was my fault."

STAND DOWN

didn't have an easy childhood—I told you that when we met—but I spared you some of the details. You were always so weighed down with your own unhappy past, I didn't want to burden you with mine. When I was ten I lived on Amberly, here in this house. There is everything and nothing for a child to do growing up on a small island like this. There was one school, one teacher, and one class for thirteen children aged between five and ten, but I was happy here. My best friend on the island was Sandy's daughter, Isla. We were the same age and we were inseparable . . ." I remember the picture on the wall in Midge's kitchen, of Abby and the blond little girl blowing out candles on a birthday cake. "So when I decided to run away, Isla decided to come with me. Unfortunately she wasn't the only one.

"There was a substitute teacher that week—a creepy old man from the mainland—because our normal teacher was ill. He always brought a flask of coffee to class in the morning and took noisy sips from the plastic cup during registration, and he shouted at anyone who dared to stare at his prosthetic hand. His idea of teaching was to wheel a trolley into the classroom with a TV and

VHS player, and let children watch films all afternoon while he sat in the pub. But he didn't go to The Stumble Inn that day.

"I was off sick and home alone the afternoon he knocked on the cottage door. I'd been taught not to open the door to strangers, but he was a teacher. A person children are taught to trust and obey. He stank of alcohol and slurred his words when he said that my mother had sent him, which I knew was a lie. He walked into this house as though he owned the place. Then he stood next to that piano, turned on the metronome, and smiled at me. I don't want to talk about what he did, or tried to do next. I got away from him and ran out of the house with a bag containing my most prized possessions: a harmonica, a book, and a Magic 8 Ball. I ran to the church looking for help, when I didn't find any I ran to find the man who was like a father to me, but he was busy working and told me to go away. So I ran to the school to find my best friend. Isla said I should ask my Magic 8 Ball what to do, so I asked out loud if I should run away and the ball said YES. The next problem was where. "Should I go to the Standing Stones?" I asked, and the screen on the ball said MY REPLY IS NO. "Should I hide in Darkside Cave?" was my next question. This time the answer was WITHOUT A DOUBT. Isla said she'd come with me but that we should keep it a secret. There is nothing more exciting than a secret when you live in a place that has none. Unfortunately the other children overheard and followed us.

"We walked out of the village, through the wildflower meadow, and along the coast road toward the bay. The path around the cliff was steep and slippery, but one by one we climbed down the giant steps until we were inside Darkside Cave. Isla handed out cookies her auntie Midge had baked—they were terrible, but we ate them anyway—but then it started to get dark. And then the seawater started rushing in. We'd all been told not to play in the cave, but we didn't know why. None of us understood that it flooded at high tide.

"We tried to leave but we couldn't, it was already too late. A wave of water reared up like a wild animal's paw and snatched the child standing nearest to the entrance. The rest of the children started screaming and crying. People say you can still hear them in the Bay of Singing Sands, and I believe them. I hear those children screaming inside my head every day. I was screaming too until the seawater filled my mouth and silenced me." She drinks the second glass of whiskey and closes her eyes.

"I remember the feeling of drowning, and letting go of my best friend's hand.

"I remember not being able to breathe and then I only remember black.

"They all died, except for me, and it was all my fault. Soon afterward I found myself living in London, with Kitty, taken away from the only place that had ever felt like home."

"That's why you don't like boats, and why you were scared of the ocean?" I ask, and she nods. "But now you're not? Beautiful Ugly is right on the beach. Your work is literally inspired by the sea."

"I guess when I finally faced my fears I discovered that I loved the thing that used to scare me. Fear can make something beautiful appear ugly."

I stare at her and she stares into the fire.

"Why did you never tell me any of this?" I ask.

"It was a version of me I wanted to forget. But I want you to understand why the women on this island are the way they are, and why I owe them so much. This isn't a *cult*, it's a community. Isla wrote a note for her mother, Sandy, before we ran away to Darkside Cave. That's how they eventually found us but it was too late. The men on this island were slowly removed after the tragedy, because if the substitute teacher hadn't done what he did, and if a woman hadn't been so desperate to leave her husband, none of it would have happened—"

"Sorry, I don't understand—"

"Men still rule this world and as a result the world is broken. Men still hold most positions of power, men control governments, men control the media, and it is always men who start wars. Men have tricked women into thinking they see us as equals, but real equality, for all women everywhere, still feels like little more than a pipe dream. The women on this island have had enough."

"What does that mean?"

"They decided it was time for men to stand down. It was a gradual process, but when someone died—like the pub landlord—the Isle of Amberly Trust would advertise for a suitable replacement. Opportunities to run a pub on a remote Scottish island are rare and surprisingly popular. The all-female board of the trust would sift through the applications and select a candidate who was best qualified to take over. And it was always a woman. Often women in need of a second chance. Same with the butchers, and the bakers, and everywhere until all of the islanders were women. An extreme example of positive discrimination but with the best of motives."

"So Arabella was the victim of domestic abuse you wrote about for the newspaper? And Cora really was in prison before—"

"It was the family of the man Cora killed who were sending me anonymous threats. They didn't like what I wrote about them. Almost everyone now living on Amberly is here because they were running away from something. Or someone. Women come here when they need to leave their old life behind and start again. It's a refuge. A safe place where they don't need to be afraid. There's no war, there's no hate, there's no crime, and there's no poverty. A handful of the women who live here now are people I met as a result of my work, people I interviewed who needed help, who Midge then read about because she collected every newspaper article I ever wrote. Cora, Alex, Mary. Arabella arrived with her whole life packed into one suitcase after her husband beat her so badly she nearly died. Her sister, Sidney, had experience running a pub and came with her. Together the islanders work hard to maintain ownership of Amberly, not for themselves but because they believe they owe it everything. As do I. The island doesn't judge you. It doesn't care who you were, or who you think you are. It doesn't make judgments based on how you look, what you believe in, what you do, or how much you think you are worth. The island treats everyone the same. The island takes what it needs from people and gives what it can. Amberly is home to women who were wronged by the world. A place of hope when all hope is lost. Everyone who lives here will do anything to protect it.

"I'm going to get another drink. Are you sure you don't want one?" Abby asks. She grabs the empty glasses and starts to leave the room.

"You said everyone on the island was running away from something or someone," I say. "So what were you running away from?"

She turns back and stares at me. "You."

TOUGH LOVE

ABBY

I pour myself another glass of whiskey in the kitchen and take a sip. I think when a relationship unravels, the way ours did, it's impossible not to look back and wonder who was to blame. To relive the good times as well as the bad and wonder *What if?* A broken record of whys regularly spins inside my head but never plays the answer.

Memory lane is a dead end but if I close my eyes I can still remember the people we used to be. I can still feel his hands on my body, pulling at my clothes, impatient to unwrap me. Those first few years when we were together were the most passionate of my life. He had this way of making me feel as though I were beautiful, even the parts of me that never were.

I never wanted to leave my husband forever, that wasn't the plan, but I knew I had to leave when I did. I have needed to put a physical distance between my past and my present more than once in my life, and sometimes there is no way back. My white lies have darkened over the years and my past caught up with me. There were things I should have said, but didn't, because they were things he didn't want to hear. But when what happened, happened, it was too late to tell him anything. I just had to go. I've always felt guilty about that—leaving without even saying goodbye—just disappearing from his life.

I know a lot about people disappearing, and not just because I did. Someone is reported missing every ninety seconds in the UK. That's 170,000 people reported missing every year, and that's just this little corner of the world. Sometimes when people disappear it's because they don't want to be found. I needed a fresh start, so I changed my name and started again, determined to become the me I knew I wanted to be. I'm old enough to know that tough love isn't real love. The truth is that my life without him was less lonely than life with him, and I know in my heart that I did the right thing.

Grady has always believed what I say. It's something I've always been baffled by—given how difficult he finds it to trust almost all other people—but I liked how it made me feel. For a while. As though he thought I was special. I've always found relationships hard to navigate, even as a child. I grew up in a home where there wasn't quite enough love to go around, so I looked for it elsewhere. And I learned most of life's lessons the hard way, but making mistakes is how we learn.

It felt strange coming back to the island after all these years. It was even stranger to visit the cabin when Grady wasn't there and to be surrounded by my husband's things. It made me miss him a little, but not enough to regret my decision to leave.

There are things I need to tell Grady tonight.

Things which will be difficult for me to say and for him to hear.

Truth is stranger than fiction and tends to hurt more too.

ORIGINAL COPY

GRADY

I wait for Abby to come back, my head too loud with unanswered questions. There are so many things I miss about my wife. Strange things. I miss the way she danced around the kitchen when she cooked. I miss her dark sense of humor and the way she would never apologize even when she was wrong. I miss waking up next to her. I miss how she said "I hope you die in your sleep" every night before we went to bed, and how I would say it back because it was our way of saying "I love you." I miss everything about who she was and who we were but now I wonder if I ever really knew her at all. This woman isn't like the Abby I knew, she's more like an original copy of the woman I loved.

"Was the baby I heard crying at The Croft and saw in the church yours?" I ask as soon as she walks back into the room.

"Yes. Holly is my daughter."

"But she isn't mine?" I already know that she can't be, but when Abby confirms it by shaking her head I still feel a strange sense of loss. I do my best to compose myself. "And are you really married to a woman?"

"Legally no—I'm still married to you—but in my heart the

answer is yes. I met Travers here on Amberly and I love her very much."

She waits for that news to sink in, but I'm not sure it ever will.

"Why did you pretend not to know me at the pottery? Was it you I saw on the ferry the day I arrived? Why are you doing this to me? Why am I here?"

"You're here to write a new book and now you have."

I hear the familiar crackle of a walkie-talkie. Abby takes it out of her pocket, places it on the table, and stares at it before looking back at me.

"Time is running out, Grady."

"What does that mean?" She doesn't answer. "You've clearly lost your mind. This *is* a cult. I don't understand what is going on here—you're all crazy—but I demand to leave."

"You can demand whatever you want, but they won't let you go. And men aren't allowed to live on this island."

"You said that already. Women only, so I'll pack my bags—"

"I don't think you've understood. Men aren't allowed to *live* on this island." The expression on my wife's face is one I've never seen her wear before, and it turns my whole body icy cold. "Have you seen the cemetery behind Saint Lucy's? I think it's rather lovely. I've always thought that a graveyard was a great place to hide a body. A place where nobody would ever think to look."

I can't quite process what I am hearing. "I don't understand—"

"I think you do. Why don't we talk about what happened the night I disappeared. You do remember that night, don't you?"

"Of course I remember," I tell her. "I loved you more than I've ever loved anyone. I've missed you every day and every night since—"

"Then tell me why?" Abby interrupts.

"Why what?"

"Why you lay down in the road, in the dark, in the rain, wearing my red coat so that I presumed you were a woman. Why you waited for me to get out of the car, knowing I would always help someone in trouble. Why you grabbed me as soon as I was close enough, held a cloth soaked in chloroform over my mouth, then dressed me in my coat, dragged me to the edge of the road, and pushed me over a cliff. Why did you try to kill me, Grady?"

WALKING DEAD

  am frozen in time. I can't move. It feels like I can't breathe.

"I loved you," I whisper.

"Someone who loved me could never do what you did. I know what happened that night, you know what happened, everyone on this island knows what you did to me. What I want to know is *why*. I've waited a long time to ask that question, face-to-face, and I think I deserve an answer. I wanted to wait until you lost everything; the house, your career, *everything* you ever cared about, because that's what you took from me when you did what you did that night. The thing I cared most about in the world was you. I loved you too, Grady. I really did, but now I *hate* you. So why did you do it? Why did you try to kill me?"

When I look in her eyes all I feel is pure terror.

I don't want to hear any more of this story. I want to delete it, rewrite it, burn it. I run out of the cottage and across the green. For once, the village is not empty. I can see them, women in the distance, women looking out of the windows, women walking down the lanes, all of them holding walkie-talkies, and all of them staring at me. I feel like one of the walking dead, as though there is a target on my back. I run past Christie's Corner Shop and

The Stumble Inn, past the church and up the hill. Despite feeling breathless, and ignoring the pain in my chest, I run until I reach the forest. I have to get Columbo and I have to get off of this island. The trees seem to block my path as though trying to stop me. The silhouettes of a thousand branches reach out like arms, slowing me down, scratching my face and tearing my clothes but I don't stop until I see the cabin in the distance. The lights are on inside and the windows look like glowing eyes. Watching. Waiting.

I push the door open and see someone sitting on the sofa with a glass of whiskey.

Someone I did not expect to see.

"Hello, Grady."

UNBIASED OPINION

———

Y ou should close your mouth; you look like a goldfish," Kitty says. "You don't mind if I smoke, do you?" My agent lights a cigarette before I can reply.

Kitty appears to have made herself at home. Columbo is sitting happily at her feet, and the wood-burning stove is casting a series of dancing shadows around the room. It looks like a cozy scene but it doesn't feel like one. It is strange seeing my agent out of her office. For years I was convinced she lived there, because that's where she was night and day, always working. It's like seeing a creature removed from its natural habitat and wondering if it can still breathe the air.

"You might want to take a seat. We have some things to talk about," she says, and I do, but only because it feels like I might fall over if I don't.

My agent was the only person in the whole world I thought I could still trust.

It feels like my whole world is ending.

Kitty must have known that Abby was alive. She must have known about this island; she's the one who sent me here. She must have known everything.

"I read the new book as soon as it arrived," she says, taking another drag on her cigarette. "I was so moved by it, I knew I had to come and see you straight away. It's the kind of writing that I don't get to read too often. The kind of story agents and publishers get very excited about. In my unbiased opinion I think it's your best book yet."

"Thank you," I mumble.

Kitty gently nudges the side of her glasses as though they aren't straight, even though they are. It was a habit I used to find endearing, but now I don't know if I knew my agent as well as I thought. I notice the silver thistle ring on her finger, the same ring that the islanders wear. My mind can't seem to catch up with what is happening. Abby must have told her what I did. Abby always told her godmother everything, and Kitty always loved Abby far more than she ever loved me, so whatever this is it can't be good. I look over at the cabin door and consider running back out of it, but where would I go? I can't trust anyone on the island and there is apparently no way to get off it.

"Why would you want to leave?" Kitty says, as though she can read my mind. "You're finally writing again. Isn't that what you wanted? I've read a lot of your stories over the years, Grady. I think it's only fair I tell you one. You see, *this* story is mine just as much as it is yours. You know that Abby is my goddaughter, but did you know she was named after me? Her mother and I became friends when we were at school together in London; back then I was called Abby too. Her mother had this wonderful town house in Notting Hill and hosted the most extravagant parties, with string quartets and a seemingly endless supply of champagne. I only changed my name when I left my husband."

EVEN ODDS

ABBY

"I was Charles Whittaker's agent long before I was yours, as you know," I tell Grady. "But for a while I was also his wife. We met on a plane—he thought I was sitting in his seat, I wasn't—and at first I was affronted by the very being of him. I guess I changed my mind because one year later we were married. Genius doesn't deserve special dispensation but tends to get it anyway.

"I was a young agent and he was an author most people had never heard of back then. I made him into who he was. He'd been writing beautiful books, literary fiction, but they weren't selling. I became his agent, persuaded him to try writing thrillers, and he became one of the most successful writers of all time in the genre. I don't think he ever forgave me.

"Our relationship worked well in the beginning. He was busy writing books, I was busy selling them, so we didn't see each other often but when we did, it was wonderful. He was the most interesting man I ever met, and it was by far the most intense relationship I've ever experienced. Things were great. Until they weren't.

"I was born on Amberly. It was my home, but unlike most people who live here I spent my whole childhood dreaming up ways I could leave. Piano lessons resulted in my mother sending me away and I got my wish. I moved to London and was raised by a woman who worked for a large publishing house in the city. She wasn't very motherly, but in many ways, the situation couldn't have been more perfect. I was sent to an expensive school—where I met Abby's mother—and given the kind of education I would never have had on a tiny island. I even had elocution lessons. My Scottish accent only comes out to play when I'm around Scottish people these days. When I was eighteen, I got myself a job as an assistant in a literary agency. Worked my way up from the bottom. I didn't have any real desire to come back to the island, ever, but then my mother got in touch after decades of not speaking to me. She wanted to see me before she died. And she wanted to confess that she once chopped off a man's hand with an axe.

"Charles came with me to visit her—he'd never even heard of Amberly until then—and I was glad of the support. She died a couple of weeks after we arrived, but there was a lot to sort out afterward, and Charles was already in love with the place so we stayed for a while in my mother's thatched cottage. He loved it so much he renamed it Whit's End.

"We had only been here for a couple of months when Abby's mother, my best friend back in London, died too. She killed herself, and the news came as such a shock so soon after losing my own mum. Abby was only ten and she was my goddaughter. She was named after me and I'd known her since she was a baby. I wanted to go back to London. I missed the city and my work, but Charlie was so happy living and writing here. He insisted that Amberly would be good for Abby—a change of scene and a distraction from the grief—so she came here to live with us and we stayed a while longer. He renovated this old cabin to write in because things were a little crowded with the three of us all living in the cottage you just visited. Charles was fond of Abby, but he never really wanted children and we spent more and more time apart. He needed quiet to write, so hid himself away here at The Edge, and Abby and I learned to stay out of his way at the cottage.

"You might have noticed the piano painted with birds when you were there? Well, the man who tried to teach me to play it when I was a little girl was a bad man. He did bad things. That's why my mother cut off his hand with an axe. I believe you found the bones beneath these floorboards—a little welcome gift. Thirty years later he was an out-of-work teacher and an alcoholic, so when an agency called him to see if he could fill in at the last minute on a remote Scottish island, he said yes. I think he came here for revenge. He came back to Amberly, he went back to that same cottage, but this time there was a different little girl living there."

"Why are you telling me this?" Grady asks, and just for a moment, I feel sorry for him. But the feelings of pity soon pass. This is my story now and I plan to finish telling it.

"Abby was always fearless and brave. Even as a child. Not like me. When that man tried to hurt her, she shoved him away so hard he fell and hit his head on the fireplace. She thought she'd killed him so she ran away. She took her most prized possessions: a harmonica, a book, and a Magic 8 Ball, and ran to the church looking for me. But she overheard me talking to someone I always thought of as the 'woman in black.' I was confiding in the Reverend Melody Bates that I wanted to leave my husband. Abby thought that meant I wanted to leave her too, so she kept running. She ran here to find Charlie, but he was writing so told her to go away. Then she ran to Darkside Cave and I think you know what happened there.

"I blamed myself for what happened to Abby, and Abby blamed herself for what happened to those children. But it was *his* fault. All of it. That man. Abby thought she'd killed him when he hit his head. But it was Sandy who did that, once she found out what really happened, and why her daughter was dead. Charles helped Sandy move the body and bury the music man in an unmarked grave behind Saint Lucy's. They bonded and became best friends after that. What they did might sound extreme, but you have to remember that all the children on this island died because of one bad man.

"Charles blamed himself for all of it. He was the one who per-suaded me to stay on the island after my mother died, he was the only reason we were still here, and he turned Abby away when she needed his help because he loved his books a little bit too much. He never forgave himself and I think that's why he stayed forever. And why he donated a large percentage of his income to the Isle of Amberly Trust set up by Sandy. It was a tight-knit community even then. Nobody wanted any more outsiders coming here, and Charlie's success meant the island needed to allow visitors for only a few months of the year. When Charles figured out that all the men on the island were being replaced with women, he thought that was a step too far. He and Sandy fell out over that, and Charlie refused to sell any more books.

"I left him here after the tragedy at Darkside Cave without even saying goodbye and I took Abby with me. I had to make a choice, and there are no even odds when it comes to hurting the people you love. I needed a fresh start for Abby and me after what happened, so I opened a new agency in London and I called myself Kitty Goldman. Kitty was a nickname only Charles called me, because my surname when we met was Kitterick. I took his surname when we got married—Whittaker— but neither felt quite right. I decided to change my surname to Gold-man, my mother's maiden name.

"I've helped countless authors come up with a pseudonym over the years. I suppose I wanted one of my own, one which wasn't tarnished by past mistakes. When I became Kitty Goldman, I became the me I wanted to be. Besides, having two people both called Abby living un-der the same roof was getting confusing.

"Charles was still a big deal in the book world and he was still my client—that was the one part of our relationship that did still work—but I took on new ones. Ten years after I started the Kitty Goldman Agency it was one of the biggest in the country. When Abby first introduced me to you, I was worried for her. I didn't want her to marry a writer—I'd al-ready made that mistake myself—but I could see how happy you made her. She asked me to represent you and I said yes, and when you got en-gaged I was happy for you both. Because I loved her. I loved you, too."

"Then why are you doing this to me?" Grady asks.

"You know why, and I haven't done anything to you. Yet. I didn't know what really happened the night Abby disappeared until a few months ago. She didn't want to tell me; said she was scared of what I might do. All I knew was that she was missing and I feared she was dead. Then Sandy invited me here, to Amberly. I am an honorary member of the Isle of Amberly Trust, and Sandy said there was something urgent that we needed to discuss in person, so I came back here for the first time in thirty years.

"It's been so long since I cried I presumed my tear ducts were broken, but I sobbed like a child when I arrived at the House on the Hill and saw that Abby was alive. Then I cried again when she told me what you did to her. By some miracle she only fell a short distance when you pushed her off that cliff. She held on to the branch of a tree that was growing out of the rock—she said it was as though the branch reached out and caught her—and she climbed back up to the road. Afraid and alone. In the dark. In the rain. She had the presence of mind to throw her red coat back over the edge, hoping that someone would find it along the coast and that you would believe she was dead. But then, instead of coming to me, she came back here. To Amberly. Thirty years after I took her away, she returned to the home she never wanted to leave. When Abby introduced me to her baby and let me hold Holly I cried some more.

"Then I dried my tears and told her that I would destroy you."

ALONE TOGETHER

GRADY

"You know I love a good revenge story," Kitty says. "Once I knew the truth about what you did to my goddaughter, Abby and I came up with a story of our own. Your life was already unraveling, all that was required was a tiny tug on the final few threads."

"Well, congratulations. Mission accomplished," I tell her.

"Oh, Grady. We're only just getting started. I think Charlie left me this old writing cabin in his will to piss me off. He said his tenth novel was his best but then wouldn't let me read it, because he was cross that I wouldn't do something to stop what was happening on Amberly. He was the only man left by then— Charlie contributed so much financially to the island that they needed him, and Sandy adored him so he was untouchable. But he became increasingly cranky about Amberly being 'overrun with women' as he put it, and I don't know whether it was the stress, or just his age, but he stopped being able to write. Didn't write a word for years, or if he did, refused to share anything with me. Then he hanged himself on that beam just there. You see, he gen-uinely lived to write and when he couldn't . . ." I see something like emotion in Kitty's eyes for the first time but it soon fades. "So when I finally got to read the infamous Book Ten manuscript after he died I was a little disappointed. It had potential, but it wasn't the masterpiece he seemed to think it was."

"So you left the book here for me to find?"

"I'll get to that part of the story when I'm ready. The island needed a new source of finance after Charlie died. Sandy and Midge liked the idea of another writer coming to Amberly, so I sent one of my authors who'd had a big debut novel but proved to be a one-hit wonder. That little experiment didn't work out, the results were very disappointing, and unfortunately he tried to leave and died in the process. He stole an old wooden rowboat without realizing it had a small hole in it and drowned about a mile off the coast. His body washed up months later. It really wasn't anyone's fault, it was an *accident*, but one which nobody needed to know about. So the Isle of Amberly Trust voted to bury him in an unmarked grave in Saint Lucy's. It's easy to make writers disappear; it's finding good ones that poses a challenge. He was like a rehearsal for you in some ways, but nothing that will happen to you will be an accident."

I stare at her in horror. "Are you saying that—"

"What I'm saying is that replacing Charles Whittaker has proved to be very difficult for the women of Amberly. So I sent you here and, I'll be honest, you surprised me. I thought you would torture yourself trying to turn Charlie's unpublished novel into something of your own, and that you would lose what was left of your mind when you failed. But I was wrong. The new book is terrific, I think it's your best. This novel really could re-launch your career, Grady. Well done."

For a moment I forget everything that she said before. My agent's opinion about my books has always meant so much to me. Too much probably. I can't help it.

"Really? Do you mean it?" I ask, sounding like a child desperately seeking praise from their favorite teacher.

Kitty smiles and nods. "I do." The smile fades. "The only problem is what you did to Abby. I need to know why."

I am my own worst enemy but I am also my own best friend. I say nothing.

"We can sit here all night if you want," Kitty says, lighting another cigarette. "I'm not going anywhere and neither are you, so—"

"I loved Abby but she was going to leave me," I blurt out.

Kitty frowns and exhales a cloud of smoke. "Why would you think that?"

"I found a pregnancy test in the bin at our home. It was positive."

"You didn't want a baby?"

"I'd had a vasectomy to make sure she didn't get pregnant, so I knew she had been cheating on me. She'd been behaving strangely for months, and was always coming home late. Abby was clearly having an affair. She was siphoning off money from our bank account, and was secretly plotting to abandon me, just like my parents did. Everyone I love leaves me in the end. I loved her so much it hurt. All I wanted was for us to be alone together."

"So you pushed her off a cliff?"

"If *she* left me, so would you have," I say.

"What do you mean?"

"Don't tell me that you would have carried on being my agent if your goddaughter divorced me. You would have abandoned me too. It wouldn't have just been the end of my marriage, Abby leaving me would have meant the end of my career. But if she *died*, if it looked like she had killed herself like her mother did, then I thought you'd feel sorry for me and be my agent forever."

Kitty's cigarette hovers in midair. She stares at me as though she thinks I am unhinged.

"I still don't understand why you thought Abby was going to leave you?"

"She was pregnant with another man's child, of course she was going to leave me."

"Oh, Grady," Kitty says, her voice dressed in disappointment. "I guess there is no cure for human nature."

"She should have been at home with me, waiting for the call about my book being a bestseller. I am sorry for what I did, more sorry than you'll ever know. I just snapped."

"I believe that you're sorry, but you didn't just snap. You planned the whole thing. You knew that Abby was recording all of her incoming calls because of the threats she had received. Those recorded calls were the biggest piece of evidence the police had, listening to her describe the person lying in the road while she was on the phone to you at home a mile away. But you weren't at home, were you? You walked to the cliff road after the call with your publishers and me. And you knew exactly where Abby was and what time she would arrive there, because of the app you installed on her phone."

"If she hadn't been 'working late' again it wouldn't have happened. She was probably with him, the father of her child. I'm not the only one to blame."

"There was no other man, Grady. Abby *was* pregnant, but she *wasn't* sleeping with someone else."

My defense briefly loses momentum, but the betrayal I felt then and now soon reignites.

"I've seen the baby and I don't think it was an immaculate conception," I say.

"The money that she'd been withdrawing from your joint bank account was for IVF, using a donor, and in secret, because she desperately wanted to have a baby before she was forty, and she knew that you didn't. Abby wanted to tell you but only if it worked, and then when it did, she didn't know how. She didn't want to spoil *your* big moment the week your book became a bestseller, so she was going to tell you the next day. Abby loved you, only you. She just wanted to give you the family you never had growing up. You had it all but you were too busy worrying about what you didn't have to notice."

I feel like all the air has been forced out of my lungs.

"I'm so sorry," I whisper.

"I'm sure you are, but I'm not here for an apology. Abby loved you. And now she hates you. And so do I," Kitty says. "I bet you've spent your whole life since then looking over your shoulder. Without a body being washed up, you must have wondered if she was out there somewhere, and worried yourself sick that all of this might come back to haunt you. And now it has. No wonder you couldn't sleep. And no wonder you couldn't *write*. Sometimes I think you've been punished enough already, that there might be another way for you to make up for what you did. Other days, I'd happily let them bury you too."

"I'm not a bad person. I just did a bad thing."

"Do you think you're a *good* person? Abby hitched rides all the way to the Scottish Highlands after you did what you did. She was pregnant, scared, heartbroken, and alone. All she had were the clothes on her back and a survival instinct, which guided her home to Amberly. The person she loved most in the world tried to kill her, and I think something got broken in her mind. She didn't want to be a journalist anymore, she didn't want to save the world from itself anymore, she just needed to save herself. She waited for the ferry on the mainland, and Sandy knew who she was the second she saw her. She and Midge took her in and helped her to start again with a new job and a new life. They helped her when the baby was born too, took her to the hospital on the mainland. And now she has a new family. I don't care if you're *good*. My client list would be rather short if I only represented good people. I only care whether you can write.

"Abby is happy here, Grady. It's her home again now. And it could be yours too, but only if you can carry on writing books I can sell. The island needs an income or they'll have to open to tourists all year long, and nobody wants that. Can you do it?"

I stare at her. "I just want to go home and for things to be how they were before."

"You don't have a home, Grady. You don't have anything or anyone anymore. Only your books. Could you write another so that the islanders can let you live here?"

A tear rolls down my cheek. "I don't know."

"That's fair enough. Nobody really knows anything. The only certainty in life is uncertainty. We're all just a bad roll of the dice away from being right back at the bottom of the ladder we spent our whole lives climbing. I do need an answer, though. It's decision time. They're waiting," Kitty says, staring at the walkie-talkie on the table.

ONLY CHOICE

Your future here isn't just for me or you to decide," Kitty says. "Ultimately it is up to the islanders whether you can stay. They've all been involved in this little experiment from the beginning. Sandy brought you here knowing exactly who you were. Cora Christie kept everyone informed of your movements with regular walkie-talkie updates, and opened any letters you sent or received at the post office. It sounds as though Midge gave a terrific performance—Hollywood was crazy not to turn her into a star—though she does sometimes stray from the script. Travers climbed one of the ancient trees to cut down a phone line when you realized that the old red phone box did in fact work. Only Morag—Midge and Sandy's elderly mother—didn't like what was happening and tried to warn you. The manuscript for Charles Whittaker's Book Ten was deliberately left hidden beneath the floorboards for you to find, and everyone else played their part until you finished writing your own version of the novel. I've told them how much money I think I could get for it, but it will be significantly more for a two-book deal—possibly enough to mean they won't have to allow visitors on the island for a whole year—and we want to make you an offer."

I shake my head. "What offer?"

"I'm speaking as your agent now, Grady. Listen carefully and *think* before you make a decision, because sometimes the only choice is the right choice. The way I see it, you've been served a triple-decker shit sandwich with a side of completely fucked, but it's exactly what you ordered. You and Charlie have a lot in common. You're both writers who like your own company. He didn't like to do interviews if he didn't have to, didn't like doing events or going to book festivals, and he wasn't interested in awards unless they were voted for by real readers—he was a writer who simply wanted to write. Like you. Which is why I think this could work. There aren't many of my clients who I could send here. Most of them have family and friends who would miss them, notice if they disappeared, but nobody even knows that you're here.

"It's been tough for the islanders since Charlie died. Without the income from his book deals, foreign rights, TV options, and royalties, they had to find other ways to fund the island. The sheepskin rugs, the pottery, and the Highland Cow candles only make a modest amount of money. The real money-spinner is tourism, but nobody wants to have *visitors* here all year round. And, as you know, they don't like *men* being here at all. It's bad enough that they have to let visitors in for a few months every summer, coming here with their bags and their burdens, their never-ending complaints and shocking sense of entitlement. Invading this beautiful island with their noise and rubbish from the mainland, polluting the place with their opinions and their hate. You could help protect the island from all of that for a whole year. I've been talking with the board of the Isle of Amberly Trust, and despite some scruples about your behavior, they would like to offer you a permanent position as resident writer."

I stare at her. "Have you lost your mind?"

"Charlie wrote fast, at least two books a year, but he rarely let anyone read them and only nine were published. He was a bit too good at killing his darlings. Charlie only wanted to publish his best work, but there were plenty of unseen, unread novels tucked away in drawers when he died, either partly completed or just in need of an edit. I thought you were finished, but you can still write. You might be struggling to find the initial sparks, the ideas, but Charles had plenty of those and you've already proved that you can bring his darlings back to life.

"This is a great opportunity for you, a chance to really focus on writing the best books that you can. You can publish *Beautiful Ugly*; I'll sell it for you. It was Charlie's idea but you've made it your own; it's your voice I hear on those pages and it's your name that should be on the cover, not his. This *arrangement* could be good for everyone. But any money you make from the books, minus my fifteen percent, goes to the Isle of Amberly Trust. It was never about the money for you anyway, was it, Grady? You just wanted to write good books."

I stare at her, wondering if she has any idea how crazy she sounds.

"Why don't you have a drop of whiskey? You're trembling and I know this is a lot to take in," she says, pouring me a glass. I drink it and she pours again.

"And if I do write another book, then what?" I ask.

"If it's good—it needs to be a bestseller—then you write another. And another one after that."

"And if it's bad? Or if I can't write? Or won't?" I ask, hearing the tremor in my voice.

"Look, the women on this island aren't *crazy*. Yes, Sandy killed the music man thirty years ago, but I don't think anyone should hold that against her. The previous writer drowning when he tried to leave was an *accident*. Burying both bodies in the graveyard was simply best for all concerned. But the islanders aren't in the habit of *killing* people—"

"Thank goodness. For a moment I thought you were saying that—"

"Unless they deserve it. There is a plot already marked out for you behind Saint Lucy's Church. It's a nice shady spot, away from the others so that you can be as alone in death as you were in life. The islanders are making an exception for you; you really ought to be more grateful. Men are not allowed to live on this island, and there's no way for you to leave. I strongly suggest you don't try; it won't end well for you if you do."

I stand up and feel dizzy. My eyes feel heavy and I realize that there must have been something in my drink. The room starts to spin, a kaleidoscope of the flames in the wood-burning stove and Kitty's face. When I try to speak my words come out slowly and slurred.

"But what about Abby?"

"It was her idea," Kitty says. "*This* was what you wanted, remember? Solitude and silence to write your precious books. Sometimes giving people what they think they want is the best way to show them what they had."

"What I want is to leave this island."

"Nobody really leaves this island, not even me. None of us can escape who we are. Do you need a little time to think about your options?" Kitty asks, looking so sincere and caring. "The way I see it, you have no money, nowhere to live, no prospects, no future, no hope. Don't you see? Accepting the offer, staying on the island, and delivering a bestseller every year *is* what you wanted. You should be happy," Kitty says. My eyelids are so heavy. I blink a few times but the world is too bright, too loud, too awful. "Why don't you sleep on it?" she suggests. "Sleeping on something always helps me to know what to do."

I close my eyes and everything fades to black.

ONE YEAR LATER . . .

VIRTUAL REALITY

GRADY

The story of my life has unfolded in ways I could never have imagined.

"Hello, Grady! How are you today?" Cora asks as I step inside Christie's Corner Shop. The little bell above the door tinkles as I close it and I smile.

"I'm very well. How are you?" I ask, taking a basket and heading off down the aisle.

"Mustn't grumble, mustn't complain—"

"Before a rainbow there is always rain," I say, finishing her little rhyme. She laughs and so do I. I carry on down the aisle, grabbing the things I need, and when I get back to the checkout I look at the selection of newspapers. They're a few days old—like everything else, they only get delivered to the island twice a week if and when the ferry sails—but I can see what I'm looking for—a three-day-old copy of *The Sunday Times*.

"Did you look already?" I ask Cora as I put one in my basket. Her smile gives her away.

"I'm afraid I did. I couldn't wait."

"And?"

"Don't you want to look for yourself?"

I suppose I do. I open the newspaper, find the relevant page, and there it is—*The Sunday Times* bestseller list. I can't help smiling when I see my name at the top of it next to *Beautiful Ugly*, which was published last week. Kitty will have known days ago, but she had no way of telling me. The phone line, once genuinely broken, never did get repaired.

"You must be so proud. I know we all are," Cora says, smiling with all of her teeth.

"Thank you," I say, folding the newspaper and paying for the rest of my things.

"It's good for you and good for us."

"It is indeed. There aren't any letters for me are there?"

I sent Kitty a new book last week, and I haven't heard back from her yet.

"Afraid not, but this came from the mainland for you," Cora says, lifting a very expensive bottle of champagne wrapped in a red ribbon onto the counter.

Columbo is waiting outside the shop and greets me with a wagging tail. My boy is looking older, but he's still the most affectionate dog in the world. I can't imagine life without him. His shiny black fur has a few gray hairs these days, especially around his chin. I have a few more gray hairs of my own. Old age sneaks up on us all like an unwelcome thief.

Sandy strolls toward us, about to head inside the shop herself.

"How are you, Grady?"

"Can't complain. How are you?"

"Never better," she says. I'm not sure she's ever forgiven me for leaving her in the cave, but I'm glad we're on speaking terms. She leans down to stroke Columbo. "You know, I always wanted a black Labrador. If you ever need someone to take care of him, I'm your woman," she adds before patting me on the shoulder and disappearing inside.

Columbo and I cross the immaculate village green and I glance over at the new church roof. It's looking good. The Isle of Amberly Trust has taken care of a lot of community issues in the last few months, mainly because *Beautiful Ugly* got a big advance.

"Hello, Grady," says Arabella coming out of The Stumble Inn. "Congratulations on the bestseller! The chef made fish-and-chips just for you," she says, handing me a takeaway box.

They all know already. Of course they do.

"Thank you, that's so kind. I couldn't be happier!" I say.

Sometimes I think we are all the unreliable narrators of our own lives.

I climb into the old Land Rover and hear the crackle of a walkie-talkie, but it's mine. I have my own these days. I'm officially a member of *the community*. I have learned a lot since I came here. A lot about myself and a lot about the world, as though this place has opened my eyes to all the things I couldn't see before. No man is an island, but a woman can be if she needs to be.

My reflection in the rearview mirror startles me, but apart from the dark circles that have made themselves at home beneath my eyes, I look well enough. I still have trouble sleeping, and my head is often filled with unfinished thoughts and conversations I never had but should have, but Dr. Highsmith prescribed some very strong sedatives. They seem to do the trick at times like this; when I'm too exhausted to function but still can't sleep. The new pills knock me out every time. I see the doctor every second Tuesday—if the weather permits the interisland ferry to sail—and she seems very keen to keep me in good health. They all do. Cora often adds green vegetables to my shopping basket when I'm not looking. I don't even have to pay for them. So long as I keep writing, I think they'll all take good enough care of me.

When Columbo and I get back to the cabin I light the wood-burning stove before slipping the pretty matchbox with a robin on the front inside my pocket. I think of that little robin as the only bird on this island, and I like to keep it close and safe. There are frequent power cuts here too, so I always keep the matches handy, and there's only one match left, so I must remember to buy more next time I visit the shop.

I open the champagne and tuck into my fish-and-chips. It feels like a real treat and I savor every sip and every mouthful. I receive a modest salary, far less money than I know my books are generating, but that's okay; it was never about the money. I just wanted to tell my stories. I'm published in forty countries these days and *Beautiful Ugly* has been made into a film. The premiere is in London next month. I was invited but won't be attending. I pick up the Magic 8 Ball that I now know was Abby's when she was a child, and ask it the question I've asked so many times before.

"Will I ever leave this island?"

DON'T COUNT ON IT, the screen tells me.

I make myself a cup of bog myrtle tea—I can't get enough of the stuff—then I sit down at my desk and look at the bestseller list again. I sometimes wonder if my readers have noticed how inactive I am on social media. Or how I never do in-person book signings or attend festivals anymore. I'm so happy and humbled and grateful that my readers loved *Beautiful Ugly*, and that they understood the story I was trying to tell. I wish I could thank them. I might be trapped inside my own virtual reality, but my readers make it all worthwhile.

Books are a bit like children for authors, we're not really allowed to have favorites, but this book was mine. Despite everything. It's a story about an author who is trapped on an island. He wants to leave, but for various reasons, he can't. So he asks his readers for help by hiding a secret message in the book. I did the same thing as my character in *Beautiful Ugly* and hid a message for my readers to find. The first word in the first fourteen chapters of the novel spells it out. Now that the book is published and out in the world,

I wonder if any of my readers have discovered the secret message yet. Maybe someone will send help if they do. Kitty would have been furious if she had noticed, but luckily for me she never did.

I pick up the small, square silver frame that was here in the cabin when I arrived, and stare at the note Charles Whittaker wrote to himself. A note so important he decided to frame it:

The only way out is to write.

Kitty said she never really understood what it meant.

I do.

Columbo is on the bed and snoring already, and I'm jealous of how easy it is for him to sleep. Anywhere. Anytime. I took a couple of the new pills Dr. Highsmith prescribed and I can barely keep my eyes open, so I follow his lead. I lie down on the bed. Then I count backward from one hundred.

I dream of the sea.

And I dream of Abby.

Then I hear her whisper.

I hope you die in your sleep.

And I am so happy because those words mean that she still loves me. It's what Abby and I used to say to each other every night. Despite everything, she is back by my side and I have been forgiven for the worst thing that I will ever do. Abby loves me again and all I want is to hold her and never let her go. I can hear Nina Simone singing in the distance "Don't Let Me Be Misunderstood," one of Abby's favorites. She must have put the record on before coming to bed.

"I love you too," I say, reaching for her, but she is not here.

She never was.

When I open my eyes, I realize that I am not where I thought I was either.

I can't see anything. I am no longer on the bed. I'm not even in the cabin. I am somewhere unfamiliar, dark, and cold. I hear the crackle of a walkie-talkie and I try to move, but it feels as though I am surrounded by invisible walls. Almost as though I am inside a human-shaped box. Everything is still and silent and black.

Abby and I often talked about the things that scared us the most.

Her biggest fear was drowning.

She knew that mine was being buried alive.

I start to panic. I twist my body and there is just enough room to reach inside my pocket for the box of matches. I feel an overwhelming sense of relief when I discover that it is still there. That relief soon fades when I remember there is only one match left. With trembling fingers I light it.

The flickering flame confirms I am inside what looks like a coffin, and it has been lined with copies of my own books.

When I hear the muffled sound of a church bell it is hard to breathe.

The robin on the matchbox comes to life and flies away, leaving me completely alone, making me wonder what I've been drugged with. The match burns my fingers before everything fades to black.

I don't scream. I don't shout. But I do cry.

Silent tears dampen my face in the darkness.

Tears for the person I was and the person I could have been.

Then I hear the crackle of a walkie-talkie again, but I can't reach it. It's getting harder to breathe and I'm so tired. I close my eyes, part of me still wondering if this is just a bad dream. Deep down, I know that it isn't. Life is a fairy tale that rarely hands out happy endings. Life is Beautiful Ugly; my wife taught me that. The walkie-talkie crackles again, it is her, and the last words I hear are the only ones I want to:

I hope you die in your sleep.

ACKNOWLEDGMENTS

With every book I write there are people I couldn't have written it without. Thank you to Daniel, Jonny, Kari, Christine, and Francesca for helping me with this one. And an extra big thank-you to Viola Hayden, who held my hand and shone a torch when I was lost in the dark.

Forever thank you as always to Jonny Geller and the whole team at Curtis Brown. With special thanks to Ciara Finan, Atlanta Hatch, Kate Cooper, Nadia Mokdad, and Sam Loader. Forever thank you also to Kari Stuart, my amazing agent in America.

This book is dedicated to my editor, Christine Kopprasch, who I have worked with for many years on many books. She is wonderful and is one of my favorite humans. Huge thanks also to the rest of the amazing team at Flatiron, my book family. With special thanks to Bob Miller, Megan Lynch, Malati Chavali, Nancy Trypuc, Katherine Turro, Marlena Bittner, Claire McLaughlin, Erin Gordon, Maxine Charles, Kate Lucas, Elishia Merricks, Maria Snelling, Isabela Narvaez, Emily Walters, Frances Sayers, Donna Noetzel, Justine Gardner, and Rhys Davies. Rhys designed the beautiful map at the start of the book. A special shout-out also to Will Staehle for this stunning cover. Huge thanks to my lovely editor in the UK, Francesca Pathak, and the rest of the team at Pan Macmillan. And thank you to all my foreign publishers who take such good care of my novels.

Thank you to the Scottish Highlands for inspiring this story. I visit Scotland every year, and if there is a more beautiful place on Earth, I have yet to find it. Getting stranded in the Hebrides sparked the idea for this book, and I can't think of a lovelier location to be trapped in. The fictional island in the story is called Amberly for my niece, Amber.

Thank you to the librarians, booksellers, journalists, and book reviewers who have been so kind about my books. And thank you to all the book bloggers. I love seeing your beautiful pictures from all around the world. Your support means so much to me and I'm so grateful, I wanted to name one of my characters in honor of book bloggers this year. Abby Endler (Crime by the Book) was one of the first bloggers I met in real life, so I borrowed her name for the character of Abby.

Thank you to Boots for being the best dog in the world, and for keeping me company in the writing shed. Thank you to Daniel for being my favorite human. The biggest thank-you is to my readers. I love you for loving my stories and I'm so grateful for all your beautiful pictures, kind reviews, and wonderful support. I wouldn't be here without you, and I hope you enjoyed this book.

ABOUT THE AUTHOR

Alice Feeney is the *New York Times* bestselling author of *Good Bad Girl*, *Daisy Darker*, *Rock Paper Scissors*, *His & Hers*, *I Know Who You Are*, and *Sometimes I Lie*. Her novels have been translated into more than thirty languages and have been optioned for major screen adaptations. Alice was a BBC journalist for fifteen years and now lives in the Devon countryside with her family. *Beautiful Ugly* is her seventh novel.